A CHARLOTTE LARUE MYSTERY

DUSTED TO DEATH

BARBARA COLLEY

WHEELER
CHIVERS

This Large Print edition is published by Wheeler Publishing, Waterville, Maine, USA and by BBC Audiobooks Ltd, Bath, England.
Wheeler Publishing, a part of Gale, Cengage Learning.
Copyright © 2010 by Barbara Colley.
The moral right of the author has been asserted.

LIBRARY OF CONGRESS CATALOGING-IN-PUBLICATION DATA

Colley, Barbara.
    Dusted to death : a Charlotte Larue mystery / by Barbara Colley.
        p. cm. — (Wheeler Publishing large print cozy mystery)
        ISBN-13: 978-1-4104-2509-6 (pbk. : alk. paper)
        ISBN-10: 1-4104-2509-6 (pbk. : alk. paper)
        1. Women cleaning personnel—Fiction. 2. New Orleans (La.)—Fiction. 3. Large type books. I. Title.
    PS3603.O44D87 2010
    813'.6—dc22   2010004448

BRITISH LIBRARY CATALOGUING-IN-PUBLICATION DATA AVAILABLE
Published in 2010 in the U.S. by arrangement with Kensington Books, an imprint of Kensington Publishing Corp.
Published in 2010 in the U.K. by arrangement with Kensington Publishing Corp.

U.K. Hardcover: 978 1 408 49108 9 (Chivers Large Print)
U.K. Softcover: 978 1 408 49109 6 (Camden Large Print)

Printed in the United States of America
1 2 3 4 5 6 7 14 13 12 11 10

DUSTED TO DEATH

To John Scognamiglio, with my sincere thanks for his support and understanding.

ACKNOWLEDGMENTS

My heartfelt thanks to all of my readers who have written me such wonderful letters about my books.

Once again, I would like to express my sincere appreciation to Rexanne Becnel and Marie Goodwin. Their input, advice, and critiques are invaluable. Thank you from the bottom of my heart.

A special thanks to Frank and Parris Bailey for so graciously allowing me into their beautiful home and answering my questions about their experiences with having their home used for a movie set.

Last, but never least, a loving thanks to my husband, David, for everything.

CHAPTER 1

"Maid-for-a-Day, Charlotte LaRue speaking."

"Hey, Charlotte, I've got some good news and some bad news. Then, I've got some more *good* news."

Charlotte bit back a groan of impatience. Bitsy Duhè, an elderly lady, was a longtime client. Her phone call had come smack in the middle of Charlotte's search for an article that she'd cut out of the newspaper. The article in the *Times-Picayune* listed the upcoming Fourth of July celebrations going on in the Greater New Orleans area, and Charlotte wanted to check out the different locations again before she settled on the one she had in mind.

"Bitsy, can I call you back in a few minutes?" Charlotte tucked the telephone receiver between her chin and shoulder to free her hands so that she could continue sorting through the stack of papers on her desk.

"This won't take long," Bitsy responded sharply, her tone petulant. "Besides, I don't have all day to sit around and wait for you to call me back."

And I do? Charlotte closed her eyes and counted to ten before speaking again. Truth be known, other than staying on the phone gossiping, watching her soap operas, and going to her many doctors' appointments, sitting around all day was exactly all that Bitsy had to do. Knowing how Bitsy could pout, though, she figured that she might as well let Bitsy have her say or Charlotte would never hear the end of it. "So what's the good news?" Charlotte asked.

"Oh, Charlotte, you'll never guess."

No, and I don't want to. Charlotte bit her tongue to keep from saying the words out loud, and guilt for being so impatient with the old lady reared its ugly head.

"They want to use my house."

Charlotte's brow furrowed. "They?"

"Mega Films — you know — the production company that's shooting that movie here in the Garden District, the one starring Hunter Lansky and Angel Martinique."

Hunter Lansky! Charlotte's mouth gaped open. Hunter Lansky was one of her all-time favorite actors. Why, even the mention of his name immediately conjured up his handsome image in her mind.

"Two days ago," Bitsy continued, "a man knocked on my door and said he was Mega Films' location manager and that he wanted to use my house for a movie. Then, yesterday, he came back with three other men, including the producer and the director. Can't remember what the fourth man's title was. Anyway, they're willing to pay me a boatload of money and said they'd put me up in the hotel of my choice while they shoot the scenes they need. I'm thinking that maybe I'd like to stay at the Monteleone. I've always thought it might be fun to live in the French Quarter — temporarily, of course."

"Why, Bitsy, that's terrific."

Louisiana, and the Greater New Orleans area in particular, was quickly becoming known as Hollywood South. Though the movie industry was good for the economy since they used locals, Charlotte had mixed feelings about the so-called Hollywood invasion. Still, it was exciting. Why, just earlier she'd read an article that mentioned that in addition to the movie starring Hunter Lansky, several more movies were scheduled for production over the next few months. She'd even had to take a different route to work the day before since part of St. Charles Avenue had been blocked off for filming. Could that be the one Bitsy was talking about?

"Yeah, I was all excited at first," Bitsy continued, "but here's the bad news. I could hardly sleep last night for thinking about it, and now I'm not so sure. I can always use a bit of extra money, but just the thought of all those strangers traipsing in and out of my house makes me nervous. Why, no telling what they'll do to my stuff."

And what on earth does this have to do with me? Charlotte thought impatiently.

Still searching through the stack of articles, Charlotte sighed. "Granted, I don't know a lot about this type of thing, Bitsy, but I would think that they would be extra careful when they use someone's home." She suddenly spied the Fourth of July article and set it aside. She should have known that it would be near the bottom of the stack.

"You're probably right," Bitsy went on, oblivious of anything but her own agenda. "But just to make sure, I called them bright and early this morning and told them that I want you to be there."

"You did what?"

12

"Well, I would have asked that young man, Dale, who you've got working for me, but since he's decided to get his master's degree, I knew he wouldn't have time."

And I do? Bitsy's audacity never ceased to amaze Charlotte.

"There would be some cleaning involved," Bitsy continued. "But between you and me, your job would mostly be to watch over my stuff. So — and this is the other good news — I insisted that they hire you to keep the house clean and organized during the shooting, and they've agreed. And guess how much they're willing to pay you for the two weeks that they'll be shooting?"

Without waiting for a response, Bitsy blurted out, "Five-thousand dollars. And believe me, I had to negotiate with them to get that much. Pretty nice, huh?"

For several moments Charlotte was speechless. No wonder making movies cost so much money. Once she finally found her voice, she said, "Ah, Bitsy, I — I appreciate the offer — I really do — and the money is unbelievable, but I do have other clients, you know. I can't just take off for that long without prior notice."

"That's what this is!" Bitsy exclaimed. "I'm giving you prior notice. And before you say no, don't forget who's starring in the movie."

Hunter Lansky and Angel Martinique. How could she forget? In spite of herself, Charlotte felt a tingle of anticipation at the chance to actually meet Hunter Lansky. *Just say no . . . just say no.* Ignoring her inner voice of reason, Charlotte hesitated. The money would be really nice and certainly more than her maid service would bring in for the two weeks. It would also be more than enough to finally have the twins' portrait done. Now that her little grandbabies were finally crawling and sitting up by themselves, they were the perfect age for a portrait.

Besides, the publicity for Maid-for-a-Day would be great, and this might be the only opportunity you'll ever get to meet Hunter Lansky.

Charlotte felt her face grow warm. Hunter Lansky had been the first movie star that she'd ever had a crush on. By now he had to be at least sixty-eight, five years older than Charlotte. She knew that because, ever since she'd been a lovesick teenager, she'd followed his career through the years. He'd been twenty when his career had taken off, and she'd collected all of the tabloid articles and pictures printed about him, not to mention seeing all of his films at least twice.

Knowing she would probably regret asking, she said, "How much prior notice are you giving me?"

"Then you'll do it?"

"Bitsy, how much prior notice?" she repeated.

"They start shooting two days after the Fourth — that's this Monday — and should be finished within two weeks."

Charlotte winced. The Fourth was on Saturday, two days away. Four days' total notice — not a lot of notice, but adequate . . . decisions, decisions. "Tell you what, let me check my schedule and see what I can do. Then I'll get back to you."

"And how long will that take?"

Lord, give me patience. At times it was all she could do to keep a civil tongue in her head when dealing with Bitsy. Finally, taking a deep breath, she said, "It shouldn't take too long. I'll give you a call just as soon as I can. More than likely, by later this afternoon I'll know something, one way or another."

"Oh, good. And, Charlotte?"

"Yes."

"Please try to work it out."

Charlotte frowned as she hung up the receiver. Something about the way Bitsy had said "Please try to work it out" gave her

15

pause. After a moment, she shrugged and reached for her schedule.

Her regular days to work were Mondays, Wednesdays, and Fridays. Since Dale worked at Bitsy's on Tuesdays and wouldn't be needed while the movie was being shot, maybe he would switch to one of her days instead.

She glanced farther down the schedule. Her part-time employee, Janet Davis, only worked once a week, on Thursdays. If she could persuade Janet to take up the slack on the other two days, then . . .

Charlotte drummed her fingers on the desktop. Janet had been an employee longer than Dale, and she really should give Janet first choice of the days to work. Even so, because of Dale's class schedule, she would have to give him first choice instead.

Charlotte glanced at the cuckoo clock on the wall behind the sofa. It was still pretty early. Had Dale left for classes yet or not? Since she couldn't remember his schedule, she reached for the telephone receiver and tried his home phone number. While the phone rang, she flipped through her Rolodex in search of his cell number, just in case he wasn't at home.

On the fourth ring he answered, and Charlotte winced when she heard his groggy voice. "Hey, Dale, this is Charlotte. Did I wake you up?"

"Yeah, but that's okay. I should have been up an hour ago."

"Are you ill?"

Dale chuckled. "No, *Mom,* I'm fine. I just stayed up too late last night working on a paper."

Charlotte grinned. "Humph, if I *were* your mother, I'd tell you to have a little more respect for your elders."

Dale laughed. "Okay, okay, sorry. So, what's up?"

Once Charlotte explained the situation, Dale readily agreed to work for her on Monday. "On Mondays my only class isn't until five. I could also work on Friday, if you need me to. The extra money would come in handy right about now."

"Great!" Charlotte grinned.

After giving Dale the addresses for her Monday and Friday clients, she quickly filled him in on their particular peculiarities. "Just so you know, my Monday client, Sally Lawson, likes all of the sheets changed. Never mind that none except hers have been slept on. Also, she has this stainless steel garbage can in the kitchen. Make sure you Windex it."

"What about the Friday client?" he asked.

"My Friday client is Joy Meadows. Joy has a couple of cats that she allows to roam everywhere, including the kitchen countertops. Make sure you wipe down those counters and get rid of all that cat hair. I swear, one of these days, Joy is going to cough up a hair ball."

"Gross, Charlotte. Really gross."

"Sorry," she apologized.

"Anything else?"

"No, I think that's about it."

After ending her conversation with Dale, she dialed Janet's number.

A few minutes later, she sighed with relief as she again hung up the receiver. Janet had also agreed to the extra day for the next two weeks, so now all she had to do was call Bitsy back and give her the news.

"No time like the present," she whispered as she dialed Bitsy's number. The phone barely rang before Bitsy answered. Charlotte figured that the old lady must have been sitting next to it, waiting. "It's all set up," Charlotte told her. "I was able to clear my schedule."

"Thanks, Charlotte. I really do appreciate this."

"So, who do I contact now?"

Bitsy cleared her throat. "Ah — well — nobody."

"What do you mean 'nobody'?"

"Now, don't get mad, but I already told them you'd do it. All you have to do is fill out the paperwork when you show up."

The heat of sudden anger burned Charlotte's cheeks. No wonder Bitsy had been so eager for her to *work it out*. As far as Charlotte was concerned, Bitsy had crossed the line. No one, but no one, made these kinds of decisions for her. Barely able to contain the anger boiling inside, she said, "You shouldn't have done that, Bitsy."

"Probably not, but I figured you'd take the job. You always come through for me."

Charlotte chose her words very carefully. "That might be true, but please don't ever do something like that again. I'm hanging up the phone now, and I'll talk to you later." Charlotte immediately dropped the receiver onto the cradle.

For several moments she glared at the phone and fumed. It was true that she always tried to help out her clients when they needed her. In fact, most times she bent over backward to be accommodating, but she truly resented anyone outright assuming that she would do something without asking her first.

"Bitsy, Bitsy, Bitsy," she murmured. "What am I going to do about you?" With a shake of her head, she sighed. There was nothing she could do about the old lady but put up with her, and what was done was done. Feeling somewhat calmer and in hopes of distracting herself, she turned her attention to the newspaper article she'd found.

After considering each location, she finally made up her mind and set the article aside. She figured that instead of fighting the crowd in Jackson Square, they could see just as well from the levee across the river at Algiers Point. Meantime, she needed to make a grocery list . . . and a hair appointment.

Where did that come from? Until she'd talked to Bitsy, she hadn't even considered getting a trim.

But you might actually get to meet Hunter Lansky.

Charlotte felt her face grow warm. Big deal. He met thousands of women all the time, so what were the chances that a bigtime movie star like him would even notice someone like her? She automatically reached up and finger-combed her hair. Still, it didn't hurt to always try to look your best.

Making a mental note to call Valerie, her hairdresser, she grabbed a pen and paper and jotted down several items she needed for the backyard barbecue that she and Louis were hosting before the Fourth of July display.

A tiny smile pulled at her lips. The whole get-together had been Louis's idea. He'd pointed out that since they lived next door to each other, why not join forces?

Charlotte got up and walked over to the birdcage by the front window. Outside was sunny, and there wasn't a cloud in the sky. According to the weather forecast, record high temperatures would be set today. Already, her air conditioner sounded as if it was having labor pains.

"I just hope it makes it through this summer," she told Sweety Boy, her little parakeet. But the heat and her aging air conditioner weren't the only things on her mind of late.

Inside the birdcage, Sweety Boy sidled over near the door, and Charlotte reached in between the wires with her forefinger and gently rubbed the back of his head. "What am I going to do about Louis, Sweety?"

She stared back out of the window. Louis Thibodeaux, her tenant and sometimes friend, sometimes nemesis, was an enigma, a Dr.-Jekyll-and-Mr.-Hyde. A retired New Orleans police detective, he now worked for Lagniappe Security, a private security firm, and just when she thought she had him figured out, he'd do something totally unexpected . . . like planning this backyard barbecue that included all of his and Charlotte's family members.

"Ever since Joyce died, I'm not quite sure what to think," she muttered. At times Louis seemed to be really sad about his ex-wife's murder. Other times, it was as if Joyce had never existed. She knew that people went through stages of grief, but she was fairly certain pretending the deceased had never existed wasn't one of those stages.

"I wouldn't think that would be one of the stages of grief," she told Sweety Boy. Suddenly, from the corner of her eye she detected movement in front of the window — Louis — followed by a sharp rap on the door.

Charlotte grinned as she reached for the doorknob. "Speak of the devil," she whispered to Sweety Boy. "Good thing I decided to get dressed early." Sometimes on her days off she didn't bother getting dressed until midmorning, but today — thank goodness — she had dressed early because of several errands she needed to get done. Of course there had been times that Louis had seen her in just her housecoat. He'd even bought her a housecoat as a gift once. Even so, for some strange reason, being properly dressed made her feel more comfortable around him.

Charlotte opened the door and smiled. "Good morning."

Louis was a stocky man with a receding hairline of steel-gray hair. He kept himself fit, and from the first time she'd met him several years earlier, she had thought that he was an attractive man for his age. Too bad he could be such a pain in the butt at times, especially when he was in one of his male chauvinistic moods.

"Good morning to you too," he said with a curt nod of his head.

Charlotte's smile faded when she noticed the small suitcase sitting on the porch beside him. "You going somewhere?" She motioned toward the suitcase.

Louis nodded. "Yeah, some unexpected business. Just an overnighter in Houston," he hastened to add. "I'll be back in plenty of time to fire up the grill on the Fourth. One of the guys got sick, and they needed someone to fill in for tonight and tomorrow morning."

Charlotte pulled the door open wider. "Want to come inside? I think I still have some coffee in the pot."

Louis shook his head. "Wish I could, but

I can't. I'm running late as it is." He reached inside his pants pocket. "I just wanted to give you this before I leave." He pulled out a money clip and removed four twenty-dollar bills. "My share of the groceries for the Fourth shindig."

Charlotte shook her head and held up a hand in protest. "Uh-uh, that's way too much. All we're having is hot dogs and hamburgers. Besides, most of the folks coming are *my* relatives."

"It's not too much," he insisted, "so take it." He reached out, and with a firm grip, grabbed hold of her wrist.

Charlotte automatically closed her hand into a fist.

"Don't be stubborn." He gently pried her fingers open, placed the money in her palm, and then closed her fingers around the money. Still holding her hand with both of his, he said, "Counting my bunch and yours, we're going to be feeding fifteen people. We will need soft drinks, paper goods, charcoal, and I'm sure there's some other stuff I haven't even thought of. Besides, this whole thing was my idea to begin with." He gently squeezed her hand. "Okay?"

After a moment, Charlotte nodded. "Okay."

"Good." He released her hand. Then from his shirt pocket he pulled out a piece of paper. "I made out a list of stuff. If you don't mind, could you pick these things up when you go grocery shopping? I'd planned to do it myself, but then Joe called."

Though Charlotte had never met Joe Sharp, she knew who he was. Joe owned Lagniappe Security, the company that employed Louis.

Curious, Charlotte glanced down at the list. A slow grin twitched at her lips.

"What?" Louis demanded.

Charlotte laughed. "Except for the badminton set, I made a list that includes most of what your list includes."

Louis shrugged. "Great minds think alike. As for the badminton set, I figured Amy and Davy would have fun with that. And if I get back in time, I'm going to pick up one of those small kiddy pools for the little ones to splash in."

Charlotte didn't want to burst his bubble of enthusiasm, but she knew for a fact that his granddaughter, Amy, who was twelve, and her nephew's stepson, Davy, who was eight, would much rather play one of their many video games. Still, miracles happened, and who knows, maybe the two kids would enjoy the badminton set. It would certainly be different from what they were used to doing. "That's really thoughtful of you, Louis."

Louis suddenly shifted his eyes downwards and a tinge of red stained his cheeks. Charlotte's mouth curved into an unconscious smile. Would wonders ever cease? Usually gruff and serious, Louis was actually embarrassed by her compliment. Go figure.

A moment later he cleared his throat and said, "Got to run, but I should be back tomorrow afternoon."

Charlotte was about to tell him bye when he suddenly bent down and kissed her. The kiss was just a quick peck on the lips, but it caught her completely off-guard. Stunned and tongue-tied, she could only stand there and watch him as he turned and hurried down the steps. By the time she found her voice, he was halfway to his car. "What in the world was that all about?" she murmured as he backed his car out of the driveway.

As if Louis had heard her, he glanced her way, winked, and with a two-fingered wave, he drove off.

The Fourth of July lived up to the weather forecaster's predictions: sunny and hot. Charlotte stepped over to the stove to check on the chili for the hot dogs. "I can't believe it's just noon, and the temperature gauge has already climbed to ninety-eight degrees."

Charlotte's daughter-in-law, Carol, nodded. "At least Louis had the good sense to put up that canopy for shade. And those fans he set up help. By the way, I love your new haircut."

"Thanks." Charlotte smiled, pleased that Carol had noticed. Thankfully, Valerie had been able to work her into the schedule late on Friday afternoon. "I thought I was due for a change — too much gray." She laughed. Up until she'd hit sixty, the gray had blended in with her honey-blond hair, but after sixty, it seemed like almost overnight there was more gray than blond.

"The shorter style really flatters you — makes you look ten years younger."

Charlotte laughed again. "Younger is good, and it's certainly easier to fix."

Suddenly, a high-pitched shriek exploded from the backyard, and Charlotte froze.

"That's just Samantha," Carol quickly reassured her. "That's her 'I didn't get what I wanted' scream. Either Hank or Judith will take care of her."

With a sigh of relief, Charlotte resumed stirring the chili for the hot dogs. It never ceased to amaze her how early kids learned how to get what they want. The twins, Samantha and Samuel, weren't even a year old yet and already they could wrap the adults around their little fingers like pretzels.

"So, when do you start the movie job?" Carol asked.

"Day after tomorrow."

"Aren't you nervous? I know I would be."

"No, not so much nervous." Charlotte rapped the spoon on the side of the boiler and placed it in the sink. After turning off the burner beneath the pot of chili, she put a lid on it. "I guess, more than anything, I'm a bit anxious. To tell the truth, though, I haven't had a lot of time to think about it." She walked over to the table to prepare a tray of buns and condiments for the hamburgers and hot dogs.

Carol grinned. "Unlike your son, I think it's sooo exciting. Sure you don't need someone to fill in for you on one of those days?"

"Then Hank would really throw a fit."

Carol giggled. "Well, we just wouldn't tell him." When Charlotte jerked her head around to stare at her daughter-in-law, Carol giggled again. "Just kidding, Charlotte. Just kidding."

Charlotte grinned, and then turned her

attention back to the task at hand. She was almost finished when the sound of children's laughter reached her ears. Smiling, she glanced out of the back window, and a warm feeling of love and contentment spread to the center of her being. All of her family and Louis's son and his family had been able to come. She'd also invited Dale and a former employee and friend, Cherè Warner, who was in town. Except for Carol, who had offered to help her bring some food outside, they were all right there in her own backyard.

Family and good friends. *Her* family and *her* good friends. Life couldn't get much better. She was truly blessed.

And what about Louis? Which category does he fit?

Charlotte closed her eyes for a moment. Where on earth did that come from? *What about him?* she answered the silent voice in her head. *He's a good friend, a really good friend.*

Just a good friend?

Well, he's not family, so what else would he be?

What else, indeed? And what about that kiss?

Ignoring the nagging voice in her head and the memory of the kiss, Charlotte opened her eyes and loaded up the tray to transport the food to the picnic table.

True to his word, Louis had returned from his overnight assignment in plenty of time to "fire up the grill" as well as purchase the small wading pool for the little ones.

Again, Charlotte glanced out of the window and smiled. While the twins splashed in the pool, Davy and Amy, much to her surprise, seemed to be really having fun playing badminton.

At that moment, Davy swung his racket and missed. Like a streak of lightning, Danielle, Daniel and Nadia's four-year old, swooped in behind him and scooped up the shuttlecock off the ground. When Davy held out his hand for it, Danielle shook her head and said something that Charlotte couldn't hear.

Just behind Charlotte, Carol laughed. "Guess that's one way to try and force them to play with her."

"Yeah, poor little thing. She thinks she's too old to play with the twins, but Davy and Amy think she's too young to play with them."

"Maybe they'll take pity on her."

"Humph! I doubt that. But —" Charlotte picked up the tray and headed toward the back door. "Maybe I can distract her — get *her* to take pity on the twins," she said over her shoulder. "The twins crawl around after her like little lapdogs."

"If anyone can, you can," Carol quipped. "Do you want me to bring that pot of chili?"

"Yes, please."

Later that night when Louis parked the car in the driveway, Charlotte opened the door and walked slowly to the porch. In the distance she could still hear the sounds of fireworks popping, and though the night air wasn't exactly cool, it was cooler than the afternoon had been.

She paused at the bottom of the steps and looked up into the sky. "That's strange," she murmured. "I've never seen that many stars out in a long time. And they all seem to be centered right over our neighbor-hood."

Though Louis chuckled, he didn't comment.

"By the way, thanks for the ride home," she told him. Though she'd ridden to the levee with Hank and his family to watch the fireworks, Louis had offered to take her home to save Hank an unnecessary trip.

"You're welcome. I don't know about you, but I'm exhausted," Louis said as he followed her up the steps onto the porch. "But it's a good exhaustion," he added.

"I feel the same way." Charlotte headed for her front door. "All in all, it was worth it. And the fireworks this year were fantastic. I have to say that, except for the heat, this day was about as perfect as they come." She unlocked the door.

"Yeah, well, don't forget the mosquitoes."

"Speaking of the bloodthirsty critters, either step inside or say good night." When he stepped inside, Charlotte quickly closed the door. With a grin she turned to face Louis. "Funny, I didn't hear anyone else complaining."

Louis laughed. "That's because the little ones didn't stay still long enough for a mosquito to land, and their parents were too busy chasing them to notice."

"And because their parents had the good sense to spray them good with mosquito repellent before we left," Charlotte pointed out.

"Yeah, yeah, whatever. Go ahead. I know you're dying to say I told you so."

Charlotte shrugged. "If the shoe fits. I did warn you to spray yourself down. And speaking of mosquito bites, if you've got some of that green rubbing alcohol, using it on the bites will help with the itching. Either that or some Benadryl cream."

"Well, unlike some people I know, I don't happen to keep that kind of stuff on hand, so guess I'll just suffer."

Charlotte laughed. "Is that a hint?" Without waiting for his reply, she said, "Hang on a minute, and I'll be right back."

Within a couple of minutes, she returned and handed him a bottle of green rubbing alcohol.

"Thanks."

"You're welcome. And, Louis, thank you for helping make this such a great day."

Louis simply nodded. "Couldn't have done it without you." Then, without an ounce of warning, he suddenly wrapped his arms around her and kissed her, again. As before, she was stunned. But unlike the brief peck he'd given her on Thursday, this kiss was a full-blown one. Surprisingly, his lips were much softer than she'd expected. Then, just as she'd made up her mind to enjoy it, Louis ended it. With a knowing smile, he released her, opened the door, and then carefully pulled it closed behind him.

For long moments Charlotte stared at the closed door. Dormant feelings within stirred, feelings that she'd long thought were gone forever with the death of her son's father in Vietnam, so long ago. Hank Senior had been her first love, and though other men had come along, none had stirred her emotions quite like Louis.

With a shake of her head, Charlotte threw the dead bolt, then turned away and walked to the bedroom.

Something was going on with Louis, and just thinking about it made her all jittery inside. She could come right out and ask him, but ask him what? How on earth did a person even phrase that kind of question? Besides, knowing Louis, he would only tell her what was on his mind when he was good and ready.

CHAPTER 2

Monday was predicted by the weather forecasters to hit a three-figure heat index, but worrying about the heat was the least of Charlotte's concerns as she drove toward Bitsy Duhè's house. For one thing, she couldn't stop thinking about Louis and wondering about his sudden need to kiss her at the drop of a hat. For another thing, she was more nervous about the job at Bitsy's than she'd admitted to either herself or Carol.

She still couldn't believe that finally, after all these years, she was actually going to meet Hunter Lansky in person. Well, maybe not "meet" him exactly. In her experience, the maid was the last person anyone paid attention to. But just the thought of being in the same room or even the same house with him was exciting.

Charlotte slowed her van to a crawl as she approached the block where Bitsy lived.

"What now?" She narrowed her eyes against the morning sun to peer up ahead. She was only half a block from Bitsy's house, and the entire width of the street was lined with barricades. As she inched the van closer to the barricades, she spotted a uniformed security guard headed her way. Tucked beneath his arm was a clipboard and he was motioning for her to turn around.

Charlotte shook her head, pushed the automatic window button, and waited for him to approach her van.

"Ma'am, you'll have to turn around," the young man told her. "Only approved personnel are allowed."

"I guess that would include me, then," she told him, noting that the logo on his shirtsleeve was Lagniappe Security, the same logo she'd seen on Louis's uniforms. "I'm supposed to be working on the movie set today."

"Name please and some ID."

"Name's Charlotte LaRue." She reached for her purse. A moment later, she showed the guard her driver's license.

The guard studied the license for a moment, and then scanned the list on his clipboard. With a nod, he said, "You're clear."

"So where am I supposed to park?"

"I'll move the barricade, and you can park anywhere on that side of the street." He motioned toward the right side. "Just don't block any driveways."

When he turned to walk away, Charlotte said, "By the way, my neighbor works for Lagniappe too. Maybe you know him. His name is Louis Thibodeaux."

The man nodded. "Yeah, everyone knows Louis. We're lucky to have him working for Lagniappe."

Once through the barricade, Charlotte drove slowly until she spotted an opening. After several maneuvers, she squeezed her van into the space, but just barely, with little room left at either end of the van.

Once satisfied that she was close enough to the curb, she cut the engine and yanked the keys out of the ignition. "Good thing I can parallel-park."

After retrieving her supply carrier from the back of the van, she locked the doors and trudged up the street toward Bitsy's house.

As she approached the house, she slowed her steps. "Keystone Cops," she murmured, her gaze taking in what appeared to be a myriad of people rushing to and fro. "Or Mardi Gras," she added.

Electrical lines were strung all over the

front lawn. Men toted in cameras; others, carrying various pieces of equipment, emerged from a huge moving van.

Charlotte searched through the crowd of faces and sighed. How on earth was she ever going to find the person she was supposed to report to, especially since Bitsy neglected to even give her the name of the person? Then, suddenly, she stopped; all she could do was gape at Bitsy's house.

"Oh, wow!" A soft gasp escaped her. Bitsy's house, a very old, raised-cottage-style Greek Revival, had never looked quite so magnificent. The peeling paint had been scraped and a bright fresh coat applied. Even the landscape had been clipped and pruned to within an inch of its life. For a moment Charlotte fancied that this must have been the way the old house had looked when it was first built, more than 150 years ago.

Still in awe of the exterior, Charlotte carefully picked her way through the people milling about as she climbed the steps up to the gallery. No one seemed to be paying any attention to her and the front door was wide open, so she kept going.

Once inside, she was again struck with awe. Though Bitsy had some nice pieces of antique furniture, Charlotte had noticed lately that the furniture had begun to look a bit dingy and worn.

Charlotte's eyes grew wide as she glanced around. From what she could see, all of Bitsy's stuff had been cleared out and had been replaced with gorgeous furnishings that looked brand-new, yet befit the era in which the house had been built.

So where was Bitsy's stuff? she wondered. The very stuff that she had been hired to watch over.

"Hey, lady, who are you?"

Charlotte pivoted around at the sound of the voice and found herself facing a rail-thin man who was just a little taller than her own five foot three and looked to be in his early-to-mid thirties.

"Ah, I'm Charlotte — Charlotte LaRue — and I was hired to help keep things clean."

The man rolled his eyes. "Hey, Jake, the maid's here," he yelled. To Charlotte he said, "Over there." He pointed toward a group of people huddled near the end of the hallway. "Jake's the tall dude with the bald head."

Once Charlotte spotted the man he'd described, she said, "Thanks." Charlotte was almost to the group when the bald-headed man broke away and met her half-way.

"You the maid?"

Still clutching her supply carrier, Charlotte nodded. "Charlotte LaRue."

The man shrugged. "Whatever. Follow me."

Whatever? No pleased to meet you, how are you, or even kiss my foot. How rude! Probably one of those high-powered lawyer types, she figured; the kind used to people snapping to attention every time he entered a room.

Dodging two cameramen and their cameras, Charlotte followed Jake back to the kitchen. When she entered the room she noticed that it looked pretty much the same as it had always looked. Either the crew hadn't gotten around to changing it or the kitchen wouldn't be included in any of the scenes.

Bitsy would be relieved. There weren't too many things that Bitsy truly valued in her home, but her vast collection of kitchen gadgets was at the top of the list, right there along with the portraits of her grand-daughters that hung in the front parlor.

Jake walked to the table and unlatched a bulging briefcase. After thumbing through several file folders, he pulled one out. "You can store your stuff in that closet over there." He pointed to the pantry. Tapping his foot, he waited impatiently until Charlotte had dutifully placed her supply carrier and purse in the bottom of the pantry and closed the door.

"Okay, I need you to sign the forms in this folder. Sign your full name wherever you see a red check mark." He rummaged through the briefcase again, then placed another form on top of the folder. "Fill this one out for tax purposes," he said, handing her a pen.

The stack of forms inside the folder was a bit daunting. She was tempted just to sign them and get it over with, but she'd learned a long time ago to never, but never, sign anything before reading it. She slid the forms over and pulled out a chair. Once seated, she began reading the top form.

"You're going to read them?"

The man's incredulous tone hit a nerve. Charlotte slowly raised her head. "That's right."

"Except for the tax forms, the rest are just release forms, lady."

Charlotte gave the rude man a saccharine smile, and in a voice that belied the smile she said, "I *never* sign anything without reading it first."

Jake rolled his eyes toward the ceiling and muttered several expletives that made Charlotte want to slap his face. "Watch your language, mister."

"My — my language? You've got to be kidding?"

"Nope. I'm as serious as a heart attack."

"Oh, sh—"

Charlotte threw up her hand, palm out, and shook her head. "Uh-uh — not that one either." From the confused look on Jake's face, it was more than evident that no one had ever attempted to correct his foul language.

"What are you?" he demanded. "Some kind of Puritan or something?"

An amused smile pulled at Charlotte's lips. " 'Or something.' Now — if you don't mind, I'll just get these read and signed."

"Knock yourself out, lady, but I've got better things to do with my time than stand here and watch you read. When you're finished, put the forms back into the file folder and leave them on top of my briefcase."

This time Charlotte was the one who rolled her eyes. "Too bad that your mama never taught you any manners."

Jake's face suddenly flushed crimson. Whether from anger or embarrassment,

Charlotte couldn't tell, but she suspected the former, especially when he suddenly pivoted and stalked out of the kitchen.

Once Charlotte had finished with the forms and placed the folder on top of Jake's briefcase, she went in search for someone who could tell her exactly what her job involved. She also wanted to find out where Bitsy's belongings were stored.

The minute she stepped out of the kitchen, she heard a deep, male voice calling her name.

"LaRue — Charlotte LaRue. Anyone seen Charlotte LaRue?"

With a frown, Charlotte headed toward the sound of the voice. "I'm Charlotte," she called out, searching for the person she'd heard calling her.

"Charlotte?"

The voice came from just behind her, and she whirled around. Standing within touching distance was one of the most gorgeous young men that she'd ever met. His hair was coal black, though just a bit long for her personal taste; yet, it seemed to fit him to a tee. But it was his eyes that held her gaze, eyes so darkly blue they were almost purple, and framed with long, thick lashes that most women would die for.

"Ah — I — I'm Charlotte," she finally

blurted out once she could breathe again.

"Hey, there, Charlotte." He shot her a dazzling smile full of perfect white teeth. "I'm Dalton, the prop manager. Nice to finally meet you."

"Same here," she said.

"Let's get you introduced around, and then we can both get to work. But first, why don't I tell you just a little about the movie?"

Charlotte grinned. "That would be great!"

"It's basically a story of an overbearing man whose wife died in childbirth, and he's left to raise his headstrong daughter alone. The story takes place during the daughter's teen years and it's basically an object lesson on the father learning to let go and the daughter learning to be more responsible."

Charlotte nodded. "Sounds, ah — interesting. And of course Hunter Lansky is the father and Angel Martinique has to be the daughter."

Dalton nodded. "Of course. But between you and me, it's not all that interesting. But then, what do I know? I'm only the set prop manager."

Silently, Charlotte agreed with him about the movie plot, but she simply smiled.

"Okay — now for those introductions." Dalton nudged her forward.

After the first ten minutes of introductions, Charlotte figured out fast there was no way that she was ever going to remember the names of everyone. Then, across the room, she saw a familiar face, and she was suddenly hot and cold all over at the same time.

Hunter Lansky.

When she heard Dalton chuckle beside her, she figured she probably looked as starstruck as she felt.

"Don't worry," Dalton told her. "He has that effect on everyone." Then, without warning, he called out, "Hey, Hunter, I've got someone for you to meet."

Charlotte felt like a giddy schoolgirl again as the man she'd once idolized turned and smiled, then headed toward them. But she wasn't a goggle-eyed teenager any longer — hadn't been for decades. And he was no longer a young, handsome movie idol. He was still handsome enough for an older man, but without the big screen and makeup, he was, after all, just a man. At least that's what she kept telling herself as he approached them.

He held out his hand, and in that deep, mellow voice that had helped to make him so famous and had once sent shivers down her spine, he said, "Nice to meet you, Charlotte." He enclosed her hand in his. "I've heard a lot about you."

Taken aback, Charlotte frowned. "You have?"

Hunter smiled and nodded. "Ms. Duhè couldn't sing your praises loud enough. And without you, we wouldn't be able to use this lovely old house."

Oh, dear Lord, there was no telling what Bitsy had told them. "Well, Ms. Duhè sometimes has a tendency to exaggerate a bit."

Hunter chuckled. "And she's humble," he said to Dalton as he squeezed Charlotte's hand. "I like that about a woman." He released her hand. "Now, if you'll excuse me, sweet lady, I think makeup is waiting for me."

"Of course." With a sigh, Charlotte watched him walk away. "Such a nice man," she said beneath her breath to no one in particular.

"Yeah, that's what they all say." Dalton cleared his throat. "Let's go upstairs," he suggested.

Jolted out of her reverie, Charlotte nodded.

As they walked up the stairs, Dalton explained exactly what Charlotte's duties would be. Though she tried concentrating on what he was telling her, her thoughts kept straying. What on earth had Bitsy said about her? Whatever it was, it seemed to have made a definite impression on Hunter Lansky, which was a good thing. At least she thought it was a good thing.

Oh, for Pete's sake, Charlotte, get a grip. The man is an actor, and everyone knows you can't believe a word they say. Besides, remember? He's just a man. He puts his pants on one leg at a time just like anyone else.

Ignoring the aggravating voice in her head, Charlotte tried harder to pay attention to what Dalton was saying as they threaded their way through busy crew members in the hallway.

"In here —" Dalton motioned toward one of the bedrooms — "is Angel's dressing room."

"I thought actors and actresses always had their own small, private trailers."

"Most of the time they do," Dalton said. "But Angel —" He shrugged. "Let's just say she's different."

The first thing that Charlotte noticed was that the bedroom, normally a guest room, had been stripped of all of Bitsy's furniture and decorations. Instead, there were racks of clothes, a small refrigerator, a chaise longue, and a couple of extra chairs along with a styling chair that was positioned in

47

front of a table and mirror that reminded her of a beauty shop setup. Also, stacked on the floor in the corner were several cases of bottled water. But it was the absence of Bitsy's things that reminded her she needed to ask about the storage of Bitsy's stuff.

The second thing she noted was the attractive, young Hispanic woman who was busy organizing what appeared to be hundreds of exotic-looking beauty items on the table.

They were all so young, she thought, as she watched the woman. With the exception of Hunter Lansky, everyone she'd met so far was young enough to be her child, which made her feel really old by comparison.

Dalton motioned toward the woman. "That nice lady over there is Heather Cortez, Angel's makeup girl. Heather, meet our cleaning lady, Charlotte LaRue."

Charlotte smiled. "Nice to meet you, Heather." But when Heather turned toward her, Charlotte's smile faded a bit. Something about Heather's face didn't quite look right. One side appeared to be larger than the other side. Suddenly, realization hit Charlotte, and she sighed. It appeared to be larger because it was swollen.

Not again, she thought. It hadn't been that long ago that she had seen something similar, one of her clients with the same type of injury. Though Heather had done an excellent job covering up what Charlotte suspected was a bruised face, there was no way to cover up the fact that it was also swollen. Like the other woman Charlotte had known, did Heather also have an abusive husband? And also like her former client, she couldn't help wondering what kind of excuse Heather would have for the bruise.

When Dalton cleared his throat and wouldn't look directly at Heather, Charlotte knew that she was right. Others had noticed as well.

"Heather will give you the lowdown about Angel's stuff — what to touch and what not to touch," Dalton told Charlotte.

Heather smiled back at Charlotte, but before she had a chance to even say hello, there was a loud commotion in the hallway, followed by raised, angry voices.

"Simon only wants the best for you," a man yelled.

"I don't care what Simon Clark wants," a woman yelled back. "I don't work for Simon. *He* works for me, so you go tell him to take that offer and shove it."

"Uh-oh, the lovebirds are at it again," Dalton muttered in an aside to Charlotte.

Lovebirds? Was he being sarcastic? Before

Charlotte could decide one way or another, a beautiful young woman dressed in jeans, a T-shirt, and tennis shoes flounced into the room. With her signature long, thick blond hair, her flawless complexion and perfectly shaped face, not to mention her large emerald-green eyes, Angel Martinique was immediately recognizable.

Unlike Hunter Lansky, Angel was just as breathtaking off-screen as on-screen. But for some reason, an old saying Charlotte used to hear her grandmother say came to mind. *Pretty is as pretty does.* And, at the moment, in spite of her beauty, Angel wasn't very pretty.

Following close behind Angel was yet another handsome young man. This one reminded Charlotte of hot sandy beaches where the lifeguards were all hunks with bleached-blond hair and bronze bodies pumped up with rippling muscles.

"Now, now, honey, don't be like that," the man told Angel.

Angel plopped down into the padded swivel chair in front of the mirror and glared at her reflection. "Don't 'honey' me, Nick Franklin," she retorted. "Now go away. I have to be on the set in half an hour."

"Can I at least tell him you'll think about it?"

Angel whirled around. "I told you to go away," she screamed at him. Then, without warning, expletives that would have made a sailor cringe spewed out of her mouth, all directed at Nick.

Charlotte froze. Every bit of PR that she'd seen about Angel had touted her as the wholesome girl next door, and without fail, all of her movies had been G-rated, family-type flicks. Either the real Angel had an evil twin or her PR people were doing what PR people do best: lying through their pearly whites.

"Okay, okay." Nick threw up his hands in surrender and backed out of the room. "Just calm down, honey, okay? Calm down."

Guess Dalton was being sarcastic after all, Charlotte decided. Surely, not even love could make someone take the kind of verbal abuse that Angel was dishing out.

The second Nick disappeared, Angel's angry gaze settled on Dalton and Charlotte. "What do you want?" she snapped.

"It can wait," Dalton answered quickly.

"Well, get out, then." Dismissing them with a blink of her eyes, Angel whirled back around to face the mirror. "Heather, now!" she demanded.

As if she'd been given a direct order by a military general and totally ignoring Charlotte and Dalton, Heather immediately snapped to attention. She quickly slipped a headband over Angel's head to hold her hair back, and began working on Angel's makeup.

Dalton gently nudged the small of Charlotte's back. "Time to go," he told her in a low voice, as he guided her through the doorway into the hall. "You'll need to talk to Heather later, but now is not a good time."

Unlike before, the hallway was almost empty . . . almost, except for the giant of a man standing next to the doorway.

Since the top of Charlotte's head barely reached the man's shoulder, she tilted her head back. The man was completely bald. Had to be shaved, Charlotte decided, since he was really too young to be bald naturally. The color of his eyes was almost as dark as his black slacks and skintight T-shirt, and his ham-hock arms were crossed against his broad muscular chest.

Mr. Clean.

A grin twitched at her lips. Yep, he reminded her of the cartoon character in the Mr. Clean TV commercials.

When Dalton nodded at the giant and said, "Morning, Toby," the giant didn't respond. Dalton gave Toby a good-natured slap on his shoulder. "Toby here is Angel's bodyguard and fitness trainer," he explained to Charlotte. Then Dalton grinned. "And he's also a man of few words."

Bodyguard? So, where was Toby when Angel was arguing with Nick? Not knowing exactly how to react, Charlotte finally said, "Nice to meet you, Toby." As he'd done with Dalton, Toby didn't respond. With a shrug, Charlotte followed Dalton down the hall.

At the top of the stairs, they both paused.

"Ah, Dalton, before I forget, I need to ask you what's been done with Mrs. Duhè's furnishings."

"No problem," he said. "Everything's been cataloged and stored in a climate-controlled storage van parked on the side of the street near the house."

Vaguely recalling the large van that she'd seen when she'd first approached Bitsy's house earlier, Charlotte nodded.

"And don't worry. I'll make sure that it's all put back exactly like we found it once we're done."

"But how will you know where it all belongs?"

Dalton grinned. "We took lots of pictures before we removed the stuff."

That made sense, she thought.

"And we have you as a backup to make

sure that we get it right." He paused a moment, then added, "One last thing, Charlotte. Don't move or clean anything where we're shooting unless I say so or without consulting me first. In fact, for right now, why don't you just hang out up here until Heather is finished with Angel's makeup? Once Angel leaves, then get Heather to fill you in about Angel's stuff."

Before Charlotte could ask Dalton exactly what he'd meant by "Angel's stuff," someone below yelled his name.

"Gotta run," Dalton told her. Turning, he hurried down the stairs.

Once Dalton was out of sight, Charlotte glanced over toward Angel's dressing room, where Mr. Clean still stood guard. Again, a grin twitched at her lips, but trying her best to keep a straight face, she reminded herself that the man's name was Toby, not Mr. Clean. She'd have to be extra careful and remember that, lest she made a slip and embarrassed herself.

So now what? Glancing around, she weighed her options. Never one who enjoyed being idle, especially if she was on a paying job, she decided that she might as well go ahead and check out all of the other rooms on the second level while she waited for Heather to finish up with Angel.

Her ears tuned in to any noise that would indicate that Heather was once again available, Charlotte inspected each of the other rooms. With the exception of the master suite, which, like the front parlor, had been completely refurbished, the rest of the rooms looked the same as the last time she'd cleaned Bitsy's house. Too bad she'd left her supply carrier down in the pantry. Though the rooms looked the same as far as furnishings went, she had noticed that they needed a good dusting.

Maybe later, she decided, as she stepped back into the hall. Glancing at Toby, she sighed. Since there was no way she wanted to wait outside the door with Mr. Clean, she headed back toward the stairs. Besides, she'd feel silly just standing there like a bump on a log. At least she could sit on the stairs.

As she eased down on the landing and leaned against the wall, below her, doors opened and closed, and occasionally, she caught a glimpse of someone hurrying past the foot of the stairwell. Then, a voice cried, "Quiet on the set," followed by, "Cameras, action." After several moments she heard the distinct rattle of dishes and concluded that the first scene was probably being shot in the dining room.

By her estimation, at least twenty more minutes passed before Angel finally emerged from her dressing room, only this Angel didn't bear a whole lot of resemblance to the one that had entered the room earlier.

Gone were the jeans, T-shirt, and tennis shoes, and gone was the mop of flyaway hair. Instead, Angel was dressed in a standard Catholic schoolgirl's uniform and resembled the sweet, girl-next-door image that she portrayed in all of her movies.

Charlotte got to her feet just as Angel and Toby hurried past her. Neither said a word nor offered a smile, and within seconds, they both disappeared down the stairs.

"Ms. LaRue?"

Charlotte turned to see Heather standing in the doorway of the dressing room. Smiling, she said, "Please, just call me Charlotte."

"Okay." Heather motioned for Charlotte to come closer. "I only have a moment, but I wanted to fill you in on Angel's rules."

"Her rules?" Charlotte followed Heather back inside the dressing room.

Heather nodded. "Angel is a very private person," she told Charlotte, "and there are certain things that no one but Toby is allowed to touch — that's rule number one." She walked over to the chaise longue and motioned toward a small object near a throw pillow. "That's one of them."

The object turned out to be a small, well-worn stuffed animal, a bulldog wearing what appeared to be a school sweater. On the sweater, embroidered in tiny print, were the words OAKDALE BULLDOGS.

"Angel is a little superstitious and calls it her good-luck charm," Heather explained. And this is another one of her do-not-touch items." She pointed toward a framed picture that had been placed on the dressing table.

In the eight-by-ten framed picture was a young girl with an older couple, and they were standing in front of what appeared to be a small country church.

"Also," Heather continued, "Angel is very particular about her drinking water." She motioned toward the cases of bottled water. "No one touches her water supply. It's a special brand she has flown in from the Swiss Alps." She turned to face Charlotte. "Rule number two. With only the exception of certain people, no one else gets inside Angel's dressing room. Those certain people include Toby Russell, her bodyguard, of course, and Nick Franklin — when he's on good behavior, that is," she added. "There's also Andre Dubois, Angel's personal chef, Simon Clark, her manager, Max Morris, the director, and Dalton." Heather grinned. "And now you."

Yeah, me, Charlotte thought, wondering if there had been some kind of mix-up. Surely, they didn't think that she'd been hired to be Angel's personal maid. "Ah, Heather, just so there's no misunderstanding, I was told that I was being hired to keep Mrs. Duhè's house clean during the shooting."

"Oh, sure — you were — but that also includes Angel's dressing room. Oh, and there's one other person I forgot to mention — Angel's chauffeur, Benny Jackson."

Charlotte frowned in thought. She'd heard that name before.

"Is something wrong?" Heather asked.

Charlotte shook her head and gave her a brief smile. "No. It's just that the chauffeur's name sounds familiar." It was right on the cusp of her memory.

"Benny's a sweetheart, and if I remember right, he's originally from New Orleans."

Like a streak of lightning, it suddenly hit Charlotte why she knew that name. "No way," she murmured. After all, what were the odds?

"Excuse me? What did you say?"

Charlotte laughed. "Sorry, I have a bad habit of talking to myself sometimes. I was just wondering what the odds were that

58

Angel's chauffeur could be the same Benny Jackson who was once friends with my son, Hank, when they were still teenagers."

Heather shrugged. "Anything's possible."

Charlotte's eyes narrowed. "How old is this Benny Jackson?"

Heather thought a moment, then said, "I'd say he's in his early forties."

Even with Heather confirming that the chauffeur was about the right age, Charlotte still had doubts that he could be the same person she'd known. The Benny Jackson that she'd known had been a troubled teenager who had come from a family known for their run-ins with the law. Considering his family background, she'd be surprised if he hadn't ended up in prison . . . or in the graveyard.

"Well, I guess that's about it," Heather said, interrupting Charlotte's thoughts. "If you have any questions, please feel free to ask me or Dalton." She reached up and lightly smoothed her fingers over her cheek.

Ordinarily, the hand motion wouldn't have attracted Charlotte's attention, but since she'd already noticed that Heather's cheek was swollen, she figured that Heather had to be checking for more swelling. Should she say something or not? If she said something, she risked being told to mind her own business, but if she didn't say anything and something happened to Heather . . .

While Heather gathered up several beauty items and placed them in a small makeup carrier that resembled a tackle box, a battle waged within Charlotte.

"If you'll excuse me now," Heather murmured, "I should probably go down and check on Angel's makeup."

Say something. Say something now.

Charlotte took a deep breath. "Heather, before you go, I do have a question."

Heather paused and stared expectantly at Charlotte.

"How did you get that bruise?"

Heather's eyes grew wide and her hand flew up to cover her upper cheekbone. Whirling around, she leaned in close to the mirror, searching her reflection for any sign of the bruise. Seemingly satisfied, she faced Charlotte. "I have to tell you that I pride myself on being a professional makeup artist. So how did you know that I have a bruise?"

"You can cover up a bruise," Charlotte told her gently, "but not the swelling. And unfortunately, I've seen this type of thing before. Oh, you did an excellent job covering the bruise, all right, but that's not really

60

the bottom line here. The bottom line is, who's been hitting you?"

"Why would you think *anyone* has been hitting me? For all you know, I could have run into a door or something. Besides, I don't see that it's any of your business, one way or another."

"No, it probably isn't, but like I said, I've seen it before, and if you believe nothing else, please believe that nothing good comes out of an abusive relationship." Though it was possible that she was wrong, Charlotte didn't think so, especially considering Heather's defensive tone. "Heather, no one, but no one, has a right to hit you."

Heather stared at her for a moment, as if pondering what to say next; then her eyes filled with tears. "He — he doesn't m-mean to. He just has a bad temper."

Charlotte was on the verge of asking who "he" was when someone near the stairs yelled out Heather's name.

Blinking back the tears, Heather sniffed. "Coming," she yelled back. With a wary, haunted look at Charlotte, she said, "I've got to go." She took one last glance at the dressing table, then froze. "Oh, no, I completely forgot," she groaned. She picked up a black velvet jewelry box off the dressing table, hesitated, and then faced Charlotte.

61

"Could you do me a huge favor?"

"Sure, I'll try."

Heather handed Charlotte the box. "Make sure that Dalton gets this. It's the duplicate pearl necklaces for the next scene," she explained. "I was supposed to give them to Dalton earlier, but forgot." She motioned for Charlotte to follow her and headed out the door.

As they walked down the hallway toward the stairs, Heather said, "FYI, we always keep duplicates of a major prop in case they have to shoot the scene over. In the upcoming scene the necklace will be broken when Hunter yanks it off Angel during an argument. According to the script, it's a necklace that Hunter's character had given his wife, and Angel's character had taken it without his permission."

By the end of shooting that first day, Charlotte wasn't sure if she was coming or going. The only thing she knew for certain was that every bone in her body ached, and if she had to go up or down those stairs one more time, she'd have to crawl. No one had bothered to warn her that, in addition to cleaning up after everyone involved in the shooting, she would be everyone's gofer as well. It seemed like every five minutes, *someone* was yelling for her to do something.

Unlike the freezing temperature inside the house, outside the sun beat down, and the hot air was so heavy with humidity that taking a deep breath was an effort. In the time it took to walk to her van, sweat had beaded on her upper lip, and the hair at the nape of her neck was wringing wet.

Just as she clicked the remote to unlock her van, she glanced in the side mirror and saw a man approaching her from behind. Something about the man made her immediately wary and she quickly glanced around to make sure she wasn't alone.

"Excuse me, ma'am," he called out. "Could I talk to you just a minute?"

Her instincts said to ignore him, to just get inside her van, lock the doors, and go home. But was it instinct or was it just leftover fear from the frightening incident that had happened to her last October? Probably a bit of both, she decided, but unlike that other time, this man looked to be only armed with a small spiral notebook and pen instead of a gun. And instead of being caught after dark in a deserted parking lot, she was out in the broad daylight with plenty of people within hollering range.

Taking a deep breath, Charlotte turned to

face the man. "What do you want?" she asked bluntly.

"Ma'am, my name is Bruce King. I'm a writer — Angel's biographer, in fact." He laughed. "And no, I'm not related to the famous Stephen King."

Yeah, you wish, she thought, not finding his silly attempt at humor the least bit funny. "Like I said, what do you want?"

"Your name is Charlotte, isn't it? Charlotte LaRue?"

Charlotte narrowed her eyes. "And just how do you know my name?"

The smarmy man laughed again. "Like I said, I'm Angel's biographer, so I know everything about what goes on when it concerns Angel."

Charlotte bit her tongue. If he knew "everything," then why did he need to talk to her, a mere maid? And another thing, no one had mentioned anything to her about Angel having a biographer. Besides, if he were the real deal, wouldn't he have been hanging out inside the house instead of accosting the maid outside? Humph! More than likely, he was lying through his teeth and was probably one of those sleazy tabloid reporters.

"For instance," he continued, tilting his head closer as if they were about to share a secret, "I heard that Angel and Nick had a knock-down, drag-out about that new script that Simon wants her to read." He shook his head. "Poor Nick. He might be Angel's main squeeze for the moment, but Simon should know better than to think he could influence Angel by using Nick."

Main squeeze? Interesting term, she thought, but not one she'd likely use.

"So, did Angel throw anything at him this time?"

Warning bells of suspicion clanged louder in Charlotte's head. Enough was enough. "Listen, mister, Angel's relationships, good or bad, are none of my business. And they're certainly none of your business. You're no more her biographer than I'm the Queen of England."

Totally ignoring her accusation, he said, "Hey, I'm just trying to authenticate my facts here. I may be a lot of things, but I don't make up the stuff that I write. I'm a stickler for the truth."

When Charlotte narrowed her eyes accusingly and tilted her head to one side, a red flush tinged his cheeks. "Well, I am," he quickly added. "No matter what, I make sure that my *writing* is the truth, the whole truth, and nothing but the truth."

"Yeah, right." Charlotte turned away. Why

was she even listening to this goofball?

"Hey, I'll prove it!" He quickly stepped in front of her, effectively blocking her path to the van's door. "In one of Angel's recent press releases, it said that she grew up in Atlanta, Georgia." He shook his head. "Not true. I did a little research of my own, and there's no record of her ever living there. In fact, there's only five other women in the whole U.S.A. named Angel Martinique, and none of them fit our Angel's description or age."

He waved his hand. "Yeah, yeah, I know Angel is probably just a stage name, but most times, an actor's real name surfaces at some point." He shook his head. "Not this time, though, and believe me, I've been doing some digging. What I'm after is her real name. And I'd gladly pay someone — pay you — for any information that you could find out." He paused for a moment. "So, how about it?"

"How about what?" Charlotte shot back.

"How about helping me out here? See what you can find out? I'd make it worth your while."

Enough was enough. "Tell you what I will do," she said between clenched teeth. "If you move out of my way and leave now, I won't call those security guards over there."

She motioned to where two of the guards were standing near the roadblocks. "But!" She pointed at him with her forefinger. "One more word and I'll start screaming my head off." He opened his mouth, but she shook her head. "Not a word! Now get out of here before I lose the little patience I have left."

To give the man credit, after only a brief moment he threw up his hands in surrender and backed off.

Charlotte quickly loaded up her supply carrier, got inside the van, and hit the automatic door lock mechanism. As she drove away, she glanced in the rearview mirror. The man hadn't moved. He was still standing where she'd left him.

Though traffic wasn't light, it wasn't bumper-to-bumper either. The first thing that Charlotte noticed when she pulled into her driveway was Louis standing on the front porch. The next thing she noticed was his suitcase beside the post nearest the steps. Another trip? So soon?

She slid out of the van and, pasting a smile on her face, headed for the steps. "Going somewhere?"

Louis nodded. "Yeah, but I didn't want to leave without letting you know."

Since when did he feel that he had to check in and out with her before he went somewhere? She certainly didn't feel that way. Besides, he could have left a note.

Charlotte trudged up the steps and winced as each step sent a sharp pain through her knee.

"What's wrong?"

"Nothing that a couple of Tylenol and a soak in a tub of hot water won't cure. Too much climbing stairs today." Not one to complain to others, Charlotte changed the subject. "So, where to this time?" She motioned at the suitcase, then walked over and unlocked her front door.

"Back to Houston. For several days this time."

Still wondering why he thought he had to wait for her, she faced him and nodded. "Well, have a good trip." She twisted the doorknob and pushed open the door.

"Wait up a minute, Charlotte."

Hesitating a moment and getting more irritated by the second, she finally pulled the door closed and faced him again. "What?"

Several seconds passed, and still he said nothing.

"Look, I've had a long day and I'm tired, so please, whatever it is, just spit it out."

"We need to talk. Have a serious talk," he

emphasized.

"So, talk, for Pete's sake."

He shook his head. "Not here and not now. I have to get on the road and I can see that you're in no mood to listen. But when I get back —"

"Okay. Fine. When you get back, we'll talk. Now, may I go inside?"

For an answer, Louis waved his hand, then picked up his suitcase. Unlike the last time he'd left, she didn't wait around, nor did he try to kiss her.

"Fine with me," she grumbled as she locked the front door behind her. "Everything's just peachy."

Only later that night, once she was in bed, did she wonder what in the world he'd meant by "serious."

CHAPTER 3

Early on Tuesday morning, Charlotte headed up the staircase at Bitsy's house. In her hand was a sheaf of papers that had script changes that she'd been told to give Angel. Halfway up the stairs she froze as the sudden sounds of screaming and cursing spiraled down. Angel's voice, easily recognizable, screaming accusations. And a man's voice yelling back. Possibly Nick, the boyfriend?

Charlotte winced; if ears could really burn from hearing profanity, hers would be smoldering stubs for sure.

What to do? What to do? She glanced down the staircase to the first floor where people were scurrying about. The only sign that anyone else was even paying attention was the occasional furtive look cast upward where she was standing.

Wasn't anybody going to do anything?

Guess not, she finally decided, but somebody needed to do something. From the sound of things, the argument was escalating fast.

With a resigned sigh and a shake of her head, she trudged up the stairs. If they were still going at it by the time she reached the second floor, then she'd . . .

What? Just what do you think you can do? Besides, it's none of your business.

Momentarily ignoring the voice of reason in her head, she kept climbing the stairs. At the second-floor landing, she froze again. Just down the hallway, standing outside the door to Angel's dressing room, was her bodyguard, Toby, Mr. Clean himself, his arms crossed and a bored look on his stoic face.

For Pete's sake, why was he just standing there? Of all people, shouldn't he be doing something? Wasn't his job to protect Angel?

Charlotte's hand tightened around the script. More to the point at the moment, what should she do?

Say something to Toby. Demand he do something.

Suddenly, there was a loud crash. Without warning, a stiletto-heeled sandal sailed through the doorway, followed by a second one. With a clunk, the first shoe hit the wall opposite the doorway and bounced back, the spiky heel coming within just inches of Toby's head. With lightning reflexes, Toby threw up his hand and caught the second one the moment it bounced off the wall. For a moment he stared at the shoe; then abruptly, quick as a wink, he turned and disappeared through the doorway.

Within seconds, the cursing stopped, and except for a distinctly male groan of pain, no other sounds came from the room. Moments later, Toby, towering over Nick, shoved the smaller man through the doorway into the hall.

Charlotte swallowed hard. With one meaty hand, Toby had Nick's arm twisted up behind his back and with his other hand he had a firm grip on Nick's shoulder.

His expression dark and angry, Nick spat out a profanity. "You're breaking my arm."

Toby's eyes narrowed and in a deep, gravelly voice edged with steel, he said, "Shut your filthy mouth or I'll break more than just your arm." As if to emphasize his point, he jerked Nick's arm even higher.

"Okay, okay," Nick cried out. "Ease up, man."

With a satisfied nod, Toby told him to "Move it" and marched him down the hallway toward the staircase. "This time I want you off the property."

They were headed right toward Charlotte, and she had nowhere to go to get out of the way, so she plastered herself against the wall. Afraid that any minute Nick would break free and there would be a brawl, she didn't dare move a muscle until the two men passed her. Only when they'd disappeared down the staircase did she remember to breathe again.

Charlotte glanced down at the script in her hand. Now what? Should she still take it to Angel?

Almost as if Angel had read her thoughts, Charlotte heard her yell, "Where is that maid? Get her in here now! And find Max. Tell him to get up here."

Within seconds, Heather Cortez appeared in the dressing room doorway. Up until that moment, it had never occurred to Charlotte that there might be someone else in the room during the brawl between Angel and Nick.

"Oh, Charlotte, there you are, thank goodness," Heather said as she hurried toward her. "Angel wants to see you." A momentary look of discomfort crossed her pale face. "But I guess you heard her, huh?"

When Charlotte nodded, Heather managed a tremulous smile in response, and Charlotte couldn't help noticing that

Heather's eye didn't look quite as puffy as it had the day before.

"I have to find Max," Heather continued. "He's the director. I'll be right back, though." With that, she brushed past Charlotte and hurried down the stairs.

Figuring there was only one reason that Angel would ask to see "that maid," Charlotte took a deep breath and let it out slowly. Finally, squaring her shoulders and reminding herself that Angel was not the devil incarnate, but simply a spoiled brat, she headed for the dressing room doorway.

When she entered the room, at first Charlotte didn't notice Angel for the clutter that seemed to cover every inch of the floor. Evidently, the shoes weren't the only items she'd thrown during her temper tantrum. The room bore no resemblance to how Charlotte had left it the day before and was a total mess. Then she spied Angel. The young woman was half hidden behind a rack of clothes and standing as still as a statue as she stared out of the window.

Charlotte cleared her throat. "You wanted to see me?"

At first Angel didn't respond. When she did finally turn to face Charlotte, her face reflected the ravages of her tantrum. In a clipped, impatient tone, she said, "Clean up this mess, and when Max gets here, tell him I'm in the master bedroom."

Charlotte nodded. "Okay. One thing, though. I was told to give you this." She held out the script. "They said that some changes had been made."

Anger flashed in Angel's eyes. Without a word, and without a thank-you or kiss my butt, she snatched the script from Charlotte and stomped out of the room.

Seconds later, Charlotte heard a bedroom door down the hallway slam shut. "Brat," she muttered as she picked her way through the mess on the floor. Once she had most of the clutter put back where it belonged, she removed the liner from the wastebasket and left to take it to the outside garbage receptacle.

On the way down the staircase, Charlotte met a wiry, bald-headed man who was on his way up. She paused. "Ah, excuse me. Are you Max, the director?" When the man nodded, she said, "I'm Charlotte, the maid."

"Yeah, I know who you are. What do you want? I'm in sort of a hurry right now."

"Sure, but Angel asked me to tell you that she would be waiting in the master bedroom."

Max rolled his eyes. "Great. Just wonderful," he responded, his voice heavy with sarcasm, as he brushed past her and continued up the stairs.

Outside the kitchen door, Charlotte deposited the trash bag into the garbage receptacle. When she turned to reenter the house, out of the corner of her eye she caught sight of Nick and Toby on the front edge of the property. Though she couldn't hear what Toby was telling Nick, she knew from the fierce expression on his face and the way he was poking Nick in the chest with his forefinger, whatever he was saying couldn't be good.

"Mutt and Jeff," she murmured. Though Nick was well built, Toby towered over him. But then Toby towered over most people.

Just as she made up her mind to go back inside, Nick suddenly drew back his fist and Charlotte froze. In a move quick as lightning, Toby grabbed Nick's fist, twisted him around, and brought him to his knees. Out of nowhere, two security guards suddenly appeared just as Toby drew back his hand to deliver what Charlotte could only speculate was a karate chop. Each security guard grabbed an arm and pulled Toby off Nick. Then the larger of the two men stepped in front of Toby and said something to him. Whatever he'd said must have worked, because with one last glare at Nick, Toby did an about-face and headed for the house. Then the security guards took hold of Nick's arms and escorted him all the way to his car.

Would this day never end?

It was only barely noon, but Charlotte's legs ached and she felt like groaning out loud as she walked down the steps of the back porch and headed for the food tent. Though she suspected that most of her aches and pains were the result of so many trips up and down the stairs doing Angel's bidding, she feared that she could be coming down with a summer cold or the flu.

Charlotte eyed the outside of the completely enclosed white tent that had been assembled at the back of Bitsy's property. Dalton had told her there would be a catered lunch buffet for the crew and that she was to feel free to help herself.

Unsure exactly what to expect, she stepped through the flaps that served as the door to the tent, and a blast of blessedly cool air hit her. Air-conditioning? In a tent? Impressive.

Glancing around, she saw that there was a long buffet table at one end of the tent for the food, while several smaller tables and chairs had been placed in the remaining space. The whole thing almost resembled a small restaurant.

By the time that Charlotte had filled her plate and selected a bottle of water from the small tub full of various types of iced-down drinks, all of the tables and chairs were occupied.

The only other shade in the backyard was beneath the back portico of Bitsy's house. In addition to the shade, there was also a fan on the ceiling of the porch. Charlotte climbed the steps. Though tempted to sit at the top of the steps, she decided that sitting off to the side was more practical, especially with people coming in and out of the house. Selecting a spot on the edge of the porch near a column, she put her food and drink down first. Then, with a groan, she lowered herself to the floor of the porch and dangled her legs off the side.

She had just settled in to eat when she noticed a man walking toward her. A frown knotted her forehead. The tall, middle-aged man was wearing a short-sleeved white shirt and black dress pants and he looked vaguely familiar. Over the past two days, she'd met a lot of the movie people, but she didn't remember him being one of them. So where had she seen him before?

Probably someone she'd met somewhere

else, she decided.

"Mind if I sit with you?" he asked, a hint of a smile on his lips.

Charlotte shrugged. "Not at all. And by the way, my name is Charlotte — Charlotte LaRue."

The man's smile grew wider, showing a mouthful of white, perfectly straight teeth. "Oh, I know who you are, and you know me. You just don't recognize me, do you?"

Charlotte felt heat flood her face. "You do look familiar," she admitted. When he busied himself settling down next to her and didn't say anything, she finally said, "Well? Are you going to tell me who you are or keep me guessing all afternoon?"

The man laughed as if she'd just told the funniest joke he'd ever heard. "I'm tempted to keep you guessing, but a really nice lady once told me that it's not nice to tease your elders."

"Humph, sounds like something I would say."

"Oh, does it, now?" He chuckled. "Hmm, maybe I'll give you a hint first. How's my old friend Hank been doing? And do you still make a red velvet cake for Hank on his birthday each year?"

"Benny? Benny Jackson!"

"Yes, ma'am."

So it was true. The Benny Jackson that was Angel's chauffeur *was* the same Benny Jackson that was once Hank's best friend when they were young teenagers.

Again Charlotte felt her face flush with embarrassment. "Oh, Benny, I'm so sorry that I didn't recognize you right away."

Benny laughed. "After the misery Hank and I put you through, you probably wanted to just forget that I ever existed."

"Yes, well, there was that — the misery part. The both of you together were certainly a handful."

Benny grinned. "Yeah, back then I was trouble with a capital T. I never told you this, and I'm glad I finally have the opportunity to do so, but I have you to thank for finally getting me on the straight and narrow. If it hadn't been for your influence in my life back then, I'd probably have ended up in jail."

Stunned and momentarily speechless, Charlotte swallowed the sudden knot of emotion growing in her throat.

"When I think back to all the sh— oops, sorry, I mean *stuff* I was doing — it was a wonder that you let me in the front door at all." Benny winked. "See, I still remember all those tongue-lashings you gave me about using proper language, especially around ladies."

Charlotte smiled and Benny paused to take a bite of the fried chicken leg on his plate. "You're really looking good, Benny," she told him. "As for Hank, he became a doctor — a surgeon. He and his wife have a set of eight-month-old twins, a boy and a girl."

"I'd heard he was some hotshot doctor but didn't know about the twins."

Charlotte grinned proudly. "Yep, I'm a grandma — finally. But listen, I know Hank would love to see you. Give him a call, why don't you? But that's enough about Hank for now. I want to know all about you."

"Well, I'm no doctor, that's for sure. But I did finally graduate from high school, even if it was by the skin of my teeth. And by the way, that's another thing I have you to thank for. All those lectures you gave me about not letting my circumstances dictate my future sank in."

Again, Charlotte choked up. Unable to look him in the eye, she lowered her gaze to stare at her plate of untouched food. She had wanted to help Benny, had tried to help him for a while, but the influence of his background and his sordidly dysfunctional family had been more than she was prepared to handle. With the exception of Benny, most of his family were alcoholics and drug addicts — people willing to sell their own son, along with their souls, for their next fix. It had all come to a head the day that Benny's mother showed up on her doorstep and demanded to know why Benny hadn't made the "drop" earlier that day. Charlotte had ended up having to threaten the drugged-up woman with the police to get her to leave. Even now, so many years later, she still felt guilty over that period of her life and the choices she'd made concerning Benny.

"Now, Miss Charlotte." Benny reached out and patted her hand. "I know that look. Don't you go feeling all guilty about none of that stuff. That's in the past. I don't blame you for running my butt off. Oh, I'll admit that I was plenty hot about it way back then, but not anymore. I lead a different kind of life now."

Benny motioned toward the untouched food on her plate. "You better eat up. If I know Angel, she'll be yelling for both of us once she finishes her lunch."

Charlotte nodded and forked up a bite of the chicken and andouille jambalaya. Fork midair between her plate and her mouth, she asked, "So, how did you end up as

Angel's chauffeur?" While Benny talked, Charlotte savored each bite of the delicious jambalaya.

"I knew if I was going to make anything of myself, I had to get out of this place," Benny told her. "Had to get away from my family. So, bright and early on the morning after I graduated, way before anyone was awake, I left town and headed for California."

Though Charlotte wondered how Benny had gotten enough money to go all the way to California, she decided, given Benny's background, it was probably best not to ask.

"I ended up in Hollywood," he continued. "Took on odd jobs here and there. Even did a little panhandling for several years just to keep a roof over my head, until I finally landed a regular job waiting tables at a really nice restaurant. I'd worked at the restaurant about a year when Angel got hired to be one of the restaurant's hostesses. With both of us being from the South and neither of us knowing anyone, we became friends. Back then, Angel was a wannabe actress trying to catch a break, and I had decided to save up enough money so that I could start taking classes at a junior college."

Benny's eyes took on a faraway look. "Those were some lean times for both of

83

us, but we hung in there. Angel did finally get her big break and I enrolled in some night classes. I'd always been pretty good with numbers and fancied myself being a CPA." He laughed. "Of course that didn't last long. Once Angel hit it big, she talked me into taking the job as her chauffeur. As the old saying goes, she made me an offer I couldn't refuse. I figured if the gig with Angel didn't work out, I could always go back to school. But — as you can see — it did work out."

Charlotte scraped the last bit of jambalaya onto her fork. All of Benny's talk about Angel's success made her think about the incident with Bruce King. "Speaking of Angel, what can you tell me about a man named Bruce King?"

Benny made a sound of disgust. "Nothing good, I'll assure you. Bruce King is a lying, low-life paparazzo who's been dogging Angel's footsteps since she made it big. Angel took out a restraining order and has had him thrown in jail a couple of times for violating it." Benny shrugged. "But all that does is egg him on. It seems his main goal in life is to dig up dirt on Angel, whether it exists or not. That lunatic is obsessed with her." He narrowed his eyes and tilted his head. "So, why did you ask about him?" He suddenly threw up his hand, palm out. "No, don't tell me. Let me guess. He just happened to be hanging around when you left yesterday."

When Charlotte nodded, Benny said, "So, what did he want?"

While Charlotte told Benny about her run-in with Bruce King, Benny finished eating. "Among other things," she said, almost finished with her tale, "he wanted me — wanted to *pay* me — to find out what Angel's real name is."

At that, Benny grinned. "Only a handful of people know her real roots and her real name, and none of them are telling. It's all part of Angel's image mystique, and besides, those who do know value their jobs too much to tell. The beauty of it is that without her real name or her Social Security number, there's no way King can find out anything about who she really is."

At that moment, a noise like a dog barking came from Benny's pants pocket. "Oops, speaking of the boss lady, I've got to run." At the look on Charlotte's face, he laughed. "The barking dog ring tone is an inside joke between Angel and me." He got to his feet, then helped Charlotte up off the porch floor. "I'll alert Security about Bruce King, but if you see him coming, go the other way.

Don't talk to him, but report him to either Toby or one of the Security crew."

Again, the barking noise came from Benny's pocket. "Gotta run now, but I'll talk to you later." He tossed his paper plate into the trash can and disappeared inside the house.

With a sigh, Charlotte dropped her paper plate and empty bottle into the trash, and she also headed back inside. The moment she entered the kitchen, she stopped in her tracks. Across the room, trapped in the corner by Angel's manager, Simon Clark, was Nick Franklin. Since earlier she'd witnessed Nick being escorted off the property with her own two eyes, she couldn't help wondering why he was back. How had he gotten past the security guards?

Not your problem. None of your business.

Doesn't matter, she silently argued with the irritating voice in her head. *No one ever pays attention to the maid anyway.*

Just keep walking, Charlotte.

For once, Charlotte decided to listen to the irritating voice, but even from clear across the room, there was no way she could miss the furious look on Simon's face, nor his aggressive stance. So, how many more people was Nick going to tick off before someone finally put him off the property permanently?

Charlotte was almost to the other door when out of the corner of her eye she saw Simon hold up a sheaf of papers and wave them in Nick's face.

"I've warned you before to stop bringing in this trash," Simon ranted, his voice growing louder with each word. Then, as if to emphasize his words, Simon stepped over to a nearby garbage can, lifted the lid, and shoved the papers inside. Immediately whirling back around to face Nick, he pointed an imperious forefinger at him. "Your little stunt this morning cost half a day of shooting. If I ever — *ever* catch you bringing Angel any more scripts, I'll make you wish you'd never been born." Then he yelled, "Security! I need someone from Security!"

Charlotte hurried through the door and into the dining area, where she was met by two security guards that rushed past her. "Oh, brother," she muttered. What was it going to take for Nick to get the message?

CHAPTER 4

Thanks to Nick and Angel's fight, shooting had been delayed, so it was almost six that evening before Dalton finally told Charlotte that she could leave. Gossip had it that Angel had been too distraught to shoot at the scheduled time and had needed some "alone time" to rid herself of all the bad vibes. Personally, Charlotte thought it was all a bunch of hooey. For Pete's sake, the woman was supposed to be an actress, wasn't she?

Charlotte gathered her stuff from the kitchen pantry and headed for the front door. The moment she stepped out onto Bitsy's front porch, a dark-haired woman dressed in a Lagniappe Security uniform approached her. Though she'd never really thought about it, Charlotte hadn't realized that Lagniappe hired women as well as men to be security guards, especially women who looked like this one.

The young woman was in her early-to-mid thirties, just a bit taller than Charlotte, and probably didn't weigh over 120 soaking wet. But even aside from her size, she had the face of an angel and didn't look tough enough to hurt a fly. Still, if there was one thing that Charlotte had learned over the years, looks could be deceiving.

"Ms. LaRue?" the woman said.

Charlotte nodded.

"Ma'am, my name is Samantha O'Reilly, and I have instructions to escort you to your van and watch you until you vacate the property."

"Vacate the property" had an ominous sound to it. *Uh-oh, am I being fired?* When Charlotte finally found her voice, she asked, "Did I do something wrong?"

"Oh, no, ma'am — nothing like that," the younger woman reassured her. "Mr. Jackson said that you were accosted yesterday by a reporter and he doesn't want you to be bothered by the man again. Besides, Louis would have my hide if anything happened to you."

Even as relief washed over Charlotte, it took a moment for what Samantha had said about Louis to finally sink in. Never mind that she hadn't been too crazy about the job to begin with; she still didn't want to be fired. Besides, it paid really well and was a nice break from her normal routine.

"So, you know Louis, huh?"

"Oh, yes, ma'am. It was because of his recommendation that I was hired last year."

Though Charlotte smiled at the young woman, her smile hid her thoughts. What on earth was Louis thinking, recommending this young woman for such a dangerous job? Why, she wasn't as big as a minute. Still . . . Louis would never recommend someone if he — or she — weren't qualified.

"So, are you ready to leave, ma'am?"

Reminding herself that what Louis did or didn't do, as long as he kept out of her business, was none of her concern anyway, Charlotte sighed, and then nodded. "Yes," she answered. "Yes, I am. It's been a long day for me. And by the way, I happen to be really partial to the name Samantha. I have a little granddaughter whose name is Samantha too."

At home, Charlotte was tempted to go ahead and change into her pajamas. "Probably should eat a bite first," she told Sweety Boy as she locked her front door and placed her purse on a nearby table.

Sweety Boy squawked, "Miss you, miss

90

you," as he sidled from one side of the cage to the other.

Knowing that his antics were his way to get her attention, Charlotte grinned and stepped over to the little bird's cage. "I missed you too, you little scamp." She took a moment to rub his head with her forefinger. "I know you'd like to get out and stretch your wings, but not tonight, Boy. Sorry."

In the kitchen, Charlotte decided to fix herself a sandwich for supper out of some leftover chicken salad. Considering the large lunch she'd had, a sandwich and a glass of milk would be plenty. She had just smeared the chicken salad on a slice of bread when she heard a loud knock at the front door.

"Who on earth?" she murmured, quickly wiping her hands on a dish towel, then hurrying to the living room. When she peeped out the front window she saw a man in a uniform standing on the porch, and in his hands was a vase of beautiful spring flowers. Looking past the man, she saw a smaller van parked behind her van. On the driver's door was the logo of a florist shop that she recognized as being local.

Shaking her head and with a frown of curiosity, Charlotte unlocked the door.

"Ms. Charlotte LaRue?" the man asked.

When Charlotte nodded, he handed her the vase of flowers. "Have a nice evening, ma'am." He backed away, gave her a smile and a two-fingered salute, then hurried down the steps.

Juggling the vase of flowers, Charlotte closed and locked the door. "Now, who in the world is sending me flowers?" she murmured. "And why?" It wasn't her birthday, she hadn't been ill, and it wasn't Mother's Day. Louis? "Not likely," she whispered as she set the vase down on the coffee table and searched for a card.

When she found the small envelope and opened it, all that was on the card inside was a single sentence: I'M A LITTLE LATE, BUT THANKS.

"Hmm, no signature. That's strange. And thanks for what?" She guessed she could always call the florist and find out who sent the bouquet. Yep, that's what she'd do, but she'd do it tomorrow. For now, though, all she wanted was a bite to eat and a good night's sleep.

According to local weather reports, Wednesday morning would be overcast, offering a small measure of relief from the heat. Although scattered thunderstorms were predicted throughout the day, on the tropical front, so far, so good. There were no signs of tropical storms or hurricanes in the Atlantic or the Gulf.

Just as Charlotte parked the van, fat raindrops began to fall, and distant thunder rumbled. By the time she'd unloaded her supply carrier and reached Bitsy's front porch, the raindrops had turned into a downpour.

Standing on the porch was Samantha O'Reilly, her arms crossed against her breasts. "Good morning, Ms. LaRue," she called out.

"Good morning to you too, Samantha. And please, just call me Charlotte." Charlotte set down the supply carrier, then shook her umbrella, folded it, and then slipped it back inside its plastic casing. Though there were a few members of the crew huddled together on the porch, there were far fewer people scurrying around than during the previous two days.

Samantha walked over to where Charlotte was standing. "Tell you what," she said. "Most of my friends call me Sam. So how about if I call you Charlotte, and you call me Sam?"

Charlotte nodded and gave Samantha a warm smile. "It's a deal." Then she motioned at the group standing near the end of the porch. "Where is everyone?"

"Big meeting in the front parlor," Sam explained. "Every other day or so, they call everyone together for a status report." She glanced away and scanned the parking area. "No sign of Bruce King, huh?"

Charlotte shook her head. "Nope. Haven't seen hide nor hair of him and hope I don't."

"Oh, he's lurking around, somewhere. You can bet on it. Bottom feeders like him aren't that easy to get rid of." Sam sighed. "Now that you're safe and sound, I've got to make my rounds. If I'm not here on the porch when you're done, just wait for me before you take off for your van. See you this afternoon."

Again, Charlotte smiled. Then her smile faded as it suddenly occurred to her that Samantha had been standing vigil, waiting for her to arrive. "Humph, my own personal security guard." Thanks to Benny, or should that be thanks to Louis? Knowing that she'd only get annoyed if the answer were Louis, she decided that she didn't want to know. With a shake of her head, she picked up the supply carrier and headed inside the house.

When she passed the entrance to the front parlor, the door was shut but she could still hear a faint murmur of voices coming through from the other side. A "big meeting," Samantha had said.

With a shrug, she headed for the kitchen. Since there was no one around to give her instructions, once she had stashed her purse inside the kitchen pantry, she decided to help herself to a cup of coffee. While she drank her coffee and stared out the window at the pouring rain, she made up her mind that today she'd start cleaning upstairs first. Though she had left it all pretty clean before she'd gone home, she figured it wouldn't hurt to give it a light cleaning again. Doing something was better than standing around doing nothing, and surely by the time she was done, the big meeting would be over.

In the habit of doing a walk-through before cleaning a house, Charlotte left her supply carrier near the top of the stairs and started down the hall with the master bedroom. While making mental notes as to what she needed to do, she thought she heard a noise, like the creak of a stair step. Going stone-still, she listened.

"Old houses, like people, creak with age," she murmured, dismissing the sound.

After finishing her inspection of the master bedroom, she moved down the hallway and inspected the other rooms as well.

A few minutes later, she stood outside the last room, the guest bedroom that had been converted into Angel's dressing room. Since the door was closed, Charlotte knocked lightly and waited a moment, just in case Angel was inside dressing. Just for good measure, she knocked again, a bit louder. Satisfied that no one was in the room, she opened the door. The first thing she noticed was that the room was in shambles again, only much, much worse than the previous day. The next thing she noticed was the smell. It was an odor she'd smelled before, one that was hard to forget.

The odor of blood and death.

A shiver of foreboding ran down her spine and her knees went weak.

"It's just my imagination, just my imagination," she chanted softly in an attempt to work up enough courage to enter the room. "There's nothing wrong, just my imagination." Finally, taking a deep breath, she stepped just inside the doorway. And she froze in place.

Just beyond the dressing table, lying on the floor, was a body. She recognized the man immediately. He was on his back, dead eyes staring up at the ceiling. Though most of the blood looked as if the rug had soaked it up, there was no mistaking the dark stains that spread out from his upper body.

Charlotte choked back a scream and her

knees went weak. Beneath her breasts, her heart pounded like a jackhammer. "Oh, dear Lord in heaven," she cried, grabbing the door frame for support.

Torn between screaming for help and checking out the person on the floor, just in case he was still breathing, she stared at the bloodstained rug. That's when she finally noticed the letter opener on the floor beside the body. From the looks of it, she figured that, more than likely, it was what he'd been killed with. For some reason, seeing it reminded her of the many times that her police detective niece, Judith, had complained about well-meaning people messing up a crime scene. Still, what if he was still alive or simply needed CPR?

Though it was the last thing she wanted to do, Charlotte forced herself to stare at him hard a moment more. Along with his open dead eyes, there was no movement around his chest area that would indicate he was still breathing. But unwillingly, her gaze kept returning again and again to the murder weapon.

What was it about the letter opener? She wrinkled her brow. Then she remembered. Unless she was mistaken, and she was pretty sure she wasn't, the murder weapon looked like the exact same letter opener that Angel had used in the final scene that had been shot the previous day.

She'd first noticed the ornate silver letter opener when she'd dusted the library. She'd mostly noticed it because she couldn't recall Bitsy ever owning one like it. When she'd mentioned it to Heather, the young woman had explained that it was one of the props. In the next scene to be shot, Angel's character was supposed to grab the letter opener off the desk and stab an intruder.

A cold feeling of dread settled in Charlotte's stomach.

Angel.

Would the police find the actress's fingerprints on the letter opener? Angel was known for her outbursts of anger. Was it possible that in a fit of anger the young woman had stabbed Nick, a case of real life imitating fiction?

"Surely not," she whispered. Surely Angel wouldn't be that stupid. Shoving the speculations to the back of her mind, Charlotte stared once more at the man's eyes, eyes fixed in that eerie death stare. With a shaky sigh, she finally decided that the man was dead, had to be, so there would be no use for her tromping through the crime scene.

She stepped back out into the hallway and pulled the door firmly closed.

Call the police. Do it now.

She automatically reached inside her apron pocket. No phone. "Great," she muttered as she realized that she'd left her cell phone in her purse downstairs. What to do, what to do?

Go get the security guards.

"Good idea," she murmured. Obeying the silent voice of reason, she turned and walked quickly down the hallway. "In fact, excellent idea." For her own sake, it would be much better if one of the security guards phoned the police anyway, especially considering the hassle she'd gone through when she'd reported Joyce Thibodeaux's murder. The last thing she wanted was to call attention to herself again.

Snagging her supply carrier where she'd left it, she hurried down the stairs. When she reached the bottom floor, she set it down beside the staircase, and glanced around frantically for someone, anyone, to help. Since the parlor door was still shut, all she could do was assume that the meeting was still in progress. No way was she going in there. The security people could make that announcement . . . if only she could find one of them. So where were they? Maybe outside on the front porch . . . or in the parking area, for sure.

Just as she reached for the doorknob, the front entry door swung open, causing her to almost collide with Samantha O'Reilly.

"Whoa, hey, Charlotte, slow down."

Charlotte grabbed hold of Samantha's arm. "Up — upstairs, in Angel's dressing room."

"Just calm down," Samantha soothed. "Calm down."

Charlotte shook her head. "No — you don't understand. You — you need to — to call the police. There's been a murder."

CHAPTER 5

"A murder? Who's been murdered?"

"Nick — Nick Franklin, Angel's boy-friend."

Samantha still didn't look convinced. "Okay, take it one step at a time and tell me what you know."

Growing more impatient with each passing moment, Charlotte shook her head. "For Pete's sake, *please* just go upstairs and see for yourself."

Samantha threw up her hands in mock surrender. "Okay, okay — but you wait right here."

After that, time seemed to stand still as Charlotte waited for Samantha to return. When she did finally return, time suddenly seemed to speed up at an alarming rate.

The security guard was talking on a cell phone as she descended the stairs and crossed over to the parlor door. Though she gave a confirmation nod to Charlotte, she continued talking as she headed straight into the parlor.

After several long seconds, an ear-piercing scream split the silence, followed by sobs of hysteria. Though Charlotte wasn't sure, she thought the scream had come from Angel. As if the scream had been the impetus, sudden chaos broke out. Shouts of disbelief followed and voices buzzed as the news spread. Then, above the noise in the parlor, the sound of wailing sirens reached Charlotte's ears.

The moment the police arrived, the whole scene was all too familiar: the uniformed officers, the detectives, the crime scene crew, and last, but never least, the news media. Just before she was herded into the front parlor with everyone else, Charlotte caught a glimpse of the multitude of reporters hovering behind the guardrails that had been erected around the perimeters of the house. It never ceased to amaze her how they found out things so fast. She slowly shook her head as she searched for an empty seat in the parlor. A pack of wolves, that's what they were. They were like a pack of ravenous wolves hungry for any juicy tidbit tossed their way.

Charlotte had just claimed an empty chair when she saw Angel, supported on either side by Heather and Toby, being escorted out of the parlor. Though the young actress had stopped crying, her face was as pale as the white walls of the parlor.

Several moments after Angel left, two homicide detectives entered the room. Charlotte swallowed hard when she recognized one of the detectives. Even worse, he spotted her almost immediately and headed straight for her.

Charlotte stretched her neck first to one side, then to the other to ease the tension she felt building in her neck muscles. Just the sight of Detective Gavin Brown stirred up unwanted memories, more specifically, her last run-in with him.

"Oh, great," she murmured as the detective approached her. "Just great."

From the expression on the detective's face, this time wasn't going to be any better than the last time that she'd butted heads with him because of a murder.

When he stopped in front of her, he glared down at her and gave her a nasty grin. "Well, well, well, we meet again, Ms. LaRue. Why am I not surprised to find you at the scene of yet another murder? Like I've said before, seems to me that you have a knack for being in the wrong place at the wrong time."

The words he used were the exact same words he'd said the last time they'd met. So, if he knew that he'd said the same thing before, why repeat it? Never mind that he was right. But just like that other time, this time wasn't *her* fault either.

"Jerk," she muttered without moving her lips.

"What was that?" he retorted, his eyes narrowing suspiciously. "What did you just say?"

Mortified that she'd spoken the word out loud, she blurted out the first thing that came to mind. "I said *work*. I'm working here."

Liar, liar, pants on fire.

Her cheeks burned from the telltale heat of the lie that she'd just told. She could always hope that he wouldn't notice or maybe he'd chalk it up to the hot flashes of an aging woman.

With a grimace, Charlotte waved her hand in front of her face, as if fanning herself. "My goodness, is it hot in here or is it just me?"

Wrong thing to do and say. From the amused look on the detective's face, he wasn't buying her act. But so what? Even if he knew that she was lying, knew that she'd just called him a jerk, what was he going to do, arrest her for calling him names? Not likely. After all, he had bigger fish to fry than her; namely, he had a murderer to catch.

From now on, keep your mouth shut. Only speak when spoken to. Only answer his questions. Nothing else.

Having dealt with the detective before, she'd known better than to antagonize him. She also knew that she should listen to her inner voice of caution and keep her sarcastic comments to herself. Never mind that the irritating detective had a way about him of getting on her very last nerve.

Gavin Brown was still staring a hole through her as if trying to decide what to say next. Then, clearing his throat, he said, "I understand that you were the one who found the body." When Charlotte nodded, he crooked his forefinger. "Come with me."

Charlotte stood and, dragging her feet with dread, followed the detective back to the kitchen.

He motioned at a chair near the breakfast table. "Have a seat." While she seated herself, he removed a small notebook and pen from his jacket pocket. "Now — tell me again what you're doing here."

"Cleaning," Charlotte told him. "Mrs. Bitsy Duhè, the owner of the house, is one of my regular clients. When she was approached by the production company about them using her house for the movie, Bitsy asked them to hire me to watch over her stuff while they shot the movie scenes."

"Spell her name for me."

Charlotte slowly spelled out Bitsy's name while the detective wrote in his notebook. "You might recall that Mrs. Duhè's husband was once mayor before he passed away," she offered.

Gavin Brown gave her a blank look. "Mayor?"

"You know — the mayor of New Orleans."

The detective shook his head. "Must have been before my time." As if dismissing the subject as unimportant, he said, "So, where is Mrs. Duhè right now?" he asked.

"Mrs. Duhè is staying at the Monteleone in the Quarter."

Charlotte suddenly groaned. "Oh, no." Only at that moment did it register that someone would have to call Bitsy and let her know what had happened. *Probably me,* she thought, unless Bitsy saw it on the news before she could make that call. Dear Lord in heaven, Bitsy would have a conniption.

" 'Oh, no' what?" the detective retorted.

"Someone needs to call Mrs. Duhè right away, before she hears it on the noonday news. She's an elderly lady," Charlotte hastened to explain, "and it would really upset her to hear it like that. Would it be okay if I called her?"

He shook his head. "No one is calling anyone until we finish our questioning. As for the media, all they know is that there has been a murder."

"But don't you see?" she argued. "That's my point exactly. It would really upset Bitsy to suddenly see her house on the noon news and hear that there's been a murder."

At first she didn't think he was going to relent, but after a moment, he finally said, "Okay. After my interview with you, you can phone her. But only tell her the bare facts. No details such as the victim's name, et cetera."

"Thank you."

He sighed heavily. "Okay, now where were we?" He glanced down at his notes. "So, when did you start working here?"

"This is my third day."

"I need to know exactly what happened this morning when you got to work."

Charlotte nodded, and while he took notes, she told him everything she'd done, beginning from the time she parked the van until her grisly discovery.

"Okay," he said, glancing up from his notebook. "Now I need you to tell me what you know about the victim — and don't try denying it. You and I both know that you hear things and see things."

Since she wasn't sure whether he'd just given her a back-handed compliment or was accusing her of being a snoop, she tried not to dwell on either possibility and concentrated on keeping her temper in check. "All I know is that he's supposedly Angel Martinique's boyfriend." That wasn't all she knew, not exactly, but the rest was just . . . Just what? Gossip? Of course there was also the little piece of information about Angel's connection to the alleged murder weapon. So why not tell him everything?

Before she had time to think of a valid, logical reason why she should or shouldn't share the rest of what she knew, he said, "Have you noticed anything else, such as the victim arguing with anyone or having confrontations with anyone?"

Oh, boy, she thought. She really didn't want to outright lie to him, but hated being a snitch. Still, given the circumstances, she didn't have a choice, did she? So, where to begin? And just how much should she tell him?

Just tell the truth, the whole truth, and nothing but the truth.

Okay, okay. "First of all, I want you to

108

know that I'm not comfortable talking about my clients."

"Didn't you say that you were hired by the production company?"

"Well, ah — yes, I guess I did."

"So the victim wasn't really your client, and neither is anyone else but Mega Films. Right?"

She nodded slowly, grudgingly. He was right; legally it was Mega Films that had hired her, but she still didn't like the idea of squealing on everyone who'd had a run-in with Nick.

Come on, Charlotte, you're making it sound like some hard-boiled detective novel back in the twenties. This is the real thing, not some book you've read.

Charlotte rolled her eyes toward the ceiling. *Yeah, yeah.* Though she hated it when that voice in her head was right, a man was dead, and there was a *real* killer running loose. No one knew better than she did that even the slightest little tidbit of information could end up being a giant clue. Besides, like it or not, she had a moral obligation to help if she could, didn't she?

With only a slight hesitation, Charlotte took a deep breath, then recounted what she'd observed during the past two days. As best she could remember, she had witnessed at least two fights between Nick and Angel; then, there was Nick's confrontation with Toby Russell, and finally, she recounted the scene in the kitchen the previous day when Simon Clark had cornered Nick and read him the riot act. In conclusion she said, "Most of the friction seemed to be over some script that Nick was pushing for Angel to consider."

The detective continued scribbling in his notebook for a minute or so more. Finally, he raised his head, and with narrowed eyes, he asked, "Anything else?"

"No, nothing else that I can recall."

Nothing except the part about the letter opener.

Yeah, yeah, but once they question the others, she silently argued, *they'll find out about that last scene where Angel used the letter opener. Besides, they'll most certainly dust it for fingerprints.*

Holding the detective's gaze without blinking, she opted to say nothing about the letter opener.

Several moments passed before he finally said, "Okay. But if you think of anything —" He reached inside his shirt pocket and handed her a business card. "Just give me a call."

Charlotte took the card and dropped it

inside her apron pocket. It would be a cold day in Hades before she ever called *him.* "May I leave now?"

The detective shook his head. "Not yet."

"Why not? I've told you everything I know."

"Yeah, well, that remains to be seen."

The implication that she'd been less than truthful stung. Never mind that he was right. Though she hadn't outright lied to him, she had purposely neglected to tell him about the letter opener scene that had been shot the day before, so she hadn't exactly told him everything she knew.

Too bad. Enough was enough. She pressed her lips tightly together, gave him a curt nod, and without looking at him, headed for the pantry, where she retrieved her cell phone from her purse. Just as she reached the door leading into the hallway, Gavin Brown called out, "Don't forget what I said about calling Mrs. Duhè. No names. Just the bare facts."

"I won't," she retorted sharply, unable to mask the irritation she felt. Not only had he implied that she hadn't told him the truth, which made her feel all the more guilty for not saying something about the stupid letter opener, but now it seemed he was intent on making her miserable. Just the thought of having to sit around most of the day with nothing to do was pure torture. Besides which, there was no earthly reason why she should *have* to stay.

Still fuming, she paused at the doorway leading into the parlor. There was no way she could go back inside that crowded room at the moment. Besides needing some modicum of privacy when she talked to Bitsy, she needed to get her temper under control.

Turning away from the parlor doorway, she walked toward the uniformed police-man standing guard at the front door. "I'm feeling a little claustrophobic," she told him. And that was the truth. "I've already been questioned by Detective Brown. Would it be okay if I went out on the porch for a few minutes? Also, Detective Brown gave me permission to make an important phone call. And I won't leave," she added quickly.

For just the briefest moment, she was afraid that the young patrolman was going to say no. Then a small grin pulled at his lips. "Say, aren't you Detective Monroe's aunt?"

Charlotte nodded. "Judith is my niece."

"I thought so. You probably don't remem-ber, but I was one of the responding offi-cers when you found that woman dead in your living room last year. Detective Monroe talks about you all the time."

Charlotte didn't remember the young officer, but then, there was a lot about that night that she'd tried her best to forget. "Sorry," she said, forcing a smile. "I'm embarrassed to admit that I don't remember you, but —"

"Hey, no problem. You were under quite a strain that night." He opened the front door. "Are you sure you want to go outside? It's pretty hot out there."

Charlotte smiled. "I'm sure. I just need a few moments and I won't leave," she assured him again.

Outside, the earlier storm had dissipated, leaving the sky overcast and the air heavy with heat and steamy humidity. Trying to ignore the commotion of the squad cars, the emergency vehicles, and the police who were dealing with the clamoring news media beyond the barricades in the street, she walked to the left side of the porch and stood staring toward the house next door.

Seeing the media was yet another reminder that she really needed to phone Bitsy, and the sooner the better. "No time like the present," she whispered. She pulled her cell phone out of her apron pocket and scanned the list of names programmed into the phone until she found Bitsy's cell number. Bitsy answered on the second ring.

"Hey, Bitsy, this is Charlotte."

"Well, I was wondering when you were going to call me."

Oh, no, did Bitsy already know about the murder?

"I've been dying to know what Hunter Lansky is like in person."

Charlotte breathed a sigh of relief. Evidently, Bitsy hadn't heard the news yet. "Bitsy, I'm afraid I have some bad news."

"Please don't tell me that they broke something, or worse, that they burned my house down."

Detecting the panic in the old lady's voice, Charlotte quickly reassured her. "No — nothing like that. But brace yourself. There's been a murder."

"Did you say a murder?"

"I'm afraid so. One of Angel Martinique's friends was found murdered in the upstairs guest room this morning — the guest room closest to the stairwell." Knowing Bitsy and how she loved to gossip, Charlotte decided against telling her that she was the one who found the body. Telling Bitsy that would guarantee that everyone in New Orleans would find out.

"Which one of her friends? Was it her

114

boyfriend? Do they know who did it?"

Charlotte closed her eyes for a moment. *Oh, brother, here we go.*

"Well, who was murdered?" Bitsy demanded.

Opening her eyes, Charlotte said, "I can't tell you that, Bitsy."

"Why the deuce not?"

"Because I was told by the investigating detective not to give out any names."

"Well, surely he didn't mean me. After all, it's my house. Hmm, maybe I should take a cab and come over there."

"No, Bitsy, don't do that. For one thing, the police wouldn't let you past the barricades, and for another thing, the media is all over the place."

"They're not in my house, are they?"

Again, the panicky sound. "No — they're being held behind barricades."

"How was this person killed? Is there blood everywhere?"

Ignoring the first question, Charlotte said, "Nothing that can't be cleaned up." Whether it was from the heat or from trying to keep up with Bitsy's scattered thought processes, Charlotte could feel the beginnings of a headache coming on.

"I certainly hope so," Bitsy retorted. "The rug in that room is an antique. I paid a fortune for it. But now that I'm thinking about it, I can't remember if I kept the sales receipt or if it got lost during Katrina. That lawyer — Jake something or other was his name — anyway, he said that Mega Films would reimburse me for any damages, but I'll need some way to verify the expense."

Sweat trickled down Charlotte's back, and her head was getting worse by the minute. If she didn't end the call soon, Bitsy would be off on another tangent. "Listen, Bitsy, I've got to go now, but I mostly wanted to let you know what was happening before you saw it on the news."

"I still think I should come over there."

Emphasizing each word, Charlotte said, "Don't — do that. I'll keep you updated — I promise. Like I said, I've got to go. Bye, now."

Charlotte quickly depressed the button to end the phone call and headed for the front door. The moment she stepped back through the doorway, the blessedly cool air inside engulfed her, and she sighed with relief. Now if only she had a glass of water and some Tylenol, maybe she could get rid of her headache.

It was late afternoon when Max Morris, the director, called everyone together and announced that, regretfully, shooting at the house would be suspended indefinitely until the police concluded their investigation. As soon as the police gave the go-ahead for the shooting to resume, everyone would be contacted.

Then Gavin Brown stood up. "All of you can leave now, but a word of caution. Don't leave town and don't talk to the news media."

Over the course of the long day, Charlotte had a lot of time to think about all that had happened. Though she'd rather chew nails, like it or not, she was going to have to talk to Gavin Brown again. At some point, she needed to clean the room where the murder had taken place. Since Gavin Brown seemed to be the detective in charge, he would be the one who could tell her when she could get back inside the house.

While everyone else filed out of the room, Charlotte hung back, waiting for the opportunity to talk to the detective. It didn't take him long to spot her, and once they made eye contact, she approached him.

"Thought of something else?" he asked.

"No, not really. I just need to know when I can get back inside to clean."

He shrugged. "That all depends on the crime scene people. Give me a call in a couple of days. Anything else?"

Charlotte shook her head no, said, "Thanks," then quickly left the room.

In the kitchen, several of the security guards were gathered around the breakfast table. When Charlotte entered the room to retrieve her purse from the pantry, the group glanced her way and suddenly went quiet.

After a moment, Samantha O'Reilly broke free from the group. "You leaving now?" she asked.

"Yes, finally."

"Wait up a sec and I'll walk you to your van."

Considering the number of police officers still on the premises, Charlotte didn't think an escort was necessary. Even so, she waited while Sam said something to one of the security officers, then rejoined her.

"This isn't really necessary," Charlotte told her as they stepped out into the wide center hall.

"Yeah, I know, but I need a break."

The young woman sounded as tired as Charlotte felt. "Guess it's been a long day for you too," she offered as she bent down and retrieved her supply carrier that she'd left near the bottom of the staircase.

"Yeah, too long, and unfortunately, before

it's over, I'm afraid some heads are going to roll. I'm just glad that I wasn't on duty last night."

Up until that point, Charlotte hadn't really thought about the repercussions for the security team. But it stood to reason that having a murder committed under their very noses would be a huge black eye for the Lagniappe Security Company. "I guess something like this could put a company out of business fast, huh?" she asked, thinking of Louis.

"I hope not. It's a really great summer job for me."

"Summer job?"

Sam nodded. "Yes, ma'am. I fill in for the regulars while they're on vacation. Otherwise, during the school year, I'm a teacher."

Later, as Charlotte entered her house, the sight and smell of the bouquet of flowers reminded her that she hadn't gotten around to calling the florist. Glancing over at the cuckoo clock, she noted that it was almost six o'clock.

"They're probably closed by now," she told Sweety Boy as she locked the front door. Then again, maybe not.

Setting her stuff down, she walked over to her desk and retrieved the phone book from the bottom drawer. Finding the number, she dialed, and to her surprise, her call was answered on the second ring.

"Ah, yes, hello," she told the woman who answered the call. After giving the woman her name and address, she said, "A gorgeous bouquet of flowers were delivered to me yesterday, but the card wasn't signed. I'm hoping that you can tell me who ordered them. I'd like to send them a thank-you note," she added.

"Hold on a moment, Ms. LaRue, and I'll check."

A few minutes later, the woman told her, "Whoever ordered the flowers paid cash, ma'am."

Cash meant the person must have ordered the flowers in person. "Do you happen to remember the person who ordered them?"

"Sorry. Yesterday was my day off. June — the owner — would know, but she's already gone for the day. You can call back tomorrow. She comes in around eight-thirty most mornings."

After thanking the woman, Charlotte hung up the phone, then turned to stare at the blank screen of the television. Curious, yet dreading what she might see and hear, Charlotte reached for the remote control, and switched on the TV.

The weather forecaster had just finished up the preliminary weather report when the camera switched to the news desk. "This just in," the announcer said. "Through a confidential source, we've learned that it was a maid named Charlotte LaRue who discovered the dead body of Nick Franklin earlier this morning in that Garden District murder."

CHAPTER 6

The second Charlotte heard her name come out of the announcer's mouth, her own mouth went dry and she began to shake. As the announcer continued giving details about the murder and Nick Franklin's connection to Angel Martinique, the rest of what he said faded beneath her fury.

"Don't leave town and don't talk to the news media." The detective's warning roared in her head. It was bad enough that her name was being broadcast all over creation. Reporters would be knocking down her door. But even worse, she was almost certain that Gavin Brown, along with the rest of the NOPD, was going to think that *she* was the one who leaked the information to the press.

Stop it! You're just being paranoid.

No sooner had the thought entered her mind than the phone rang. Sure enough, the caller ID read "Gavin Brown."

"So, I'm being paranoid, am I?" She jerked up the receiver. "I didn't do it," she told him.

"Yeah, we know," Gavin Brown said.

How could he know?

As if he'd heard her silent question, he explained. "I have to admit that at first I didn't trust you to only give Ms. Duhè the bare-boned facts, so, to make certain, I called her about an hour ago. But when I spoke to her, she assured me that you hadn't said a word about being the one who had discovered the body." He chuckled. "In fact, she was pretty indignant about the whole thing. Anyway, I was mostly calling to warn you in case you didn't see the broadcast, and I'm hoping that you might have some idea of who might have leaked the info."

Still angry, Charlotte drummed her fingers against the desktop. "I wish I did know who the blabbermouth was. But considering how angry I am at the moment, it's probably best that I don't know, or else you might have another murder on your hands. I don't want or appreciate my name being broadcast over the airwaves, especially in connection with a murder."

What about Bruce King, that awful paparazzi fellow?

Charlotte frowned. Why on earth would

his name come to mind? Unless the man was Houdini, there was no way he'd be able to sneak inside the house or know any more than the rest of the media. Still, he had tried unsuccessfully to bribe her for information, so it stood to reason that he could have found someone willing to feed him dirt. And if he did, he could have leaked her name on purpose, out of spite — payback for not taking his bribe.

"I don't blame you for being ticked off," the detective said. "But one thing — you might want to consider staying somewhere else for a few days. Reporters will be camping out on your doorstep now."

"Great! Just wonderful," she added sarcastically. "Thanks for the warning, but barring a hurricane, I have no intention of letting anyone run me out of my home."

Unbidden, again the name Bruce King came to mind. Should she or shouldn't she mention the tabloid reporter? It only took a moment for her to decide. "Listen, now that I'm thinking about it, you might want to check out a reporter who was hanging around on Monday. I was leaving when he approached me and tried to bribe me to give him information about Angel. Of course I refused, but someone else might have decided to take him up on his offer.

He could have someone on the inside feeding him information."

"So, are you going to give me his name or keep me guessing?"

"Oh — yes, of course. His name is Bruce King."

"Okay, thanks."

With Bruce King still on her mind, Charlotte slowly hung up the receiver. By all accounts, when it came to Angel, the sleazy man was relentless. Could he also be desperate, desperate enough for something sensational about Angel that he would create his own so-called news?

What? By committing murder? Don't even go there.

Immediately dismissing the idea as yet another case of having an overactive imagination, Charlotte headed for the kitchen to see what she could find for supper.

The first thing Charlotte did on Thursday morning was peek out her front window in search of anyone who didn't belong there. "So far, so good," she told Sweety Boy, and she stepped outside onto the porch to retrieve the morning newspaper from the front steps. Back inside, she headed for the kitchen, where she settled down at the table with a fresh cup of coffee and the news-paper.

Sure enough, an article about Nick Franklin's murder made the front page. She briefly skimmed it. When she'd finished, she breathed a sigh of relief that her name hadn't been mentioned.

After breakfast she headed to the bedroom to get dressed for the day. As she passed through the living room, the sight of the bouquet of flowers gave her pause and reminded her about phoning the flower shop.

"It should be open by now," she murmured. Her call was answered on the third ring. "Hi, is this June, the owner?"

"Yes, this is June."

"June, I'm looking for some information on a bouquet of flowers that was delivered to me Tuesday afternoon."

"Name, please," June asked.

"Charlotte LaRue and I live on Milan Street."

"Just a sec while I check my records." Several moments passed; then June said, "Ah, yes, here it is. Was there a problem with the flowers, Ms. LaRue?"

"No, no problem, except that the card wasn't signed. I'm hoping that you can tell me who ordered them. They're so beautiful and I want to send a thank-you note."

"Hmm, let me see . . . No, sorry, no name was given. I see from my records that the flowers were a cash purchase."

Charlotte sighed. "Yes, well, do you happen to remember the person who bought the flowers?

There were several moments of silence before June finally said, "Sorry, I don't. Tuesday was an exceptionally busy day for me and I was in the shop by myself."

"Phooey," Charlotte whispered, even more puzzled.

"Like I said, ma'am, I am sorry that I can't help you."

"That's okay, but if you do remember something — anything — or if he comes back in and you recognize him, could you please give me a call?" Suddenly, another thought occurred. "Or, if anyone else comes in with a cash order for me, could you make sure you get their name?"

"Sure. Give me your phone number."

"Thank you so much." Once Charlotte gave June her phone number, she thanked her again and hung up the phone.

Shaking her head and even more puzzled than before, Charlotte continued on to the bedroom to dress. Maybe it was Louis who sent the flowers. He had been acting a little strange of late, and it would be like him to just assume that she would know he sent the bouquet. But what on earth would he be thanking her for?

She could always call him and find out. Or she could simply wait until he got home and then ask him. She'd wait, she decided.

On Friday morning, Charlotte was headed out the door when the phone rang. "Murphy's Law," she murmured as she marched over to the desk. "What can go wrong will go wrong," she added, glaring at the CALLER UNKNOWN on the phone ID display screen. Usually CALLER UNKNOWN only popped up when someone was calling from a cell phone, didn't it? No, that wasn't exactly right, but at the moment she couldn't remember.

Probably Mega Films. "I should have known this would happen," she told Sweety Boy. "Should have known that the moment I promised Carol I would babysit the twins for a couple of hours, that would be the time they would call for me to come back to work."

Still and all, maybe it was simply a wrong number, or someone looking for a maid, or . . . "Oh, for pity's sake, just answer it," she whispered. With a sigh, she picked up

128

the receiver. "Maid-for-a-Day, Charlotte speaking."

"You'll never guess what I just found out."

Great! Bitsy!

"The police have arrested Angel Martinique for murdering that boyfriend of hers," Bitsy continued without waiting for Charlotte to comment. "I believe the boyfriend's name is Nick Franks or Franklin, something like that. But then you probably already know that, don't you?" Without waiting for an answer she continued. "They say that Angel stabbed him with a letter opener, of all things. Do you think she did it on purpose or was it an accident?"

When Charlotte didn't answer, Bitsy said, "Oh, never mind. Anyway, not only did they find her fingerprints all over the letter opener, but there's been some talk that Angel and this Nick person have a history that goes way back to when they were teenagers."

For several moments, Charlotte was too stunned to speak. Even though she'd witnessed two separate altercations between Nick Franklin and Angel, and one had even been a bit violent, she just couldn't picture Angel stabbing Nick.

"Well, aren't you going to say anything?" Bitsy demanded.

129

Charlotte took a shaky breath. "First of all, is this just gossip or facts? And second, if what you've just told me is true, where did you get your information? There was nothing on the morning news about any of this."

"No, it's not 'just gossip.' I don't gossip."

Charlotte rolled her eyes. *Yeah, right, and I'm the Queen of England.*

"I'll have you know," Bitsy retorted, "I have my sources. I may be old, but in case you've forgotten, I still have connections to City Hall."

Oh, boy, now she'd gone and insulted the old lady . . . again. She knew she should be ashamed for being so impatient and judgmental, but Bitsy had a way of getting on her last nerve.

"And by the way," Bitsy continued, obviously still miffed, "while I'm thinking about it, you should have told me that you were the one who discovered the body."

Dear Lord, give me strength. "Bitsy, I've already explained to you why I couldn't do that." Charlotte forced herself to soften her tone. "I just want to know who told you about the arrest."

"Well, if you must know, my neighbor called me. Don't you remember? She's the one whose son works over at the jail. She's also keeping me informed about the goings-on around my house while I'm gone."

Charlotte was still trying to wrap her mind around the idea of Bitsy having a snitch when the old lady said, "So, what do you think? Did Angel do it? I figure since you've been around her for a couple of days, surely you have some kind of opinion about it."

Charlotte had no intention of discussing her own speculations about Angel's guilt or innocence with Bitsy or prolonging the conversation, for that matter. Purposely ignoring the question, she said, "Bitsy, I really appreciate the information and I hate to cut this short, but I was on my way out the door when you called. I promised Carol that I would babysit Samantha and Samuel this morning."

For several moments, the only sound Charlotte heard was heavy breathing, then, "Humph! When you finish *babysitting,* call me." The next sound Charlotte heard was a loud click.

Charlotte pulled the receiver away from her ear and stared at it. "I can't believe it. She hung up on me." She shook her head. "Guess there's a first for everything," she told Sweety Boy as she picked up her purse and headed for the door. Just as she reached for the doorknob, she remembered the detective's warning about reporters camping out on her doorstep. "Might be a good idea to check first," she told the little bird as she stepped over to the window.

Sure enough, there was a strange van parked across the street from her house. "Great!" she muttered. "Now what?" Finally, after staring at the vehicle a few moments more, she straightened her shoulders and lifted her chin. Might as well get it over with.

"Now, you be a good little birdie, and I'll be back later," she said to Sweety Boy, then firmly closed the door behind her and locked it.

She was almost to her van when a man emerged from the driver's side of the parked vehicle. "Hey, lady," he called out, walking quickly toward her. "Wait up a minute."

Charlotte hopped inside her van, slammed the door shut, and hit the automatic door-lock. Then, after cranking up the van, she turned to see where the man had gone. The sight of his face on the other side of the window gave her a start, and fear mixed with anger spurted through her.

"Sorry about that," he said loudly as he backed away. "Didn't mean to scare you, but are you Ms. Charlotte LaRue?"

"Who wants to know?" she asked pointedly.

"I'm a freelance reporter, ma'am, and I need to talk to Ms. LaRue."

Torn between telling the man to get off her property and calling the police, Charlotte simply glared at the man.

Remember, you can catch more flies with honey than with vinegar.

Or, in this case, maybe she could get rid of the pesky reporter easier by being nice rather than being nasty. It was worth a try and she knew just exactly how she was going to do it.

Pasting on the sweetest little-old-lady smile that she could conjure, she said, "Sorry, young man. I know all of my neighbors and none of their names are LaRue." It wasn't a lie . . . not exactly. She did know all of her neighbors and none of them but her had the last name LaRue. "You must have the wrong street."

The reporter didn't argue, but he did give her a funny look as he backed away. Then, with a shrug, he finally turned and headed for his van. "That should work for a little while," she said aloud to no one as she shifted into *Reverse* and backed out of her driveway.

Putting thoughts of the reporter aside for

the moment, she mulled over Bitsy's phone call while she drove to her daughter-in-law's house. If it were true, if the police had arrested Angel for murder, how would that affect the movie? Would they shut down production permanently? She figured that without one of the main stars, they wouldn't have a choice.

By the time that Charlotte got home that afternoon, she was well ready for a little peace and quiet . . . and she was bone-tired. What she needed was a cup of coffee.

She headed for the kitchen, fixed the coffeepot, and turned it on. While the coffeepot gurgled and sputtered, reminding her that it was past time to give the machine a thorough cleaning, she stared out the window over the sink. She dearly loved the twins and loved spending time with them, but being around them when their mother was there to referee as opposed to having the full responsibility of being the referee was an entirely different thing.

Smiling with the lingering memories of her morning, she poured herself a cup of coffee and headed for her desk in the living room. As she settled at the desk, though, her smile quickly faded. She'd rather eat worms than have to fool with the monthly bookkeeping chores for Maid-for-a-Day. Too bad, though. It was a dirty job, but somebody had to do it.

It was times like these that she wished she could simply hire her sister to keep the books for her. Several years back Madeline had started her own small accounting firm, and now she had more clients than she could handle. Even so, Charlotte had been reluctant to let her sister handle the books for Maid-for-a-Day, the main reason being that she didn't really want Madeline, or anyone else for that matter, knowing all about her business. Besides, Madeline charged her clients a lot more than Charlotte was willing to pay, which left little choice but for her to do it herself.

Charlotte reached down and removed her business ledger from the bottom drawer. From another drawer, she removed a large manila envelope full of receipts. Just as she flipped the ledger open, there was a loud knock on the front door.

Uneasiness spiced with irritation swept through her. Since she wasn't expecting company, thoughts of the reporter who had been parked in front of her house earlier that morning immediately came to mind.

Charlotte stood and tiptoed over to the front window. If the man had returned, she'd simply pretend that no one was at home.

And what about your van parked in the driveway?

Oh, yeah, the van. "Too bad," she whispered. In that case she would simply ignore the man.

The first thing she spotted was the long white limousine parked in her driveway. "What on earth?" she murmured as her gaze shifted from the limo to the man standing on her porch.

"Well, for Pete's sake," she exclaimed. Reaching for the deadbolt, she quickly unlocked the door and threw it wide open. "Hey, there, hon." She gave a sweeping motion with her hand. "Come on in."

Though Benny Jackson nodded and gave her a wan smile, the smile didn't quite reach his bloodshot eyes. Dressed simply in a pair of jeans and a T-shirt instead of his chauffeur uniform, he looked much younger and more like the young man who used to hang around her house so many years ago.

"Sorry to barge in on you without calling first," he said as he stepped inside.

"No problem. Can I offer you something to drink? I just made a pot of fresh coffee. Iced tea?"

"Iced tea would be great, if it's not too

much trouble? I'm up to my eyeballs in coffee."

"No trouble at all," she replied. "It won't take but a minute."

Benny followed her back to the kitchen and seated himself at the kitchen table. Once she'd served him the tea, she sat down opposite him with her cup of coffee. "So, what brings you over to my neck of the woods this afternoon?"

Benny lowered his gaze to the sweating glass in front of him. "Angel's been arrested for murdering Nick Franklin."

Charlotte nodded. "That's what I heard."

At that, Benny glanced up. "It's on the news already?"

Charlotte shook her head. "No, I don't think so. Not yet. One of my clients knew that I was working on the set, and she called me early this morning." Charlotte shrugged at Benny's puzzled look. "Don't ask. All I know is that she's well connected in the city — she knows just about everyone." Boy, was that an understatement! "And she has very reliable sources."

"So, what did this client of yours tell you?"

While Benny listened thoughtfully, Charlotte summed up her conversation with Bitsy. When she'd finished, Benny nodded. "Yeah, that's about right. But one thing your friend either didn't mention or didn't know was that in addition to Angel's fingerprints being the only ones on the letter opener, Nick's blood was also found on a pair of her jeans. Even worse, Angel doesn't have an alibi for the time frame in which Nick was murdered. She was tired that evening and had me drop her off at the hotel. On top of that, now she's been denied bail. The prosecutor claims that because she's a celebrity, she's a slight risk. Not only that, but it looks like her manager, Simon Clark, as well as the studio, has abandoned her."

Charlotte frowned. "I find that hard to believe, especially considering what a big star she is."

"Yeah, well, Simon Clark is the type who only looks out for number one. As for the studio, if you can believe it, there's actually a morals clause in her contract that makes it easy for them to ditch her. Never mind that she's innocent."

When Charlotte raised a speculative eyebrow, he gave a slight shake of his head. "She's innocent," he repeated. "I've known Angel for a long time now, and I swear to you, there's no way she could kill anyone. She can be a real pain, and yeah, she's a bit of a prima donna, but it's all mostly an act.

No matter what they say, she's no killer."

For several seconds Benny stared at Charlotte as if willing her to believe him; then with a sigh, he picked up the glass of tea and drank almost half of it before he finally set it back down. "You still make the best iced tea I've ever tasted."

"Thanks, but you didn't come by to just drink my tea."

Benny sighed again. "No, ma'am. You're right. I came by to ask for your help."

"My help?" she sputtered.

He nodded decisively. "I trust you and don't know where else to turn. Angel's hired some high-priced attorney from Hollywood, but I don't trust him."

Charlotte frowned. "I don't understand."

"I overheard one of the detectives talking about how you've solved several murder cases, and I'm hoping that you can either help me prove Angel's innocence or at least point me to a good private investigator we can trust."

For several long moments Charlotte was speechless. Since Gavin Brown was the only detective at the murder scene that she knew, that's who Benny had to be talking about. Go figure. Out of everyone she'd met at the NOPD, Detective Gavin Brown was the last person that she'd ever expect to hand her a compliment, especially considering that he always acted like such a jerk around her.

Taking a deep breath, she said, "Benny, I'm sure that Angel's attorney probably has his own investigator."

"Yeah, well, like I said, I don't trust him, but I trust you. So, do you think you can help me?"

Could she? Did she even want to? "I — I don't know what to say," she responded honestly.

While it was true that she had solved several murder cases in the past, she hadn't realized that the police thought of her as anything but a pest or an aggravation at best.

When Benny's face fell with disappointment, Charlotte hurriedly added, "I do admit that when I heard that Angel had been arrested, my gut reaction was the same as yours. I just don't see her as a killer — more like a spoiled brat. Sorry. I know she's your friend, but that's how she comes across." When Benny just shrugged she continued. "Do you think it's possible that she's been set up? I mean, like, could the studio have wanted an excuse to break the contract and — no!" She shook her head. "Forget that. They could always write off the movie as a loss on their income taxes, or I suppose they could hire another actress since they had just started shooting." She shook her head again. She was rambling. "Wrong track. But how about this? Is there anyone else you can think of who would resort to murder to get her out of the movie? Maybe another starlet? Or perhaps someone out to make some headlines, like that sleazy reporter Bruce King?"

"Yeah, sure, I guess anything's possible. There are lots of people out there who are jealous of Angel's success. But there are also plenty of people who would like to see Nick out of her life permanently too."

Well aware that she was fast approaching the point of no return, Charlotte mentally chewed on Benny's answer for a moment while she took a sip of her coffee. If Angel was innocent, then it was obvious that someone meant for her to take the fall for Nick's murder. Just thinking about an innocent person, any innocent person, being set up for a murder and the real killer getting off scot-free was enough to make her blood boil. Of course just thinking about any human being murdering another human being made her angry too.

At best she figured she had two choices: she could either just say no to Benny, or she

could help Benny and Angel as best she
could.

Mind your own business. Just say no.

*Yes, you can say no, but remember, every-
thing happens for a reason.*

Charlotte lowered her gaze to stare at the
wisp of steam rising from her coffee cup,
but the silent warring voices in her head
couldn't be ignored. There had been other
times that she'd been faced with the same
dilemma. One time in particular stood out
from the rest. After much agonizing about
getting involved and after continuously asking herself, "why me?" she had finally
concluded, "why not me?"

Raising her gaze, she looked straight into
Benny's hopeful eyes and said, "Look, I'm
not promising anything, but I'll do what I
can."

The grateful look of relief on his face gave
her pause. "Just so you know," she warned,
"I'm not a professional by any stretch of
the imagination. But I do have my resources,
and, like I said, I'll do what I can."

Benny grinned from ear to ear. "Thanks,
Ms. LaRue. Thanks a lot. And just so *you*
know, I'm not expecting miracles, but I do
want to know the truth."

Charlotte hesitated, but then said, "Even
if it turns out that Angel is guilty?"

"She's not," he quickly retorted. "But other than my gut feelings, I have no proof. I just know she's not guilty."

"Well, in that case, pour yourself another glass of tea while I get a pen and pad to jot down some notes."

At her desk, Charlotte eyed the financial ledger. Too bad, she thought. It would just have to wait. Grabbing up a tablet and a pen, she returned to the kitchen.

Back in the kitchen, she poured herself a fresh cup of coffee. Once they were both seated at the table again, she tapped her pen against the pad of paper and said, "Okay, now I need you to tell me anything that you think could be relevant, no matter how small. Why don't we start with Angel and Nick's relationship? How long have they been together and just what is their relationship?"

Benny leaned forward, wrapped both hands around his glass, and rested his forearms on the table. "To tell you the truth, I'm not sure what their relationship is, but I'm pretty sure it's not romantic. It's almost like he's holding something over her head. In fact, I've often wondered if Nick could be blackmailing Angel."

A soft gasp escaped Charlotte. "Blackmailing?"

"I should explain," Benny said. "You see, right after Angel made it big, Nick suddenly showed up on her doorstep out of nowhere one day. Even though she introduced him as an old friend from her hometown, she didn't seem exactly overjoyed to see him. In fact, she seemed almost —" He shrugged. "Almost scared or nervous or something." He shrugged again. "But what's even more weird is that even though she didn't much like him just showing up, she let him move in and stay."

"But what could he have on her to blackmail her?"

"I always figured it had something to do with when they were kids. Once, I even asked Angel about it, but she just shook her head and said for me to leave it alone."

"Do the police know this?"

"Not unless Angel said something to them, and since that would be even more motive for her to have murdered him, I don't think she would say anything. She's not exactly the sharpest knife in the drawer, but she's not stupid either."

"Okay, good. So, tell me what you know about Nick. Like, who, besides Angel, might want him gone for good?"

"That's easy. I guess I'd put Simon Clark at the top of the list. Like I said earlier, Simon looks out for *Numero Uno*. I kinda got the feeling that he viewed Nick as a threat to his business relationship with Angel. They were always at odds over Angel's career."

Charlotte nodded, remembering the confrontation that she'd witnessed in Bitsy's kitchen between the two men.

"Yeah, good old Simon wanted Angel to continue in the PG-rated movies she'd been making, but Nick kept bringing her scripts for other, racier movies."

Suddenly, Charlotte frowned. "But why would Simon go to the trouble of killing Nick, and setting Angel up for the fall, then dropping her when she got in trouble? Wouldn't that be like killing the goose that laid the golden egg? Why wouldn't he simply ditch her to begin with?"

Benny shrugged. "Who knows? Probably because he's such a sleazebag."

Deciding that Simon as a suspect just didn't make sense for now, Charlotte said, "Okay, so who else would want Nick dead?"

"I don't know that it means anything, but for a while there was this man who was stalking her. There are all kinds of crazed fans in this business. Anyway, right before we came to New Orleans this man and Nick had a really nasty altercation one evening at a restaurant. Nick had him thrown out of the restaurant, and convinced Angel to get a restraining order against him. I thought it was over, but now I suspect the guy followed us here. There have been a couple of times that I thought I saw him hanging around out on the street."

Charlotte nodded as she jotted down what Benny had said. She didn't mention it out loud, but again, why kill Nick, then frame Angel for the murder? "Anyone else?"

Benny suddenly took a deep breath and let out a sigh. "There's me."

CHAPTER 7

"You?" Charlotte stared at Benny.

Benny lowered his gaze and stared at the glass in front of him. "Yeah, me. Heather and I were seeing each other for a while. Then Nick stepped in. I really cared about her — still do. I tried to warn her that Nick was no good, that he just used people, but it took him smacking her around to make her finally realize that he was bad news."

Charlotte tensed. "So Nick was not only two-timing Angel, but he was the one who gave Heather that black eye. What a jerk!"

"Yeah, he was." Benny raised his gaze to stare at Charlotte, and there was a lethal calmness in his eyes. At that moment, she could believe that he *was* capable of murder.

"When I saw that shiner he gave her," he continued, "I wanted to kill him. If I could have gotten my hands on him at the time, I would have. But I didn't. Someone else beat me to it."

Though Charlotte believed Benny was capable of killing Nick, she also believed that he didn't do it. But even if he had killed Nick, he'd have no reason whatsoever to frame Angel for the murder. Still, his admission brought up another point to ponder. "I hate to point this out, but what you just told me also gives Heather motive as well."

Benny stiffened and his eyes lit up with fire. "Heather didn't do it," he snapped. "Don't even go there. Besides, she broke up with Nick the day before he was killed."

Charlotte sighed, then reached out and gently patted Benny's balled fist. "Just calm down," she soothed. "No one, least of all me, is accusing Heather of anything."

After a tense moment, Benny finally relented. "Sorry," he whispered. "It's just that —" His voice trailed away and he gave a one-shouldered shrug.

"It's just that you're in love with her."

"Heather is a nice woman who wouldn't hurt a flea."

For whatever reason, it was clear that he didn't intend to answer her question, so she figured it was time to change the subject. "So — back to suspects. Anyone else?"

"Just a couple more that I can think of right now. I know that Nick had some gambling debts, but that was back in California, and then there's Bruce King. Nick and King had a run-in day before yesterday."

Charlotte nodded as she jotted down the information. When she'd finished she stared out of the window for a thoughtful moment, then turned back to Benny. "What about Angel's bodyguard, Toby Russell? Angel and Nick were having a knock-down, drag-out fight Tuesday morning until Toby stepped in and forcibly escorted Nick off the premises."

Benny shook his head. "Naw, Toby was just doing his job. Or following Angel's orders," he added. "Believe it or not, he's a pretty okay guy."

Charlotte suddenly laughed, but then sobered quickly. "I know it's no laughing matter, but it seems to me that just about everybody that Nick came in contact with had a motive to kill him."

Benny chuckled. "Yeah, it does, doesn't it?"

"Only problem," she pointed out quickly, "what would any of these people on this list gain by framing Angel?"

For an answer, Benny simply shook his head. "I don't know," he admitted. "I've thought about it and thought about it, but come up with a big fat blank."

Charlotte drummed her fingers against the tabletop as she mentally sorted through the suspects. "As I see it, the only person who could possibly want Nick dead *and* want to frame Angel would be that reporter, Bruce King. He'd be getting a double whammy of a story." She shook her head. "But even that theory has flaws."

With a puzzled frown, Charlotte glanced down at the notes she'd made. The word *blackmail* kept jumping out at her, and after a moment, she underlined it. "I know you've already said that you didn't know," she said, still staring at the notes she'd made, "but your blackmail theory bothers me. We need to find out if Nick *was* blackmailing Angel and why. I can't help but think that something like that could be the root cause for Nick's murder."

Charlotte lifted her head to stare at Benny. "What if I simply asked Angel?" As soon as the words left her mouth, another thought suddenly struck her. She narrowed her eyes. "Angel does know that you intended to come to me for help, doesn't she?"

"Yes, ma'am, she knows."

She nodded. "Good, because I could get into a lot of trouble for sticking my nose into her business without her blessings, so to speak."

Benny smiled. "No problem. I assure you, I discussed talking to you with her. As for outright asking her about the blackmail business, you can try, but I doubt she'll tell you any more than she told me."

"Probably not, but there's only one way to find out, which presents a problem. They won't let just anybody visit prisoners, especially a prisoner who's being held for murder."

"Yeah, that's a problem." He paused; then, after a moment he said, "What if you went in with her lawyer? He could say that you were his assistant or something."

Charlotte nodded. "But would he do it?"

"If Angel told him to do it, he would. Let me see what I can do, and I'll get back to you."

"Ah, Benny, there's just one more thing that's bothering me."

"Just one?"

When he chuckled, Charlotte smiled. "Yeah, well, several, if you want to get technical. But the one I'm talking about is the letter opener. I can understand how easy it would be for blood to be on a pair of Angel's jeans. The jeans could have been left in her dressing room. But if our theory is right, and Angel was set up, how did the killer stab Nick without smearing Angel's fingerprints on the letter opener? Surely, even if he used gloves, some of the fingerprints would have been smeared. Then again, if Angel did stab him, her fingerprints could be smeared anyway."

Benny thought a minute, then shrugged. "You got me on that one. Maybe some of them were smeared, but you'll have to ask your detective friend about that. I wouldn't hold my breath, though, if I were you. The police think they already have the killer in custody, so they're not going to be inclined to poke holes in their case."

Especially not on the word of a mere maid, Charlotte thought. Besides, just the thought of having to ask Detective Gavin Brown anything gave her the heebie-jeebies.

He did warn you about the news media, and he paid you a compliment about solving a couple of past murders.

Yeah, but like Benny had said, he probably wouldn't appreciate someone poking holes in his investigation. But there was one person she could ask. If anyone could find out, Judith could. But would her niece do it? was the big question.

After Benny made sure she had his cell phone number and he left, Charlotte put in a call to Judith.

After several rings, Judith answered,

"Monroe."

"Hey, hon, this is Aunt Charlotte."

"Hey, yourself, Auntie. What's happening?"

"I know you're probably working, so I'll keep this as brief as possible. I need a favor."

There was an ever so slight hesitation; then Judith said, "What kind of favor?"

This time Charlotte hesitated. In the past Judith hadn't approved or condoned Charlotte's interference in a murder investigation; in fact, just the opposite. So, how to approach her this time was the big question.

Just say it and be done with it. All she can say is no.

Charlotte cleared her throat. "Now, before you say no, please hear me out. I need some information concerning the fingerprints on the murder weapon that killed Nick Franklin."

Judith groaned. "Now, why in hell would you —"

"Judith Monroe! You know I don't like that kind of language."

"Sorry." Judith sighed. "But why would *you* need to know something like that?"

"It's a long story —"

"That I don't have time to listen to," Judith interrupted. "Besides, it's not my case."

"But you could find out."

"No, Auntie, I couldn't, not without raising a few eyebrows around here. Besides, my own caseload is heavy enough without snooping into other cases."

Getting more frustrated with each passing moment, Charlotte blurted out, "I need to know if the fingerprints were smeared. Angel is a small woman and plunging a letter opener into Nick would not only take a lot of strength, but I'm sure her grip would slip, therefore smearing some of her prints. If her prints aren't smeared, then that would help prove that she was set up, wouldn't it?"

Judith didn't bother to answer. "Can't do it," she shot back. "Look, I don't know why you've gotten yourself involved in this, and I don't care, but I'm telling you here and now to butt out. Leave it alone. Let the police handle it."

Disappointment washed through Charlotte. "Should have known," she grumbled.

"I'm not kidding, Auntie. You know that I love you, and I don't mean to be rude, but for Pete's sake, *please* mind your own business. I have to go back to work now, but we'll talk some more about this later."

Without warning or even so much as a good-bye, Judith disconnected the call.

For several moments, Charlotte simply sat there and stared into space. Then, finally, she replaced the phone receiver.

"*. . . I'm telling you here and now to butt out. Leave it alone. Let the police handle it.*"

"Easier said than done," Charlotte muttered to the empty room.

Early on Saturday morning, Charlotte accompanied Angel's lawyer, Barry James, inside the building where Angel was being held. According to what Benny had told her, James was supposed to be some hotshot criminal attorney out of Hollywood. He certainly looked the part. Though she figured he was probably in his early forties, his evenly tanned face was free of wrinkles, and his dark hair was perfectly styled — not one hair out of place. He was fit, probably worked out in some high-class gym every day, and the suit he wore looked expensive and custom made. No department store sales racks for Mr. *GQ*.

Come to think of it, now that she'd met the lawyer in person, she was pretty sure that she'd seen him before on TV; if she remembered right, he'd represented a whole bunch of big-name stars. Not that she made a habit of keeping up with such things, but there was no way a person could totally ignore stuff like that, especially with the media spreading every tidbit of news from here to kingdom come, over and over, ad nauseam.

So why didn't Benny trust Barry James? She never had come right out and asked him. Later, she'd have to ask him, she decided, but for now, first things first.

Charlotte glanced around and shuddered. Just walking down the hallway of the jail made her claustrophobic. Right then and there, she decided that being incarcerated in jail was something she hoped she never had to experience.

Inside the bare, tiny room where they waited for Angel, the only furniture were a table and three chairs — two chairs on one side of the small table that was bolted to the floor and the other chair on the opposite side. Charlotte seated herself and stared at the door leading into the room.

Barry James chose to pace the length of the room. "This is highly irregular, you know," he told her. "And a waste of time."

It was the same thing he'd said when they'd met just outside the entry to the jail. And he'd said nothing else since. Besides, why on earth would he care about wasting time? He was probably making more money per hour than she made in an entire week or even a month. Tempted to say so, she bit her bottom lip instead.

Just remember that you can catch more flies with honey than with vinegar.

Yeah, yeah, whatever.

But she had to say something, if for no other reason than to shut him up. Taking a deep breath and trying not to choke on the words, she said, "Irregular or not, I really appreciate you doing this." No sooner had she uttered the words than the door opened and Angel, shackled in handcuffs and chains and accompanied by a guard, entered the room.

Charlotte noted that Angel's face was bare of makeup. Tresses of her signature long blond hair hung as limply around her pale face as the ill-fitting orange jumpsuit that she wore. Orange was definitely not a good color for the starlet, Charlotte decided. It made her skin look kind of sallow. Of course the poor lighting in the room could be to blame as well, but all of it combined made Angel look more like a sick, homeless orphan than like a woman who was admired by millions of movie fans.

As Angel shuffled across the room and was directed to sit in the one chair opposite Charlotte, what really got to Charlotte the most were her eyes. Her beautiful emerald-green eyes were bloodshot and rimmed with dark circles. From lack of sleep? Or from crying? Probably from a bit of both, she decided, as something deep within tugged at her heartstrings. In spite of her misgivings about Angel and about getting involved, unbidden sympathy for the young woman washed through her.

Yes, Angel came across as a spoiled brat, a diva, but Charlotte reminded herself that, according to Benny, Angel had also worked hard to get to the top of the entertainment heap. If there was one thing Charlotte understood and respected, it was hard work. And if there was one thing she detested, it was someone being wrongly accused of anything, especially murder.

Charlotte smiled encouragingly at the young woman. "How you doing, hon?"

"Just how do you think I'm doing?" Angel shot back. But the instant the harsh retort left her mouth, a glazed look of remorse spread over her face. "Sorry about that," she said, her voice low and subdued. "Sorry," she repeated. "That's no way to treat someone who's trying to help you."

Charlotte sighed. "No, I'm the one who should apologize. Considering the circumstances, that was a pretty stupid question. I do have a not-so-stupid question for you, though."

Angel frowned. "Yeah, well, Benny said that you could help, but —" She shrugged. "I'm not sure anyone can help me." Tears filled her eyes. "One thing I want you to know, though." She blinked back the tears. "I did *not* kill Nick."

Charlotte wasn't sure what she had expected from Angel's attorney, but sitting like a bump on a log and saying nothing encouraging to his client was just not right. With a glancing glare at the lawyer, Charlotte said, "And one thing I want you to know. I believe you. But whether you killed Nick or not wasn't my question. Like I told Benny, I'm no professional by any stretch of the imagination, but I will do what I can." Ignoring the rude snort from Barry James, Charlotte said, "So, back to my question. Was Nick blackmailing you, and if so, why?"

That Angel shifted her gaze downward to stare at the tabletop was telling, but Charlotte couldn't help but note that her question had captured Barry James's interest. The lawyer suddenly sat up straight and stared at Angel.

Guess that got his attention, Charlotte thought. But when Angel finally responded, she said, "No, he wasn't blackmailing me." She lifted her gaze and stared hard into

159

Charlotte's eyes. "But even if he was, why would I admit such a thing? Admitting it would give the police even more ammunition against me."

"I'm not the police," Charlotte said bluntly. "Anything you tell me goes no further."

Angel gave a one-shouldered shrug. "Look, Ms. LaRue, no offense. I know that Benny trusts you and I respect that, but right now, I don't trust anyone."

"Except me, of course," her lawyer quickly injected.

Angel snapped her head around and glared at him. "Yeah, well, the jury is still out on you, so to speak," she retorted. "And, unfortunately, it's still out on me as well."

Back at home, Charlotte sat down at the kitchen table and looked over the notes she'd taken down from her conversation with Benny. Though she had been disappointed that Angel wasn't more forthcoming, the visit wasn't a total bust. Now, more than before, she was convinced that Nick Franklin had been blackmailing Angel.

At the bottom of the page of notes she wrote the word *blackmail* and added several question marks behind it. Then after the question marks, she wrote, *Angel is lying, but why?*

Whatever the reason for the blackmail, Charlotte understood the starlet's reluctance to admit such a thing. Even so, she had to wonder what in Angel's background could be so terrible that she could be blackmailed to begin with.

"O-kay," she murmured, drawing the word out after staring at the notes for several minutes. Charlotte had always held the theory that there was more than one way to get past an obstacle in her path. If she couldn't go through it, then there had to be a way of going around it or over it.

She tapped her pen against the pad of paper. So, besides Angel, who was the most likely suspect?

Bruce King's name immediately popped into her head. The man's whole mission in life seemed to be digging up dirt on people, especially Angel. Since he'd been barred from the set and couldn't get near her because of her bodyguard . . . "And couldn't bribe the maid to cooperate," she muttered. Maybe, like she'd told Benny, he'd decided to create his own dirt. What better dirt or scandal was there than for Angel to be accused of killing her boyfriend?

Maybe it was time for her to find out more about Mr. Bruce "Tabloid Journalist" King.

Charlotte shuddered at the thought of having to even come near the sleazy man again. But there were other ways without actually confronting him.

Charlotte stood and walked to the telephone. After punching in a phone number she waited. On the fourth ring, the phone was answered.

"Maddie, it's me," she said into the receiver. "Are you busy right now?"

"No, just trying to decide what I'm going to fix for tomorrow's lunch after church."

For years it had been a family tradition that Charlotte and Madeline alternated hosting a lunch for their combined families after church services. With everything that had happened that week, Charlotte was grateful that this Sunday was Maddie's turn to furnish lunch.

"I can't decide whether to fix a roast or gumbo," Madeline continued. "I'm leaning heavily toward a chicken-andouille gumbo, though, since gumbo is much better cooked ahead of time than a roast."

Charlotte didn't want to hurt her sister's feelings, but Maddie's gumbo left a lot to be desired. "Gumbo is always good," she said diplomatically, "but you do fix a mean roast."

"Hmm, yeah, well, we'll see. So, what's

going on with you?"

Charlotte felt like telling her, Nothing much, just a murder that needs solving, but figured it would be best to explain in person. "I need some help with a little project I've taken on."

"O-kay, what kind of help?"

At her sister's reluctant tone, Charlotte felt a smile tugging at her lips, and just to aggravate her, she said, "I'll tell you when I get there. Be there in about fifteen minutes."

"What kind of project?" Maddie demanded.

Charlotte's lips curved into a full-blown smile. "See you in fifteen," she said, and quickly hung up the receiver.

CHAPTER 8

"So, what did you decide about lunch tomorrow?" Charlotte asked her sister fifteen minutes later when she entered Madeline's living room.

Madeline narrowed her eyes, then closed the door. Ignoring the question, she said, "Right after you hung up on me, I suddenly remembered that you're supposed to be working at Bitsy's house this week while that movie is being shot. Your so-called project wouldn't happen to have anything to do with the murder of that movie star's boyfriend, would it?"

"Yes, but he wasn't her boyfriend — not exactly."

Madeline groaned and shook her head. "I should have known. Now I'll end up having to play peacemaker between you and Judith again."

Less than a year earlier, there had been another murder that Charlotte was involved in solving, and Madeline had the unfortunate experience of being present when she and Judith had a heated conversation over Charlotte's involvement.

Charlotte shook her head. "No, I promise you won't end up in the middle this time. I'll make sure of it. Besides, I've already talked to Judith."

With a suspicious look on her face, Madeline crossed her arms over her breasts. "Yeah, and I'll bet she told you to mind your own business."

Charlotte shrugged. "And your point?"

Madeline groaned. "Never mind. I give up. You always have been one stubborn woman."

"Again, and your point?"

"Grrr — stop that!"

Charlotte snickered. "Okay. I'll stop if you will. Truce?"

"Truce," Madeline answered. "Now, about this project."

"What I need is your computer expertise," Charlotte told her.

"For what?"

While Charlotte explained about Bruce King, Madeline led the way back to the bedroom that served as her home office. "I need you to do one of those search thingies —"

"It's called Googling," Madeline explained with a roll of her eyes as she sat down in front of her computer and powered it up.

Charlotte waved a dismissive hand. "Whatever — anyway, *Google* everything you can about Bruce King, especially any articles that he's already written about Angel."

"You know that Hank would set you up with a computer if you asked."

"Yeah, he's mentioned it a time or two."

"So what's the problem?"

Charlotte shrugged. "Part of me really wants to learn how to operate one, but another part of me balks at even the thought."

"Old age," Madeline quipped. "The older some people get, the less they want to learn."

"I am not old," Charlotte insisted. "Not that old anyway."

"Okay, sister dear, then drag up that chair over there and pay attention."

"Aw, come on, Maddie, do I have to? Can't you just do it for me, then show me the results?"

"Do you want my help or not?"

"Oh, okay," Charlotte grumbled. Over the next half hour her sister gave her a crash course on how to turn on the computer, what a mouse was and how to use it, how to access Google, and what to do once Google popped onto the screen.

"I'll never remember all of that," Charlotte complained. "And what if I mess it up or something?"

"Yes, you will remember it," Madeline insisted. It's like riding a bicycle. Once you've learned it, you'll always know it. As for messing something up, you won't. That little back arrow in the upper-right-hand corner is the key and will take you back to the last thing you looked at. Now —" Maddie stood and indicated that Charlotte should sit in her chair. "I want you to try it. And stop looking like you just sucked a lemon."

Knowing that Madeline wouldn't give up until she did it, Charlotte, with a sigh of resignation, stood and they exchanged chairs.

Two hours later, after scrolling through page after page of articles written by King, Charlotte was almost ready to give up when the word *murder* jumped out at her. She quickly placed the cursor on the link like Maddie had showed her, and clicked on it. After a moment, the Web site of a tabloid called the *Hollywood Tattletale* popped up.

"Now, that's strange," she murmured as

she noted that the date of the article was the same day that Angel had been arrested. At first she skimmed the article; then she started over and read it more slowly. When she had finished, she stared at the computer monitor. How could he have gotten the article out so fast? Not only that, but where had he gotten his information, details that she was fairly certain that only the police would know? King was either a *really* fast writer or he was psychic.

"Or he's as guilty as sin and wrote the article ahead of the actual murder and arrest," she whispered. Since she didn't figure anyone could be that fast of a writer and didn't believe in psychic mumbo jumbo, that left guilty.

Her thoughts racing, after a moment she finally decided that there might be another explanation. If King hadn't set up the whole thing and done the murderous deed himself, what if he'd made a deal with the devil, so to speak? What if he knew who the real killer was and had prior knowledge of what was about to happen?

Only one way to know for sure, she decided. Find Bruce King, find the answers.

After Charlotte left her sister's apartment, she decided that the best place to start was

Bitsy's house, just on the off chance that Bruce King might be hanging out with the rest of the media. She figured that by now, most of the media had probably left, but there might still be a few still hanging around, hoping that they could get an exclusive from someone.

Once she'd turned down Bitsy's street, though, she wished she hadn't. What if she did see him? What would she do then? Question him? And if she questioned him, what on earth would she ask him? There was no way she could just come right out and ask if he'd killed Nick and set Angel up to take the fall.

Worrying about an encounter with Bruce King turned out to be unwarranted. As she drove slowly by Bitsy's house, as far as she could tell, Bruce King was nowhere to be seen. Bitsy's front entrance door was still sealed off with crime scene tape. The only people there were a couple of policemen patrolling the perimeters of the property and what appeared to be a few gawkers.

"Makes sense," she decided. Either way — whether he'd actually committed the murder or knew who had — he wouldn't want to hang around.

A few minutes later, the first thing that Charlotte noted when she pulled into her driveway was that Louis's car was still gone. With everything that had happened over the past few days, she hadn't really had time to dwell on Louis or the mysterious discussion he wanted to have with her.

Charlotte's stomach growled loudly as she unlocked the front door to her side of the double and went inside. Eyeing the blinking light on her answering machine, she deliberately ignored it for the moment and headed straight for the kitchen. Already it was past her regular lunchtime, and she really needed to eat. After she'd decided on a ham sandwich and leftover potato salad, she fixed a plate and took it back to the living room so she could watch the noon news and weather.

Before turning on the television, she took a moment to bow her head and say a prayer of thanksgiving. After asking for her meal to be blessed, she prayed about the weather, specifically that there would be no tropical activity out in the Gulf of Mexico to worry about. What with first, Hurricanes Katrina and Rita, then, a mere three years later, Hurricanes Gustav and Ike, she prayed that the tropics would be quiet and mild this hurricane season, and that no one would have to contend with damaging weather.

With a firm "Amen," she picked up the remote control and turned on the TV. By the time the news and weather were over and she'd satisfied herself that there was nothing new about Nick's murder or Angel's arrest, Charlotte had finished her meal.

Again she eyed the blinking answering machine light. "Guess now is as good a time as ever," she murmured. After she set her empty plate on the coffee table, she walked over to the desk to listen to her messages.

The first message was from Louis. "Hi, Charlotte. Guess your new job played out, what with the main star being arrested for murder, huh?" There was a long pause. "Not quite sure how to say this except just to come right out and say it. Stay out of it. Let the police handle it. Anyway, enough said. Looks like I'll be in Houston longer than I'd planned. If you don't mind, would you collect my mail for me? I would appreciate it. Oh, and in case you need to get in touch with me, just call my cell phone. See you in a few days. Bye."

Stay out of it? Charlotte fumed. Just who did he think he was? What was it with him? A few kisses and he thought he could dictate what she could do and what she couldn't do?

Don't you think you're overreacting a bit?

Ignoring the aggravating voice of reason, she muttered, " 'Enough said' indeed," and immediately dismissed his so-called advice. Until he started paying her bills, he could mind his own business and stay out of hers.

Louis's message ended with a beep, and the second message began. "Charlotte, this is Bitsy. Where the devil are you? I tried your cell phone and left a message, and this is the third time I've called you at home. What's going on at my house? No one will tell me anything."

A beep sounded, and the mechanical voice of her answering machine informed her, "You have no more messages." Frowning, Charlotte dug inside her purse for her cell phone. "Great," she whispered. "I didn't even turn the ding-dang thing on this morning." So how many more messages had she missed?

Charlotte turned on the cell phone. After determining that Bitsy's call was the only one she'd received, she turned the phone off again and dropped it back inside her purse.

Still aggravated over Louis's call, she marched into the kitchen and placed her dirty dishes into the dishwasher, all the while telling herself to take a few deep breaths and calm down. By the time she returned to the living room, she felt somewhat better.

Stopping by her desk, she stared at the phone and the financial ledger that was still exactly where she'd put it. Charlotte sighed. There was still Bitsy to contend with and she still needed to catch up on paperwork for Maid-for-a-Day.

Charlotte sighed again. Dear Lord, she dreaded calling Bitsy almost as much as she dreaded the boring task of posting receipts to the ledger. She'd much rather check in with Benny and see if he knew where she could find Bruce King.

"First things first," she murmured. The ledger could wait a while longer, but if she didn't call Bitsy, she'd never hear the end of it. So first she'd return Bitsy's call, and then she'd phone Benny. Even if Benny didn't have any information on King, she'd bet her bottom dollar that he'd know someone who did.

Half an hour later, Charlotte hung up the telephone receiver and once again had to take several deep breaths to calm down. Though she had tried repeatedly to reassure Bitsy that her house and her possessions were under lock and key with policemen patrolling the grounds, the elderly lady kept insisting that Charlotte needed to check it out for her. Of all things, Bitsy was still worried about the blood-soaked antique rug.

When Charlotte explained that the crime scene team had taken the rug with them, Bitsy had a conniption fit. "What about the wood floor beneath the rug?" she'd whined. Then she'd started a tirade about how she'd have to have the floor sanded and refinished. Never mind that a man had been murdered, and never mind that an innocent woman was being held for that murder. Since Bitsy didn't know them personally, none of that really mattered to her. All she could think about was her ruined rug and floor.

"You could get inside the house if you wanted to," Bitsy had declared. "It may not be too late to scrub up the bloodstains. Get that niece of yours to let you inside."

The only way she'd been able to finally end the conversation was to promise Bitsy that she would at least ask Judith about getting inside the house.

"I swear." Charlotte shook her head. At times, talking to Bitsy was like talking to a brick wall. The elderly lady had been her client for several years now, and it seemed that the older Bitsy got, the more stubborn she became.

Be careful. That's kind of like the pot calling the kettle black. Judge not, lest ye be judged. You're no spring chicken, you know, and you're getting older as well.

174

"Yeah, yeah," Charlotte muttered, recalling what her sister had said about "old age" earlier that morning. "Guess everything's relative," she whispered. She thought of Bitsy as being old, and Maddie thought of Charlotte as being old.

"Enough already. Right, Sweety?" she called out. But Sweety Boy ignored her. Probably pouting, she decided, since it had been days since she'd let him out of his cage to stretch his wings. After the time he'd flown into the shower and after his adventure outside several months earlier, now she always made sure that she could watch him when he was out of the cage. Maybe she'd let him out once she'd talked to Benny.

After a brief futile search of the top of her desk for Benny's cell phone number, she remembered that she'd scribbled the number at the bottom of the list of notes she'd taken when they had discussed the suspects.

Once she'd retrieved the notepad, she dialed the number. After the fourth ring, Benny answered. "Hello, Benny Jackson here."

"Benny, this is Charlotte."

"Hey, Miss Charlotte. Any luck with Angel?"

"No, but I could tell that there's definitely something that she's hiding. I think you're right about that blackmail business. But listen, one of the reasons I'm calling is in hopes that you might know how we could locate Bruce King."

Charlotte went on to explain about the article written by King that she'd found. "Besides being the best suspect we have at the moment," she continued, "I think we should explore all of the possibilities. He seems to know a lot about a lot of things. Even if my suspicions about him don't pan out, it just might be possible that he stumbled onto something about Angel and Nick. I thought he might be hanging around the house where the movie is being shot, but when I drove by, I didn't see him."

"Finding King might be helpful," Benny offered, "but it's not likely that he's going to confess or give out any information. Besides, if he knew anything about the blackmailing business, don't you think he would have included it in his article?"

Charlotte drummed her fingers against the top of the desk. "Yeah, I suppose you're right. Then again, he might be afraid that if he wrote something like that, he'd attract the attention of the police. Hmm, guess we'll have to try something else."

"I've been thinking about that. There just may be another way to find out if and why

Nick might have been blackmailing Angel. Remember me telling you that only a very few people know Angel's real name and where she comes from?"

The drumming of Charlotte's fingers slowed, then stopped completely. Of course! If anyone knew the truth about Angel's name and background, it would be Benny. "And you're one of those people," she shot back.

"Yes, ma'am, I am, and I think that's where we have to start. I really hate to discuss this sort of thing over the phone — you never know who might be listening — but I guess it doesn't really matter right now. What matters is getting Angel out of jail."

When Benny hesitated, Charlotte said, "If it makes you feel any better, I can't imagine why anyone would be listening in to either of us. For one, the police think they've solved their case, and secondly, the real killer thinks he's in the clear, what with Angel in jail."

"Yeah, you're probably right. After all this time I tend to be paranoid where Angel is concerned."

"Being paranoid is not necessarily a bad thing, especially in circumstances like this

177

one. Believe me, I know. So, tell me what you know about Angel."

CHAPTER 9

Benny sighed deeply. "Well, here goes nothing. Her real name is Martha Pate — Marti, for short. Believe it or not, her father was a Baptist preacher."

"Was?"

"Yes, ma'am. He was killed in an accident the summer after Angel graduated from high school. From what she's told me about him, he wasn't exactly Father of the Year. Nope, not a nice man at all, considering his profession. From everything that Angel's said about him, he was one of those uptight, strict, controlling types."

Though Charlotte was surprised about Angel's background, after she thought about it a moment, she decided she shouldn't be. That Angel was actually a PK, a preacher's kid, made perfect sense. The strain on the children and wives of ministers was tremendous. They were expected to be perfect, which of course was ridiculous. No one but Jesus Christ was perfect. But because of the high expectations, there were many PKs who ended up rebelling by being real problem children. Of course there were also many that turned out to be just fine.

"She grew up in a small town in Mississippi called Oakdale," Benny continued. "Actually, it's not that far from Jackson, about halfway between Hammond and Jackson. Before we began shooting, Angel had me take her to Oakdale to visit her mother."

Charlotte wrinkled her brow in thought. She couldn't recall the town, so why did the name Oakdale sound so familiar? Where had she heard that name before? Then, suddenly, she remembered. Not heard, but seen. She'd seen the name on the sweater of the stuffed bulldog in Angel's dressing room — one of the do-not-touch items that Heather had told her about.

"Angel is a little superstitious and calls it her good-luck charm."

A knowing smile pulled at Charlotte's lips. Heather had called it being "superstitious," but now that she knew more about Angel's background, Charlotte suspected it was nostalgia, Angel's one connection to her real identity. That, along with the other do-not-touch item, the eight-by-ten framed picture of an older couple and a little girl standing in front of what appeared to be a church. Angel and her parents. No, not *Angel,* not then. Then, she was *Marti,* Marti Pate.

"Miss Charlotte? Are you still there?"

With a slight shake of her head to clear out the cobwebs of speculation, Charlotte said, "Yes, I'm here. Sorry, guess I was lost in thought there for a moment."

"Well, how about it?"

Uh-oh. Guess she'd been more lost in thought than she'd realized. "Sorry, how about what?" she asked.

"What say you and I take a little trip to Mississippi and see what we can find there?"

"I say that sounds like an excellent idea. I've already cleared my schedule for two weeks anyway, and I don't think they'll be resuming shooting any time soon."

"Could you be ready to leave in the morning?"

"The sooner the better."

"Great! I'll pick you up around eight. Oh, and pack a bag, at least for a couple of days."

"Good idea. See you in the morning." Charlotte hung up the receiver. Her mind on packing a suitcase, she headed for the bedroom. Halfway there, she remembered Louis's message about checking his mail and did an about-face. At the front door, she glanced over at Sweety Boy's cage.

181

"Hmm, two days," she murmured. She should probably have someone come in and feed Sweety Boy. Maybe Madeline? No, not Madeline. For one thing, Sweety didn't like Madeline. Every time she came near his case, he squawked and thrashed around inside the cage like a wild thing. For two, she'd learned a long time ago that her sister wasn't that dependable.

Judith or Carol would be her best bet. Of course then she would have to explain about where she was going and why. After a moment she shook her head. Sweety could get by okay for just the couple of days that she and Benny would be gone, especially if she left extra helpings of food and water, and an extra cuttlebone. After all, when she'd first discovered the little bird in her former, deadbeat tenant's half of the double, as best she could calculate, the tenant had been gone at least a week and Sweety had survived then. Barely, but he had survived. With extra food and water, he'd be just fine. At least that was what she kept telling herself as she went out onto the porch.

Louis's mailbox was stuffed, and so was hers. With everything that had happened during the week, mail was the last thing on her mind.

She'd often thought about having a mail

slot installed in both front doors, but never seemed to get around to it. Besides, she found the thought of having a hole in her door that anyone could push open and see inside unappealing, to say the least.

Inside again, she squashed the temptation to sneak a peek at what type of mail Louis received. After separating the envelopes from the magazines, she shuffled all of it, and placed it in a neat stack on the coffee table. Once she'd separated her own mail into bills and junk mail, she placed the bills on her desk and threw the junk mail into the trash can.

Glancing around, she tried to think of anything else that needed doing.

Nothing but packing.

Packing. Right! Doing an about-face, she once again headed for the bedroom.

The sleepy little town of Oakdale reminded Charlotte of a town in North Louisiana called Minden, only smaller. She and her family had evacuated to a small community near Minden during Hurricane Katrina, and again more recently during Hurricane Gustav. Minden was a really nice town, and from the looks of Oakdale, she figured it was probably a really nice town as well.

"It's almost lunchtime," Benny said as

they drove slowly through the streets of the downtown area. "Are you hungry?"

Charlotte nodded. "I could use a bite."

"If I remember right, there's a pretty nice local restaurant just on the other side of town — not fancy, but good food. And not far from there is a Holiday Inn. I figure that we should probably check in to the motel first, then go eat."

"Sounds good to me," she told him, but her mind was stuck on the word *fancy* as she took in the old-fashioned storefronts, mostly constructed with bricks. There were a couple of banks, a drugstore, several antique shops, a dress shop, a florist, and even a barbershop, complete with an old-fashioned barber pole.

Charlotte couldn't help grinning as time after time, heads turned and people stared openly at them. Talk about fancy, from the expressions on the faces of the townsfolk, evidently not too many limousines drove through town. Either that or they were trying to figure out what celebrity was being squired around and why.

If only they knew, she thought. Wouldn't they be surprised to learn that the only person being chauffeured around was a maid?

No one could have been more surprised

than she had been when Benny had pulled up in her driveway earlier that morning in the long white limousine that was leased to Angel for her stay in New Orleans. Charlotte couldn't remember the last time, if ever, that she'd ridden in a limousine. When she'd protested, Benny had simply shrugged and told her that the limo was the only vehicle he had to drive. Of course she had immediately offered her van for the trip instead, but he'd insisted that since they were on a business trip, for Angel, they would use her limo.

Not knowing what else to do or say, she'd finally given in. It was when he had opened the back door and motioned for her to climb inside that she'd balked. She'd told him that there was no way that she was going to ride in the backseat all by herself like some highfalutin society lady while he chauffeured her all the way to Oakdale, Mississippi. Either she rode up front with him or they took her van.

"That's the restaurant," Benny pointed out as they passed an older redbrick building. "And here's the motel," he added, a few minutes later.

The motel looked to be fairly new, and the rooms were clean and nicely decorated in earthen tones. After checking in and unpacking their suitcases, Charlotte suggested that they walk to the restaurant instead of driving, and Benny agreed.

When they entered Karen's Café and Catering, Charlotte's mouth watered at the delicious aromas wafting through the air. "It smells wonderful," she told Benny. "Either that or I'm hungrier than I thought."

From what she could see from the foyer entry, the restaurant was small with a homey, yet slightly formal atmosphere. An attractive, middle-aged woman dressed in a black silky pants suit greeted them. Smiling, she said, "I'm Joanne, your hostess. Table for two?" When Benny nodded, she showed them to a nearby table covered with a white linen tablecloth, linen napkins to match, a full setting of china, what appeared to be crystal glasses, and a complete layout of silverware. In the middle of the table was a small bouquet of fresh flowers arranged around a lone candle.

Within seconds of their being seated, a young waitress dressed in a black-and-white uniform appeared. "I'm Sally," she said with an unmistakable Mississippi drawl and a smile as she handed each of them a menu. "And I'll be your waitress." Sally suddenly frowned at Benny. "Say, don't I know you?"

she asked. Without waiting for his answer, she said, "Aren't you that guy who was in here with Marti Pate a few weeks ago?"

When Benny nodded, she grinned, and in an aside to Charlotte, she said, "Marti and I went to high school together. In fact, speaking of high school" — she turned to Benny — "I hope you can help me persuade Marti to come to our ten-year reunion this October. I mentioned it to her when y'all were here before, but she never gave me a definite answer. I think it would be a real hoot if she showed up."

Though Charlotte simply nodded and smiled, her mind raced. Persuade was a good word. Maybe, just maybe, with the right kind of persuasion, Sally might prove to be a wealth of information about Angel's background, especially if she thought she would be helping out the town celebrity.

Sally winked at Benny. "So, how is she?" she asked. "Working on some big movie, probably, huh?" She suddenly froze. "Hey, I've got an idea!" she exclaimed. "I need a date, so why don't you come with her?"

After a moment of stunned hesitation, Benny said, "Thanks for asking, but a lot will depend on her schedule."

"Well, next time you see her, be sure and say hello for me and try to talk her into coming. Everyone here in Oakdale is proud as punch of her success. Oh, and be sure and tell her that her secret is safe with us. Everyone here thinks it's a hoot that all of those paparazzi types are chasing their tails trying to find out who she really is and where she's from. It's like a conspiracy-type thing, but a nice one. And best of all, the whole town's in on it."

Again Benny nodded. "I'll tell her."

Charlotte stared at Sally for several moments. Was it possible that no one in this little burg even knew about Angel's arrest yet? She glanced over at Benny, but his expression confirmed her thoughts. He seemed as shocked as she was. A smile tugged at her lips. Or maybe he was just shocked that the waitress had asked him to be her date for the reunion.

Sally didn't seem to notice, though. "Even if Marti can't come, maybe you could." She winked at Benny, then whipped out two smaller drink menus and handed one to each of them. "Now, what can I get you folks to drink? We have a nice selection of house wines."

Charlotte shook her head and handed the smaller menu back. "Just unsweetened iced tea for me, please."

Benny handed his back as well. "I'll have

the same."

After Sally left to get their drinks, Benny leaned toward Charlotte and, careful to keep his voice low, said, "Can you believe that?"

"What? That the waitress would hit on you? Of course I can believe it."

Benny grimaced. "No, not that. I meant, you know, about them not knowing. How is that even possible?"

Though Charlotte grinned, enjoying teasing him, she scanned the tables surrounding them and noticed that the couple at the next table seemed to be interested in what they were saying. She gave a slight nod of her head in their direction. "Maybe we should discuss that later," she whispered. "When so many eyes aren't watching and so many ears aren't listening."

Benny cut his eyes to the table next to them. "Yeah, I suppose so. I sure don't want to be the one to tell them."

But we will have to at some point, Charlotte thought, as she looked over the menu. If, as Sally had indicated, the whole town were helping keep Angel's secret of her origin, surely they would want to help her out in her time of trouble?

When Charlotte spied the Panne' Chicken on the menu, she closed it and placed it beside her plate. Panne' Chicken, if it was cooked right, was one of her favorite entrées.

Evidently, having also chosen what he wanted to eat, Benny closed his menu and placed it on the table. "According to my *friend,* this place has been here for ages," he said.

Friend? Oh, for pity's sake, she thought, with a quick glance at the nosy couple. Now they were reduced to using code words.

Don't be so testy.

Yeah, well, people should mind their own business.

You're one to talk about minding your own business.

"In fact," Benny continued, interrupting her silent argument, "she was a waitress here for about a year before she took off for California."

Though Benny had already told her that Angel had worked as a hostess in a restaurant in California before she made it big, it still stunned her a bit trying to imagine the spoiled brat that she'd met a few days earlier waiting on tables here in her hometown. From preacher's kid to waiting on tables, to hostess, to having a full-time chauffeur and personal chef was quite a step up in the world.

While soft classical music, punctuated with the occasional laughter and the clink of dishes, drifted in the air, Charlotte glanced around, trying to picture Angel in the midst of the local patrons. Most of the restaurant's customers were dressed in what Charlotte liked to call their Sunday go-to-a-meeting clothes. And since it was Sunday, she figured that the majority of them had probably come straight from church services.

Nope, she couldn't do it. Though the restaurant was nice enough by most people's standards, Charlotte simply couldn't imagine Angel even eating there, and found it impossible to imagine her waiting tables.

Once Sally brought their lunch, Charlotte and Benny, by mutual silent agreement because of the nosy couple nearby, stopped talking and concentrated on eating.

"That was delicious," Charlotte said as she folded her napkin and placed it on the table.

"Yeah, my steak wasn't half bad."

Both declined a dessert and coffee. After Benny paid the check and left a generous tip for Sally, they headed back toward the motel.

Outside, the sky had grown overcast, and as they walked slowly back to the motel,

Benny said, "Looks like it might rain."

"Maybe not," Charlotte offered. "So, where to now?"

"I think a good place to start asking questions might be Angel's mother."

Charlotte nodded. "I agree."

"There's something you need to know, though," he said. "Laura, Angel's mother, was diagnosed with Alzheimer's about a year ago. Sometimes she's almost normal, but other times, she's —" He shrugged.

"I understand," Charlotte told him. "That's a terrible disease."

"Yeah, Angel was all broken up about it when she first found out, and it was even worse when she had to put her mom in the nursing home."

"If this happens to be one of her bad days, don't forget that our waitress Sally could be helpful."

"I don't know," he said. "After what she said about the entire town keeping Angel's secret —"

"I think she could be persuaded, especially if she knew the circumstances."

"Maybe, but why don't we use her as a last resort? I still can't believe that no one here knows what's going on. It's almost like stepping into a whole different world, one where no one knows what's happening in the real world."

Charlotte laughed. "I've got news for you. This *is* the real world." Like her, Benny had always lived in a big city and had no idea how insular or protective a small town could be, especially toward one of its own. Though it was hard to believe in this modern age, not everyone had access to cable television, and those that tuned into the news on the local channels mostly watched the weather segment. "Small towns, you gotta love 'em."

"Still hard to believe," Benny said as they approached the motel. "The limo is over there." He motioned toward the spot where he'd parked the car.

"I'm wondering," Charlotte said. "Do you think we'll have any problems getting in to see Angel's mother? Some places have an approved visitors' list. Unless you're on that list, you don't get in."

Benny shook his head. "I don't think that will be a problem. Besides, I don't remember anyone checking when I was here before with Angel. We just walked right in. Also, being that it's Sunday and most people visit on the weekends anyway, it should be easier today."

By the time they drove to Oakdale Nursing and Care Center, the sky had grown even darker, and a breeze had kicked up.

"It sure is a lovely place," Charlotte offered as Benny parked the limo.

The center was located just on the edge of town and surrounded by huge draping oak trees. The outside of the facility looked to be well maintained and had a beautiful garden off to one side overflowing with flowers in full bloom. Nestled between the beds of flowers were wooden benches where the patients could sit and enjoy the view.

Inside the facility, Charlotte noted that the floors were spotless as she walked alongside Benny. Another thing that she noticed was the lack of the heavy cleaner odor that she'd found in other facilities she had visited; instead, the air had a fresh, clean scent.

Since Benny had been there before and seemed to know his way around, Charlotte let him take the lead through the maze of hallways.

Another plus for the center, as far as she was concerned, were the nurses and the patients. All of the nurses that they passed in the hallway had welcoming smiles on their faces, and the patients they encountered looked neat and well groomed. Some even looked happy.

Of course, as Benny had pointed out

earlier, today was one of the prime visiting days, so it stood to reason that the patients would be happy about that. As for the staff, it just made sense that they would want to present a good face for all of the visitors.

For Pete's sake, stop being such a cynic. Maybe for once things are exactly as they seem. Maybe the staff and the patients are contented.

Charlotte winced and felt duly chastised by her conscience. While she didn't always agree with the little voice of reason in her head, this time she did. She *was* becoming a cynic, and she needed to stop it. *"Do right and you'll feel right,"* she'd once heard her pastor say during his sermon. It was a lesson on positive thinking and action that she certainly needed to work on.

"Her room is that one." Benny interrupted her thoughts, pointing to a door that was standing wide open. After a brief knock he stepped into the doorway. "Mrs. Pate, may we come in?"

Laura Pate didn't answer right away, but Benny stepped just inside the room anyway, and Charlotte followed. Once again, Charlotte was impressed with the cleanliness and neatness of the place. No dust on any of the surfaces that she could see, and the floors appeared to be dust and dirt free as well.

But it was the middle-aged woman resting in the bed who drew her attention.

Even if she hadn't known that Laura Pate was Angel's mother, she would have recognized her immediately. Except for the obvious age difference, her hairstyle, and the blank look in her eyes, Mrs. Pate was simply an older version of her daughter.

Laura Pate suddenly frowned. "Do I know you, young man?"

"I'm Benny, ma'am." He stepped closer to the bed. "Benny Jackson — Marti's chauffeur."

Without acknowledging Benny, Angel's mother turned her gaze to Charlotte and frowned. "You're not Marti."

Charlotte shook her head. "No, ma'am, I'm not, but I'm a friend of your daughter. My name is Charlotte LaRue."

Laura Pate turned her gaze back to Benny. "Where's Marti?"

Benny smiled and gently patted Laura Pate's hand. "Marti couldn't come this time, so she asked me and Miss Charlotte to come instead. But she will come again next time."

Charlotte thought for a moment that Laura was going to say more, but she closed her eyes instead. "She does that," Benny explained to Charlotte. "But she usually opens them within a few moments."

Sure enough, only a minute or so later, Laura opened her eyes again. "Who are you people? Why are you in my room?" She suddenly frowned. "Where am I? Do you know where I am?" she asked, turning her gaze to Charlotte.

"Yes, ma'am," Charlotte answered softly. "You have some medical problems and you're in the Oakdale Nursing and Care Center."

Laura's frown deepened. "Am I ill? I don't remember being ill." Tears welled in her eyes. "Where's Marti? I want to go home." Then, louder, "I want to go home."

At that moment, a young nurse entered the room. Noting Laura's distress, she hurried over to the bed. "Now, now, Mrs. Pate. You're okay, sweetheart." She smoothed Laura's hair back, then blotted the tears from her cheeks with a tissue. "It's Dawn, sweetie."

"Dawn?" Laura asked, her face an effigy of confusion.

"Yes, ma'am, Dawn Sanders, your nurse. Remember? Marti hired me personally to take care of you while you're here. Just relax now. That's right, just close your eyes and relax."

After a moment, Laura's breathing evened

out, and only then did Dawn turn to Benny and Charlotte. "I don't recall seeing you here before. Are you family?"

Benny and Charlotte both shook their heads. "Friends of the family," Benny explained. "Friends of her daughter, Angel — I mean Marti," he added.

Dawn nodded that she understood. "She's resting now, so you should probably leave."

Benny glanced down at Laura, then back to the nurse. "Would it be okay if we come back later this evening?"

"Tomorrow would be better," Dawn told him. "But even then there's no guarantee that she'll be any better, or even remember that you visited today."

"We understand," Charlotte said. "And thank you for taking such good care of her."

The nurse shrugged. "It's my job, and it's a privilege. Mrs. Pate is a really nice lady." The nurse managed a tremulous smile, but her eyes held a wealth of sadness. "Up until I got to the fifth grade, she was my Sunday school teacher. It was because of her influence on my life that I became a Christian and later became a nurse."

Though it was still overcast outside, the rain had held off when they emerged from the nursing home. Benny was suspiciously stoic and silent during the short drive back to the motel, and Charlotte's throat was too tight with emotion to speak. Even if she could say something, she feared that she might burst into tears at any moment. She'd been around seriously ill patients before and had felt deep sympathy for them, but for some reason that she couldn't explain, Laura Pate's predicament seemed somehow different, seemed much, much worse.

Complete loss of control, she decided. At times the poor woman didn't even know where she was. Charlotte couldn't begin to imagine what that would be like, how frightening that would be. One rare minute Laura could remember who she was and where she was, and the next, nothing, an entire lifetime wiped out. Even sadder, there was no hope that she would ever get better, only a lot worse.

Then another thought hit her and she swallowed hard and blinked back tears. If Angel was railroaded into a murder conviction, then who would there be to look after Laura? Benny hadn't mentioned Angel having any siblings or other relatives.

Charlotte glanced at Benny. "What will happen to Laura if Angel is convicted of murder? Does Laura have other relatives?"

Benny's lips tightened into a thin line and

e shook his head no. For a moment Charlotte didn't think he was going to say anything; then he cleared his throat and said, "After Angel's father died, him being a preacher and all, there was no retirement money or savings to speak of. The only income they had was a hundred-thousand-dollar life insurance policy and a small monthly check from Social Security.

"One of the first things Angel did after she made her first big-hit movie was set aside enough funds to make sure that her mother was taken care of for the rest of her life. One of the deacons who served under her father in their church is also an attorney, and Angel gave him power of attorney if something should happen to her."

Once Benny parked the limo, they headed, by silent, mutual consent, for their rooms. When they reached Charlotte's room, she turned to face him. "So, what do you think? Should we try again tomorrow?"

Benny cleared his throat and sighed deeply. "I think we should try at least once more. If not for Angel's sake, for her mother's sake."

Charlotte nodded. "I agree. Now, if you don't mind I think I'll rest a bit before supper. And speaking of supper, since we had such a big lunch, I'd be perfectly satisfied with just a hamburger or a salad."

Benny nodded. "Sounds good to me." He glanced at his wristwatch. "What say we meet in the parking lot about six?"

"Great. See you then," she told him over her shoulder as she unlocked the door to her room and went inside. After she made sure the door locked again, she kicked off her shoes, then stretched out on the bed. Just as she closed her eyes, she heard the ring tone of her cell phone."

"Oh, for pity's sake," she groaned as she rolled into a sitting position and scooted off the bed. "Live and learn," she muttered, hurrying to where she'd left her purse across the room. Next time she'd make sure she put the silly phone next to the bed instead.

She dug the phone out of her purse and flipped it open. "Hello?"

"Hey, Charlotte."

Louis. Just hearing his voice did funny things to her insides, and for a second she was too stunned to respond. Why on earth was Louis calling her?

Chapter 10

There was only one way to find out. Clearing her throat and taking a deep breath, Charlotte said, "Hey, yourself. Is anything wrong?"

"Humph! I was about to ask you the same question. I've been calling your house off and on most of the afternoon. I know you usually go to church Sunday mornings, and I figured you probably ate lunch at your sister's."

"Why didn't you just call my cell phone when you didn't get an answer at home?"

She heard his deep sigh. "If I remember right, you normally don't even turn it on, not on Sundays."

He was right . . . as usual. Several months ago she'd made the mistake of forgetting to turn it off during the morning worship hour, and it had rung right in the middle of the pastor's sermon. Now everyone in the whole church knew that her ring tone was the song "God Bless the U.S.A." To top it off, the call she'd received was a wrong number. She'd later joked with the pastor's wife that perhaps everyone in the church should switch to the same ring tone of the song "Amen."

"So why this Sunday?" he asked. "What's going on?"

"Well, ah, nothing — not exactly."

"What does 'not exactly' mean?"

It was Charlotte's turn to sigh. Louis knew her too well. Even worse, she knew him well enough to know that he wouldn't approve of what she was doing . . . if he knew. Maybe she could change the subject. "When are you coming home?"

"Now I know something's going on," he said, his voice heavy with suspicion.

Oops!

"You know that if you don't tell me, I'll just call Judith, and she'll tell me." His voice rose. "So stop trying to change the subject. Knowing you, you probably completely ignored my advice and got yourself involved in another stupid murder investigation. And let me guess," he added sarcastically. "It wouldn't happen to have anything to do with that movie star's boyfriend, would it?"

Stung more by his condescending tone of voice than what he'd actually said, Charlotte felt her temper flare. "Call Judith!" she retorted, her voice rising in anger. "Be my guest! Or call your watchdog, Samantha O'Reilly."

"Samantha?"

"Oh, yeah, I know all about your little spy. Go ahead. Call her."

"But Samantha isn't —"

Charlotte cut him off. "Not that what I do or don't do is any of your business. In fact, call anyone you please, but do *not* call me again."

Her heart pounding in her chest, she pulled the phone away from her ear, then snapped it closed, effectively ending the call. "Serves you right," she said, glaring at the phone. Almost immediately, it rang again. This time, when she flipped it open, she pressed the button that would turn the phone off.

"So there, take that!" she muttered as she dropped the tiny phone back inside her purse. Still angry, she stomped over to the bed, threw herself down on it, and covered her eyes with her forearm.

Outside, thunder boomed, and the sound of rain beating against the windowpane reached her ears. "Perfect," she grumbled. "Just perfect." Nice that the weather outside fit her mood inside, she thought sarcastically.

As she lay there, listening to the thunder and rain, the thought that she had totally overreacted flitted through her mind, but she immediately squashed it. What she didn't understand, though, *couldn't* understand, was why Louis thought he had the right to run her life. Sure, they were friends, sorta, kinda, on again, off again. And while it was true that she was attracted to him in most of the ways that counted and she truly respected him, none of that gave him the right to keep track of her like she didn't have the sense God gave a goose.

For more years than she cared to remember, she'd run her life just fine, thank you very much, without a man's help, without help from anyone but the good Lord above. What on earth made Louis think that she wasn't capable of doing so now? If anyone was capable, she was. For Pete's sake, she owned her own business, a lucrative business that employed several other people. Not only that, but she was debt free; she outright owned her own home, and owned her van.

And what about Hank? Did Louis ever stop to think that she'd raised a son, all by herself, and had even helped put him

through medical school?
You're overreacting, don't you think?
No! she silently argued.
Yes, you are, and you know why.
Leave me alone. Go away.
The truth hurts, doesn't it?
"Yeah, yeah," she whispered. Truth was, if she were honest enough to admit it, she cared about Louis, cared about him more than she had cared about any man since her son's father. Oh, there had been other men in her life. A woman couldn't live for as many years as she had without making male contact somewhere along the way. But none of the others had ever measured up to her memories of her son's father, Hank Senior, the ultimate love of her life . . . until Louis came along.

Charlotte sighed, and for some reason, Laura Pate came to mind. Maybe, once again, it was that control thing. Was it possible that she'd been in control of her own life, her own destiny, for so long that she wouldn't be able to relinquish that control to anyone else? And why should she have to? Unlike poor Laura Pate, who didn't have a choice in the matter, she did have a choice.

Charlotte sighed again. Was that the choice? And if it was, why did it have to be that way? Why couldn't she have both? Why couldn't she control her own life *and* enjoy life with Louis? While it was true that she didn't want to spend what was left of her life all alone, she didn't want to spend it kowtowing to a male chauvinist either.

"Humph! Better alone," she murmured, "than with someone telling you what to do or what not to do all the time."

But as she lay there thinking back over the past few years, she kept remembering how her life had been before she'd met Louis and how it had been since.

Charlotte turned over onto her side and rolled into the fetal position. Just because he'd been rude didn't mean it was okay to be rude back. She probably owed him an apology. Maybe later, she decided. Later she'd call and apologize . . . well, not apologize exactly. Instead, maybe she should try and explain why she'd lost her temper.

Then another thought struck her. Why had Louis been trying to call her to begin with? He never did say. Of course in all fairness, she didn't give him much of a chance to say why.

Charlotte turned over onto her other side. Some conversations were better face-to-face. Maybe she'd wait until she got back home to talk to him. Besides, at the moment, she had more pressing issues to take care of. She needed to concentrate on the reason she was in this little town to begin with: namely, who really killed Nick Franklin?

On Monday morning, the evening storm had passed, leaving the air muggy with heat and humidity. After Charlotte and Benny ate an early breakfast at a nearby Shoney's Restaurant, they drove back to Oakdale Nursing and Care Center.

This time when they approached the doorway to Laura's room she was sitting up in a chair watching television. From the sound of the program she was tuned to, Charlotte figured it had to be one of the many cable cooking shows. How sad was that? In all probabilities, Laura Pate would never cook another meal.

Benny leaned close to Charlotte. "I think you should do most of the talking. I figured that she'll be more inclined to open up to another woman than a man."

"I agree," she said, but though what Benny said made sense, at the moment she didn't have the foggiest idea how to even start a conversation.

"Ready?" Benny asked.

"As ready as I'll ever be," she replied.

When Benny rapped lightly on the door

frame to Laura's room, Laura glanced up from the television and smiled.

"What a nice surprise," she said. "Come on in here." She glanced curiously at Charlotte as she pointed the remote control toward the TV and muted the sound. Then she turned her attention back to Benny. "If I remember right, your name is Benny, isn't it? You're Marti's chauffeur. Is Marti with you?"

Benny nodded and Charlotte followed him inside. "Yes, ma'am, I'm Benny." Then he shook his head. "Sorry — Marti couldn't make it this trip. But —" He motioned toward Charlotte. "I brought someone else along to visit you. Her name is Charlotte — Charlotte LaRue."

"Are you one of my Marti's friends too?"

Charlotte hesitated a moment, then simply smiled. She couldn't really call herself Marti's friend, but explaining their relationship was more complicated than Laura needed to hear at the moment.

Avoiding the question, Charlotte said, "You must be very proud of your daughter and all that she's accomplished."

Laura's entire face lit up. "Oh, I am proud of her, but —" Abruptly, her expression grew tight with strain. "At the same time I worry about her. I've tried over and over to teach her that fame and fortune don't guarantee happiness, but I guess that all I can do now is hope and pray that she paid attention to what I tried to teach her."

Charlotte nodded. "That's all that any parent can do."

"Do you have children?"

"Yes, I do," Charlotte answered, relieved that Laura seemed lucid and also relieved that she was the one who opened up a topic of conversation. How had she forgotten that one thing all mothers had in common with other mothers was their children? "I have a son and two grandchildren."

"Oh, you have grandchildren! I'd love to have grandchildren. I keep hoping that Marti will decide to settle down one of these days and give me some, but so far, she doesn't even have a boyfriend." Laura blinked several times; then her eyes suddenly clouded over.

For long moments, it took every ounce of willpower that Charlotte possessed to hold her smile in place, when what she really wanted was to cry. In light of Laura's medical condition and Marti's present circumstances, there was more than a good chance that Marti would never marry and have children and that Laura would never get to hold a grandchild on her lap.

When Laura abruptly lowered her gaze to stare at the floor, Charlotte's heart sank. As seconds dragged into minutes, Charlotte feared that they had lost her, feared that once again she had retreated into that foggy never-never land.

Then, without warning, Laura lifted her gaze to Charlotte and like a magician's sleight of hand, the clouded look had disappeared. "Sorry." Laura frowned. "Now, what was I saying?"

"We were talking about children," Charlotte gently prodded.

"We were?"

Charlotte smiled and nodded.

Laura shrugged. "Humph, I don't know why, but it seems like lately, I keep having these blackouts. Then, when I try to remember, all I remember is the past."

Charlotte swallowed the huge lump of emotion lodged in her throat. Blackouts? Was it possible that Laura didn't remember that she had Alzheimer's? Come to think of it, not once yesterday or today, so far, had Laura even mentioned having Alzheimer's. How could that be? Then again, maybe that was a good thing. Except for the confusion and panic at the beginning of the disease, maybe not remembering that she had the dreaded disease was a blessing in disguise.

"Ah, speaking of the past, I'd love to know about your daughter."

At that, Laura smiled. "My Marti was a wonderful child, beautiful and smart as a whip. Never gave me a minute's worry, at least not until her senior year of high school."

"So what happened in her senior year?" Charlotte gently probed.

Laura frowned and slowly shook her head. "Not all parents are as blessed as I have been. At least I still have my Marti."

Afraid that Laura was going off on a tangent, Charlotte prompted, "You were going to tell me about her senior year."

"I was? Oh, yes, of course I was. Why, I remember it like it was only yesterday. It was when one of our most prominent families in town — the Scotts — lost both their daughter and their son." She slowly shook her head. "Such a tragedy — a terrible tragedy — especially in a small place like Oakdale. Their daughter was accidentally run over. The whole thing was so upsetting for Marti and for the rest of her class as well."

Charlotte's interest suddenly peaked, and though it might not have anything to do with anything, she found it intriguing that Laura mentioned the "tragedy" in conjunction with having problems with Marti. "You said that the Scotts lost both their children, so what happened to their son?"

Laura frowned. "Whose son?"

"The Scott family," she gently reminded her.

Laura slowly shook her head from side to side. "Terrible tragedy . . . terrible. Most people around here blamed the parents for leaving the kids unsupervised, but I try not to judge. After all, Alex was eighteen, a senior in high school, plenty old enough to take responsibility. But boys will be boys, or so I'm told. Guess the temptation was too great, what with his parents being out of town and all. Did your son ever do anything like that?"

"Like what?"

Again Laura's eyes grew cloudy and she frowned. "I — I don't know."

"You were telling me about Alex, the Scotts' son."

"I was?" For a moment, she seemed lost in thought; then, "Oh, yeah, now I remember. It seems that he decided to throw his own senior party, without chaperons, or so they say. Of course I'm not supposed to listen to gossip — my husband would disapprove — but it was also in the newspaper and that's not gossip. According to the newspaper, Alex got drunk and accidentally ran over his own sister, killing her. And if that wasn't bad enough, a jury ended up convicting him of — of —" She frowned a moment, and then her expression brightened again. "That's it. Now I remember. They convicted him of criminal vehicular homicide and sent him away to state prison." Laura sighed. "Poor Betty Jean — that's Alex and Jackie's mother."

Jackie? Jackie must be the name of the Scotts' daughter, Charlotte decided.

"Some say she had a nervous breakdown," Laura continued, "and has never been the same since. Can't say as I blame her. Who knows how any of us would act under those circumstances? All I know is how hard Marti took it, just being in the same class and all. Why, for days I couldn't get that girl to hardly eat. I can't imagine what poor Betty Jean went through."

Hoping that Laura's memory wouldn't play out before she revealed a bit more, Charlotte said, "So, why do you think Marti was so upset about it? Was she good friends with either of the Scott children?"

Laura shook her head. "No, not good friends. We didn't run in the same social circles as the Scotts, and they weren't members of our church. But Marti has always been the sensitive type. Of course back then, I had strong suspicions that there was more to it than she admitted. In fact, I strongly suspected that she and that boyfriend of hers were there at that party. Of course she denied it, but I could always tell when she wasn't telling me the truth about something. Mothers know those things. And besides, when I washed her clothes the next day, her jeans and sweater reeked of alcohol. Alcohol was strictly forbidden in our household. Why, if her daddy had even suspected she'd been drinking he would have whipped her within an inch of her life. Sometimes I wonder if we were too strict."

Though Charlotte listened with half an ear, the words *that boyfriend* stuck in her mind. Could it be? Was it possible? Though she was pretty sure she already knew the answer, she asked anyway. "Marti had a boyfriend back then?"

The sad look on Laura's face disappeared, and she smiled, then nodded. "Lots of boys came around after my Marti. She's a beautiful girl. Do you know my Marti? Have you ever met her?"

Charlotte prayed for patience. "Yes, I have," she answered kindly. "And you're right, she is beautiful. But you were going to tell me about the boyfriend she had when

Alex Scott gave that party."

"I was?" Laura frowned, then suddenly smiled. "Oh, yeah, I was. Out of all of Marti's boyfriends, I guess I liked him the least." She shook her head. "Those Franklin kids were the rowdiest kids in my Sunday school class, and Nick was the worst of the bunch."

Bingo!

"There were four of them, you know. But bless their little hearts, they couldn't help it if their daddy was a no-account drunk, a mean drunk at that. Why, it near broke my heart to see those little ones come in with bruises on their arms and legs." Laura suddenly covered her mouth with her hand and looked as if she were in pain. After a moment, she lowered her hand, and with her face still etched in pain, she said, "Lord, forgive me. There I go gossiping again . . . and judging. The Bible says, 'Thou shalt not judge, lest ye be judged.' Mr. Pate will be angry if he knows. You won't tell him, will you?"

Charlotte swallowed hard against the tightness in her throat. Not only had Laura forgotten that her husband was dead, but she still feared his reproach. Charlotte reached out and patted Laura's hand. "It's okay. I won't tell. We all tend to be judgmental at times."

Laura stared at her a moment, then suddenly yawned. "My goodness, I'm tired." When she struggled to her feet, Benny rushed to her side to steady her. "Maybe I'll take a little nap before lunch," she told them, and with Benny's help, she climbed into bed.

Benny pulled the cover over her, and without apology, she promptly closed her eyes. Within mere seconds Laura was softly snoring.

Benny moved closer to Charlotte. In a low voice he said, "So, what do you think?"

"I think we should probably leave for now and let her rest. Even with what she's told us, there's still nothing concrete — no proof of anything." She shrugged. "No reason, so far, from what Laura said, that Nick would have to blackmail Angel — I mean, Marti."

With one last glance at Laura, who was still sleeping, they headed for the door. Just outside the door, both came to an abrupt halt when they found themselves face-to-face with Laura's nurse. From the stern expression on her face, Charlotte figured that they were about to get a lecture for tiring out her patient. Best to get it over and done with.

Charlotte plastered a smile on her face. "Hi, there. You're Laura's — I mean, Mrs.

217

Pate's nurse, aren't you?"

The nurse nodded. "Dawn Sanders," she replied.

"Oh, yes, now I remember. I think that Dawn is such a pretty name. Just so you know, your patient is fast asleep now. I guess I should apologize. I'm afraid that our visit tired her out. But don't worry, we were just leaving."

"Yes, I know." A momentary look of discomfort crossed her face. "I guess I should apologize too." When Charlotte frowned questioningly, she rushed on, "I'm afraid that I shamelessly eavesdropped on most of your conversation with her." She paused, and then said, "But now I'm glad that I did. By chance, have either of you seen the front page of the *Oakdale Weekly* this morning?"

Charlotte shrugged. "I haven't."

Looking more uncomfortable with each passing moment, Benny chimed in, "Neither have I. Why? Is there something we should know?"

Dawn shot him a sly but knowing look. "I'm pretty sure that you already know, and after listening to your conversation with Laura, I'm positive that you knew before you came here. And now, after that front-page article, the whole town knows."

Charlotte's heart sank, but just to be sure that Dawn was talking about Nick's murder and Angel's arrest, she asked, "What, just exactly, is the article about?"

"It's about Nick being murdered and Marti being arrested for his murder. Y'all knew it all along, didn't you? That's why y'all came here to begin with."

Smart lady. Charlotte nodded. "Yes, it is. But we didn't set out to purposely deceive anyone," she hastened to add. "It's just that everyone we've talked to is so proud of Angel — I mean Marti — and once we realized that no one knew about it yet, we didn't want to be the ones to bring the bad news."

"Just one thing," Dawn said. "Are you trying to help Marti or hurt her?"

"Help her," Charlotte and Benny immediately replied in unison.

"That's what I thought — had hoped — but I had to make sure. Still, if you think that Nick was blackmailing Marti, and it proves to be true, wouldn't that hurt her?"

Out of the corner of her eye, Charlotte spotted two nurse's aides within hearing distance. From the looks of them, they were soaking in everything that was being said. At the other end of the hallway, nurses bustled in and out of patients' room. Too

219

public, she decided, much too exposed to talk here.

Charlotte shook her head and lowered her voice. "Not necessarily. If you have a few minutes, we'd love to explain, and maybe even ask you a few questions, but not here. Too many curious ears around, if you get my drift." She tilted her head in the direction of the aides. "Is there somewhere else we could go and talk in private?"

Dawn shifted her eyes to the aides, then back to Charlotte. "I understand, and you're right. How about I meet you at the Coffee Corner in about fifteen minutes or so? It's a coffeehouse not far from here," she explained. "There shouldn't be a lot of people there this time of the morning, and" — she smiled — "Mr. Harper, the owner, is half deaf."

"That would be great," Benny said, "but you'll need to give us directions."

"I also need to make sure that one of the other nurses will keep an eye on Laura — Mrs. Pate — for me too."

After giving Benny directions to the Coffee Corner, Dawn rushed off toward the nurse's station near the junction of two hallways, and Charlotte and Benny headed for the limo.

"Did you get the feeling that Dawn Sanders wants to tell us something?" Charlotte asked as Benny pulled out of the parking lot onto the main road.

Benny nodded. "Yes, ma'am. Let's just hope it's something that will help Angel."

"Maybe she can enlighten us a bit more about Angel and Nick's early relationship. And about that party that Laura mentioned. Interesting that even back then, Laura didn't like Nick hanging around."

"Good intuition," Benny replied. "Nick was a piece of trash as far as I'm concerned. And believe me, I know trash when I see it."

Given all that she'd learned so far about Nick Franklin, Charlotte had to agree with Benny's assessment. Even so, Benny's vehemence and brief reference to his own past was a bit unnerving, as well as telling. She only wished there were some way she could help him move past the deep resentment he still harbored against his family.

The Coffee Corner turned out to be half of a quaint, small shotgun double that had, like Charlotte's home, probably been built in the 1920s, but had been meticulously restored. The other half of the double was obviously an antique shop since the sign above the door read THE ANTIQUE STORE.

"Catchy name, huh," Charlotte said,

tongue-in-cheek, when Benny opened her door.

"Now, now, someone once told me that 'if you can't say something nice, then you shouldn't say anything.' "

Charlotte rolled her eyes. "I swear, do you remember everything that I told you?"

Benny grinned. "Yeah, most of it — at least the good stuff. And by the way, you also said that I shouldn't swear either."

By the time they entered the small building, they were both laughing. Charlotte breathed deeply. "Don't you just love the smells of a coffeehouse?" She glanced around, taking in the quaint café. There were several individual small tables with chairs, but there was also a conversation area that consisted of a small sofa, a couple of easy chairs, and a coffee table, along with a bookcase full of books.

"It does smell good in here," Benny replied.

As Dawn had predicted, there weren't but a few customers inside the Coffee Corner. There were two men busy typing away on laptops at separate tables. At another table a woman was talking on a cell phone.

Since the older man behind the counter was wearing a hearing aid, Charlotte figured he must be Mr. Harper, the owner. When they approached the counter, the man greeted them with a big smile. "Morning, folks." He reached across the counter and gave each of them an enthusiastic handshake. "Name's Joe Harper. What'll you have?"

Charlotte smiled back and quickly scanned the menu posted on the wall above the counter. "Café au lait for me," she told him.

"The house blend will be fine for me," Benny added.

By the time they paid for their coffee and had chosen a table that would afford the most privacy, Dawn arrived.

"Your usual, honey?" Mr. Harper asked her, his big smile still in place as he hurried around the counter to give Dawn an affectionate hug.

Talk about your friendly proprietor, Charlotte thought. Maybe a little too friendly.

"Yes, sir," Dawn responded, hugging him back and kissing his cheek.

Charlotte sighed. Maybe she was just being an old fuddy-duddy.

Or an old prude.

I'm not that old, she silently argued with the aggravating voice in her head. *And I'm certainly not a prude.*

When Dawn joined Charlotte and Benny,

Charlotte commented, "Nice, friendly place here," putting the emphasis on "friendly."

Dawn nodded as she seated herself. "Yes, ma'am, and Mr. Harper is a real sweetie pie." Then, as if Dawn knew exactly what Charlotte had been thinking, she grinned. "And just so you know, he also happens to be my stepfather. My own father died before I was born, and Joe raised me since I was two."

The heat of embarrassment burned Charlotte's cheeks. Clearing her throat, she forced a smile. "No wonder you recommended this place."

Still grinning, Dawn nodded again. Then her expression grew serious. "About Marti — why do the police think that she killed Nick? Not that I'd blame her if she did," she added.

Charlotte winced. "I hope you'll pardon me for saying so, but you sound a bit bitter."

"Not so much bitter as guilty," Dawn admitted. "I heard you mention something about the possibility of Nick blackmailing Marti. Well, Nick was certainly capable of doing that and more. Suffice it to say, he was not a nice man. I could tell you lots of stuff about him, only I'm afraid that anything I tell you might only hurt Marti more."

"I understand," Charlotte replied. "But just keep in mind that we're the good guys. We want to help her. What we're trying to find out is if there's any reason Nick would have a hold over Marti."

Dawn shrugged. "Maybe, but mind you it's only hearsay, and I can't prove anything."

"It doesn't matter. Right now, we're just trying to gather as much information as we can." Charlotte paused a moment. Ever since they had talked to Laura Pate, what Laura had told them about the wild party given by Alex Scott had stuck in her mind. Though it might not have anything to do with Angel and Nick's relationship, Charlotte had a feeling that there was something fishy about the whole thing.

"Ah, Dawn, Laura mentioned something about a wild party that a boy named Alex Scott gave and how she suspected that Marti had been to that party. Do you know anything about that?"

"Maybe. You see, back in high school during our senior year, Nick and Marti were dating, but —" Dawn's face flushed and she lowered her gaze to stare at her cup of coffee.

"But what?" Charlotte prompted.

"I can't tell you how embarrassing this is and how ashamed I am, but at the time, Nick was two-timing Marti." She paused, then lifted her gaze to stare directly at Charlotte. "He was two-timing her with me." She grimaced. "I was so stupid back then. Not only stupid, but also naive. I thought that Nick was my ticket to becoming one of the popular kids."

Charlotte frowned. "I don't understand. According to what Laura told us, she strongly suspected that Nick and his brothers were abused by a drunken father. Usually kids like that aren't in with the popular crowd."

"It's true that his father was a mean drunk, but he was also the president of the only bank in town."

"So what you're saying is that Nick's family had lots of money?"

"If living in one of the biggest houses in town, belonging to the country club, and wearing only the best clothes counts, then I guess they did, or so everyone assumed."

Charlotte thought about that for a moment, mostly because it didn't quite fit her preconceived idea of Nick.

"Just goes to show that not everything is as it appears to be, though," Dawn explained. "It wasn't long after we graduated that Mr. Franklin was found dead in the parking lot behind the bank. The police think it was a robbery gone bad. According to the gossip around town, the robber tried to force Mr. Franklin to open the bank vault after hours, Mr. Franklin refused, and the robber beat him to death." She shrugged. "They never did find who killed him. But after that, Nick's mother lost everything and moved back to Jackson, where she had family. It seems that her husband didn't have any life insurance and their big house was mortgaged to the hilt. Their whole lifestyle was a sham. They fooled everyone for a while, though, especially me."

But Nick hadn't fooled Laura Pate, thought Charlotte. And from what Charlotte had learned so far, the apple didn't fall far from the tree where Nick Franklin was concerned. But when it came down to it, nothing that Dawn had said so far was going to be any help. "So, about that party," Charlotte said, trying to steer Dawn back on track. "Were you at that party?"

Dawn shook her head. "No, ma'am. Like I said, back then I wasn't exactly what you'd call one of the in-crowd — you know, one of the popular kids — so I wasn't invited. I really didn't know anything about the party until later, and that's what I wanted to tell you. Not long after Alex Scott was tried and convicted — and this was before Nick's father was murdered — Nick wanted to go up to Jackson to a rock concert. Marti's parents wouldn't let her go, so he invited me. Afterward, he got drunk and said some things that made me believe that he and Marti, not Alex, were the ones who had taken Alex's car for a joyride the night that Alex's sister was killed."

Dawn shuddered, and after a moment, she took a deep breath and said, "Nick, not Alex, was the one who ran over Alex's sister. Nick was the one driving the car."

CHAPTER 11

Momentarily stunned, Charlotte stared at Dawn. "But wait!" she exclaimed, once she found her voice. "I don't understand. Wasn't Alex — the girl's brother — arrested *and* convicted?"

When Dawn nodded, Charlotte said, "But how can that be? If Nick was the one who was driving, then surely there had to be evidence in the car, fingerprints and such."

Dawn shook her head. "Nick bragged about wiping off all of their fingerprints and fooling the cops."

"But surely there must have been witnesses. Some of the other kids at the party must have seen something."

Dawn shook her head. "All the kids were in the back around the swimming pool. The car was out front on the driveway."

Before she thought it through, Charlotte blurted, "So, once you knew what really happened, why didn't you go to the police?

For that matter, if it was an accident, why didn't Nick or Marti go to the police?"

Dawn shook her head. "Both of them had been drinking that night. Nick had already had a couple of run-ins with the law and had spent time in a juvenile detention facility. A hit-and-run conviction could have landed him in prison for most of the rest of his life. Also, with Angel's father being a minister and all, a scandal like that would have ruined him. As for me, I thought about going to the police. I wanted to go," she stressed, "but it would have been my word against both Nick and Marti's — my word against the bank president's son and a minister's daughter. Who do you think the cops would have believed?"

Dawn could be right about the police not believing her, but — "Why didn't you at least tell your parents?"

Dawn sighed. "Then I would have to have told them about my trip to Jackson with Nick. I knew they didn't want me dating him and I also knew that if I had asked to go with him to that concert, they would have said no. So I didn't ask. I lied and told them I was spending the night with a girlfriend. By the time I'd worked up enough courage to tell my parents, Nick had sobered up and realized what he'd told me.

He threatened to kill me and my parents if I ever breathed a word of what he'd said to anyone." Dawn's lips quivered. "And I believed him," she whispered.

Dawn blinked several times, but a tear slipped down her cheek anyway. "The whole thing has bothered me for years, especially the thought of Alex serving time for a crime he didn't commit. I can't tell you how many times I wanted to tell someone, but I'm ashamed to admit that I'm a coward at heart. Then, today, when I read that article on the front page of the newspaper, I knew that I could finally tell the truth. Not that it really matters anymore or helps Alex. Nick is dead and Alex got out of prison a couple of years ago. Still, it doesn't seem right that the truth will never be known."

Charlotte was at a loss for words as she sat there, staring into space, trying to make sense of everything that Dawn had revealed.

"Guess y'all think I'm a pretty rotten person, huh?"

Dawn's quivery voice drew Charlotte's attention, and she immediately reached out to pat the young woman's hand. "No, of course not," she soothed. "You were just a kid and got caught up in a no-win situation. It took a lot of courage for you to finally share this."

Out of the corner of her eye, Charlotte spotted Joe Harper headed their way. From his grim, bordering on angry expression, Charlotte figured he'd noticed Dawn was upset and probably thought that she and Benny were the blame.

Glaring at Charlotte and Benny, Joe placed a protective hand on Dawn's shoulder. "Dawn, honey, what's going on? Are you okay?"

Dawn turned her head and looked up at him. "I'm okay, Daddy." She glanced at Charlotte, then at Benny. Finally, giving Joe a shaky smile, she said, "There's something I need to tell you." She shoved her chair back and stood. To Charlotte, she said, "If y'all need anything else, you can find me at the nursing home."

Charlotte smiled encouragingly at the young woman. "Thank you for your help. Also, I don't think it's in anyone's interest, especially Marti's, right now to go to the police."

"Police?" Joe sputtered.

Ignoring him for the moment, Charlotte continued. "Like you said earlier, Nick is dead, and Marti certainly isn't going to risk incriminating herself further at this point. Without proof, it's just hearsay."

"I'll keep that in mind."

Charlotte reached inside her purse and pulled out her business card. She held out the card to Dawn. "Just in case you think of anything else, please give me a call."

Dawn took the card and nodded. Then she turned to Joe. "Daddy, it's almost lunchtime. Why don't you close the store and let me take you to lunch, for a change? I've got a story to tell you."

"What now?" Benny asked a few minutes later, his hand on the door handle of the passenger side of the limo.

Charlotte frowned in thought. "I'm not really sure. It seems that we've certainly opened up a can of worms here. One thing I am sure of is that if what Dawn says is true — and I do believe her — then that's our proof that Nick was blackmailing Angel. At least now we know why Angel was so tight-lipped about Nick. Proof that he was blackmailing her would only be more motive for her to kill him. Even so, and if for no other reason than clearing that Scott boy's name, I think we need to find out for sure."

"No!" Benny shook his head.

"What do you mean, no?"

"That would be like nailing the lid closed on Angel's coffin. In fact, we need to tell

Dawn and her stepfather to keep their mouths shut about this."

Benny's dark angry expression sent a shiver up Charlotte's spine, and she didn't like it one bit. What she needed was to calm him down before things got out of hand. "Whoa, Benny," she said evenly, but with force. "Take it easy." She reached up and gently squeezed his upper arm. "I'm on your side, remember? And I did suggest to Dawn that it wasn't in Angel's best interest right now to go to the police. At the moment this all seems like it's really bad news, but I don't intend to do anything that's going to hurt Angel. We came here to *help* her, and I have to believe that once the whole truth comes out, in the end, Angel will be exonerated."

At the moment, she wasn't sure whether she was trying to convince Benny or herself. All she knew was that she had to keep a lid on things, especially Benny's temper, and hope and pray that everything worked out for the best.

She paused a minute to let what she'd said sink in. For long minutes, Benny silently stared past Charlotte into space. From his agonizing expression he seemed to be fighting some inner demon. Then, out of the blue, it came to her. Why, oh why, hadn't she seen it before? It was right there in front of her nose the whole time. Benny's protectiveness of Angel went way beyond mere friendship or even their employer-employee relationship. At some point he'd fallen in love with her.

But at what point? And what about Heather? He had already confessed that he was in love with Heather. Charlotte thought on that a moment. The logical answer was that Benny had been in love with Angel from the beginning, a love that, in his mind, was hopeless. After all, she was a big movie star and Benny was only the chauffeur. Maybe Heather had been his second choice, right up until the time that Nick had interfered.

"Yeah, for all the good that does me."

Benny's words echoed in Charlotte's head. Evidently, because of Heather's fixation on Nick, she hadn't felt the same way about Benny as he had about her. Poor guy just couldn't seem to catch a break in his love life.

Bottom line, once again, whether on Heather's behalf or Angel's behalf, she had to ask herself if Benny was capable of murder. As before, she came up with the same answer. Back when he'd been a troubled teenager, when he'd been surrounded by people who would kill for their next drug fix, such a thing might have been possible. Anything might have been possible then, but not now. Benny had changed. He'd broken away from that environment and severed all the ties with his horrible family. Now he was a completely different person, a good person, so the answer was a resounding no. Besides, there was that other little problem called motive. Though Benny might have had cause to want to murder Nick, he had no motive to frame Angel for that murder.

Charlotte squeezed Benny's arm again. Emphasizing each word, she repeated her earlier statement. "Benny, I'm not going to do anything that will hurt Angel." She held her breath, waiting for his response. For more than one reason, she needed his co-operation, the least of which was transportation to get back home again. Several tense moments passed, but he finally nodded.

Breathing a quiet sigh of relief, she said, "Well, okay, then. Tell you what, it's lunchtime and I need to eat. Why don't we find a nice fast-food restaurant, like that place we saw near the Oakdale Nursing and Care Center? I don't know about you, but now that all of Oakdale probably saw that article in the newspaper about Angel and Nick, I'd just as soon not run into anyone who might ask questions. In fact, if it's okay with you, we could use the drive-through and take the food back to the hotel."

Once again, Benny nodded. "Sounds good to me." He opened the passenger door and motioned for her to get inside.

Though the day was warm, there was a nice breeze blowing, so by mutual consent, Charlotte and Benny ate their food outside by the hotel's pool area. It was a really nice setup, complete with a small diving board, a slide, and bright yellow and blue umbrella-covered tables. Best of all, no one was using the pool at the moment, so they had the area all to themselves.

Benny had ordered hamburgers and fries, and Charlotte, ever mindful of her diabetes, had settled for a side salad and chicken nuggets.

The lunch was a quiet affair, with little conversation, and both were content to simply enjoy the meal beneath the shade of one of the umbrellas. Even so, once Charlotte finished eating, she felt the need for some time alone to think things through.

As she stuffed the napkins, the plastic salad bowl, and the cardboard container into her sack, she said, "Benny, I'm feeling a bit drained. If you don't mind, I think I'll go up to my room for a while and rest." She glanced at her watch. "Why don't we meet up again about three o'clock, and then decide where to go from there?"

Benny gathered up his food wrappings and napkin, then stuffed them into a sack. "Sounds good to me," he told her. "I need to gas up the limo anyway and check the tires, so I'll see you back here at three." They both stood, and he reached for her bag of trash. "I'll dump these in the garbage on the way out."

Once inside her hotel room, Charlotte made sure that the door locked behind her. Kicking off her shoes, she stretched out on the bed. As she stared up at the ceiling she thought about everything that both Laura Pate and Dawn Sanders had told them, and she thought about Benny. None of what they'd learned so far would help prove Angel's innocence. In fact, like Benny had said, all of the information that they had gathered could very well nail the lid shut on her coffin.

Charlotte squeezed her eyes closed. So why, no matter how hard she tried, did she keep coming back to the blackmail thing? And why the nagging need to confirm what Dawn had said about Nick's drunken confession, as well as the things that Laura had told them?

Then there was the Scott boy to consider. If what Dawn had said was right, he was yet another one of Nick Franklin's victims. And like Angel, didn't Alex Scott also deserve justice?

Startled by the thought that suddenly flashed through her mind, Charlotte froze. Beneath her breasts, her heart pounded like a jackhammer. Yes, Alex Scott deserved justice, but maybe, just maybe, he or someone close to him thought he deserved revenge.

CHAPTER 12

Charlotte sat straight up in the bed, her heart still pounding. One of the problems all along had been the lack of motive to frame Angel. All of the suspects that she and Benny had come up with had a motive to kill Nick, but none of them had a motive to kill Nick *and* frame Angel for the murder. None until now, none except Alex Scott. According to what they had learned, Alex Scott had a motive to kill Nick and a motive to frame Angel: Nick, for committing the crime that Alex had been convicted of, and Angel for not coming forward with the truth.

Charlotte climbed off the bed and, hands on her hips, paced the small hotel room. She needed to remember exactly what Dawn Sanders had said about the Scott boy. Something about Nick being dead now and . . .

"Alex got out of prison a couple of years ago."

"Yes!" she murmured, doubling her fist and pumping her arm in a triumphant gesture. That was it! According to Dawn, Alex Scott had been a free man for two years or more, plenty of time to plot revenge. And what better revenge than to kill the man who had murdered his sister and, at the same time, frame the woman who had been his so-called accomplice.

But how did he do it? Even if it was true and even if it made perfect sense to her, the information they had now was not enough to take to the police. What did the prosecution on *Law & Order* call it? Was it hearsay or circumstantial evidence? Whichever, that's what she and Benny had right now. What they needed was proof — real proof.

"But how to get it?" she murmured, dropping back down on the bed. As she lay there staring up at the ceiling and pondering what to do next, once again she mentally reviewed all of the suspects that she and Benny had discussed. They had talked about Angel's manager, Simon Clark, Angel's makeup girl, Heather Cortez, her bodyguard, Toby Russell, and last but certainly not least, Bruce King, the sleazy tabloid reporter.

Charlotte frowned. Seemed like there was

someone else as well. Her brow furrowed in thought, she finally remembered that Benny had mentioned Nick having some heavy gambling debts. She shook her head. "No way," she whispered. There was no way that his gambling debts had anything whatsoever to do with this particular scenario.

Charlotte rolled onto her side and stared at the flowery print hanging on the wall. There was another problem as well. So far, none of the suspects were Alex Scott; else Nick or Angel would have recognized him.

Once again, something niggled at the back of her mind, something that Benny had mentioned, but what? Something about a stalker or a crazed fan, if she remembered right. Even so, if, and that was a big if, the stalker had been the Scott boy, wouldn't Nick or Angel have recognized him?

Charlotte sighed, and after a moment she decided that granted, it was a bit far-fetched, but still possible that maybe they did recognize him. Hadn't Benny said something about Nick having an altercation with the stalker in a restaurant, and about convincing Angel to take out a restraining order?

Charlotte shook her head from side to side. Too many questions and not enough answers. First things first, she decided. And the first thing she needed to do was somehow confirm the story that Dawn had told them.

But how?

Find Alex Scott.

Again, how? she wondered. So far, the only lead she had was Dawn Sanders.

Charlotte eyed the clock on the bedside table. Then her gaze strayed to the telephone. Dawn had said if they needed anything, she would be at the nursing home, hadn't she? There was still an hour left before time to meet up with Benny.

"Plenty of time to make a telephone call," Charlotte murmured as she sat up, then scooted to the edge of the bed. After a brief search through the drawers in the bedside table, she located a local telephone directory. She thumbed through it until she found the telephone number for Oakdale Nursing and Care Center and dialed it.

"I'd like to speak to Dawn Sanders," she told the receptionist, then added, "She's the nurse who takes care of Mrs. Pate."

"Who's calling, please?" the receptionist responded.

"Charlotte LaRue."

"Can you hold a moment, Ms. LaRue?"

"Yes, I can."

For several moments, Charlotte was subjected to a recorded advertisement for the nursing home; then the message stopped and she heard a ringing in her ear. On the third ring, a woman's voice answered, "Mrs. Laura Pate's room. How may I help you?"

The voice sounded so formal that at first Charlotte wasn't sure it was Dawn. "Dawn? Is this Dawn Sanders?"

"No, sorry. Dawn called in sick today."

"Oh, I see. Could you give me her home phone number?"

"No, ma'am. That's against the rules."

With a sigh, Charlotte said, "Okay. But if you talk to her before I reach her, could you please tell her that I called?"

"Sure, what's your name?"

"Charlotte LaRue, and thanks."

Charlotte hung up the receiver and reached for the phone directory again. After a moment, she closed the directory. There was no listing for a Dawn Sanders. Was it possible that she still lived with her parents?

She picked up the directory again and found the number for the Coffee Corner. She dialed the number and waited. On the fourth ring, a gruff male voice answered, "The Coffee Corner."

"Ah — hello. Is this Joe Harper?"

"Yes, it is."

"Mr. Harper, this is Charlotte LaRue, and

I'm trying to get in touch with your step-daughter Dawn."

"Sorry, Ms. LaRue, but Dawn took a few days off and went out of town."

"Oh . . . well, do you know how I can reach her? Maybe a cell phone?"

"No, I don't, and she doesn't have a cell phone."

"Well, ah, thank you anyway."

Strange, Charlotte thought as she hung up the receiver. Very strange indeed, especially since the woman at the nursing home had said Dawn was sick, and now here was Dawn's stepfather telling her that Dawn had gone out of town for a few days.

With a shrug, Charlotte reached for the telephone book again and turned to the S listings. She'd hoped that Dawn could help her, but there was more than one way to track down a person. Surely Alex's parents would know where he was.

The listing for the Scott family was easy enough to find. There was just one Scott family listed in the whole town of Oakdale. Relieved that she'd only have to make one call, she tapped out the phone number.

"Scott residence," a pleasant female voice answered.

"Hi, is this Mrs. Scott?"

"No, I'm the housekeeper."

Charlotte cleared her throat in preparation for the lie she was about to tell. "I'm an old friend of the Scotts, just in town for a short visit, and I thought I'd say hello. Is Alex at home?"

"Nooo." The housekeeper drew out the word, her tone suspicious. "He isn't home."

"When do you expect him?"

"Is this a reporter?"

"Oh, no. Like I said earlier, I'm an old friend of the family." *Liar, liar, pants on fire.* Charlotte winced. She hated lying and only hoped that the ends would justify the means.

"Well, Mr. Alex doesn't live here any longer; he hasn't been home in years. And I don't expect him to visit any time soon."

"What about Mr. or Mrs. Scott? Could I please speak to one of them?"

"Sorry, but no. They're out of town on an extended business trip, but I'll be glad to let them know that you called. What did you say your name was?"

The last thing Charlotte wanted was to leave her name. Instead of answering the question, she said, "Do you happen to know where Alex is living now?"

The housekeeper hesitated a moment, then said, "You sound like a reporter. Are you sure you aren't one?"

"No — I promise — I am not a reporter."

At least that much was the truth, she thought.

"Well, no one knows where Mr. Alex is now, but the last time we heard from him, he was living somewhere in California."

California. Nick and Angel lived in California.

Yeah, but California is a big place.

Charlotte swallowed her disappointment. The fact that all three lived in California didn't mean anything. Not really.

"Thanks," she told the housekeeper. "Sorry to have bothered you." Charlotte quickly hung up the receiver before the housekeeper could ask for her name again.

Now what? she wondered, as she stared at the telephone. She still needed information, but where else could she look? Where else could she find information about Alex Scott?

She supposed she could always start by checking a telephone directory in and about Hollywood or she could call directory assistance, just to see if he happened to be living in that area.

A few minutes later with disappointment sinking deeper inside, Charlotte hung up the phone receiver again. According to the operator, there were no less than fifty Alex or A. Scotts living in the greater Hollywood area. To get a listing of all of the telephone numbers, the woman suggested that she could either go online or go to a library, since many libraries had a collection of directories from other cities.

Frustrated, Charlotte sighed. To look something up online would require a computer, along with someone who had expertise using a computer. Though she had learned a little bit about search engines and such from her sister, by no means did she feel competent for the job.

As for the library, she doubted seriously if the local Oakdale, Mississippi, library would have any telephone directories at all for California, much less Hollywood.

"Dead end," she muttered. Glancing at her watch, she decided that by the time she freshened up a bit, Benny would be knocking at her door.

In the bathroom, she fluffed up her hair, then brushed her teeth. As she applied a fresh coat of lipstick she thought back on what she had learned in the past hour. "Humph! Not much," she muttered, other than the fact that Alex was living somewhere in California.

Charlotte shook her head, and wondering if the local library had computer access, she put away her lipstick and walked back into the main room to wait for Benny.

Outside the only window in her room, there was a great view of the pool area. While she watched two young children frolicking in the pool, an idea popped into her head. Even if the local library didn't have a Hollywood phone directory or a computer for its patrons, most libraries did keep back copies of old newspaper articles, if not on a computer, then on microfiche. She might not be able to locate Alex Scott now, but more than likely she could read about the death of his sister and his subsequent trial. Who knew? Maybe something somewhere would lead to a clue that would help locate him. At the very least, she could get the whole story on what had happened back then.

Eager to get started, she glanced at her watch. It was ten past three, so where was Benny? Frowning, she thought back to their last conversation. Though she didn't think so, maybe she was supposed to meet him downstairs in the lobby.

Just as she made up her mind to go down to the lobby, there was a sharp rap on her door. Charlotte rolled her eyes and as she collected her purse on the way to the door, a little song from the *Bullfrogs and Butterflies* CD album that she'd bought for the twins played through her mind. The name of the song was "Have Patience." Though the peppy tune was meant for little children, Charlotte thought that a lot of grown-ups, including herself, could benefit from listening to it as well.

When she opened the door, Benny grinned. "How about a cup of coffee down in the diner?"

"Sounds good," she told him, "but I have an errand I'd like to run first, if that's okay with you?"

Benny shrugged. "Sure, whatever you want. Where to?"

"The local library, wherever that is. I'm sure someone from the hotel staff can give us directions, and we need to go now, just in case they close early."

On the way downstairs to the front desk, Charlotte told Benny about the phone calls she'd made and explained to him the reason she wanted to go to the library.

"You don't happen to know your way around the Internet, do you?" she asked as they stepped out of the elevator into the hotel lobby.

"I'm not what you'd call a computer nerd or anything." Then he nodded. "But I know my way around good enough to get what we need. And if the library doesn't have public access to a computer, then I'm sure the hotel can accommodate us."

"Let's check out the library first."

The library, like most everything else in town, was only a few blocks from their hotel and was located in a beautiful old antebellum-styled home that, according to the hotel manager, had been donated to the town for the express purpose of housing a library. Charlotte figured that the house had to be at least 150 years old, yet had been kept in pristine condition.

During the short drive, Charlotte and Benny came up with what they thought was the most probable year that Alex's sister had been killed. Just in case their calculations were a bit off, though, Charlotte decided that she would ask for copies of the local newspaper for both the previous and the following year. Since there was only one weekly newspaper in town, she figured the library should have every copy ever printed. If not, then she could always pay a visit to the local newspaper office.

Inside the library, much to Benny's delight, the front parlor was solely dedicated to media, including a bank of state-of-the-art computers.

Charlotte was truly impressed with the entire facility as well as the eager, gracious staff. "Is there something in particular you're looking for?" the librarian at the information desk asked with a smile. "Not being nosy, mind you. It's just that I was born and raised here and know just about everything that's happened in the past forty years."

A smile pulled at Charlotte's lips. The woman was a perfect cliché of a little old lady librarian, complete with blue-gray, bouffant-styled hair and horn-rimmed glasses.

Shades of Bitsy Duhè.

Like Bitsy, Charlotte had no doubt, she made it her business to know everything that went on in Oakdale.

Confiding in the woman would probably speed up her research process, and though she was sorely tempted, after a moment's hesitation, Charlotte shook her head. "Thanks, that's very kind of you. But what I'm looking for is the type of thing that I'll recognize when I see it, if you know what I mean." Which was the truth, sorta kinda. Besides, for all she knew, the librarian could be best friends with Alex's mother, or worse, a relative of the Scotts. One thing that she'd learned about Oakdale, the citizens seemed to stick together and protected their own. Nope, best not to go there or stir up that hornet's nest.

While Charlotte scanned headline after headline of the weekly newspaper, and learned more than she'd ever wanted to know about Oakdale, Benny searched the Net at one of the computers for anything he could find about Alex Scott.

An hour later, Charlotte felt the need to stretch, as well as take a much-needed bathroom break. Then she hit pay dirt. Their time reference had been close, but what she'd found came at the end of the year before their calculated year. It continued through that year, and on into the following one.

Enthralled, she scanned through article after article that detailed every aspect of the murder, Alex's arrest, and his trial.

According to one article, the prosecution insisted that, because of the Scotts' prominence in the community and the local publicity, any jury chosen would be biased in Alex's favor. He'd filed a motion to have the trial moved to Jackson, and the judge had granted his motion.

So that's why, she thought. She'd wondered why a town so tightly knit would convict a member of one of its most prominent families, with what appeared to be circumstantial evidence, especially since there were no witnesses.

In the next article she read, Alex's car was found parked near the street-end of the long driveway; his sister's body was found a few feet in front of the vehicle.

Throughout the trial, Alex had vehemently denied killing his sister. He had testified that the last thing he remembered that night was feeling sick and going inside the house to the bathroom to throw up. He claimed that he must have passed out, because the next thing he remembered was waking up on the bathroom floor to the sound of police sirens. Only problem, a couple of the kids who had been at the party testified about hearing Alex and his sister arguing about his promise to give her a ride to a girlfriend's house.

There were pictures of Alex's parents, his sister, and even a shot of their home. But the picture that got to her most was one of Alex being led away from the courthouse in handcuffs. It was a huge color picture that took up almost a third of the front page.

Nice-looking kid, she thought as she stared at the skinny boy with his thick mop of blond hair. In the picture, two burly policemen who towered over Alex were leading him away from the courthouse. The teenager's shoulders were slumped in defeat, and there was a tortured, hangdog expression on his pale face as he stared back over his shoulder at someone. Probably his parents, she figured.

There was no mistaking the lost look in his dark eyes, and Charlotte felt her heart breaking just thinking about what must have been going through his mind at that moment. Poor kid. Yes, he was eighteen at the time, but from personal experience in dealing with her own son, Charlotte knew that eighteen didn't automatically mean he was a full-grown, responsible, mature adult. In fact, in many cases, it meant just the opposite. In Charlotte's opinion, the years between fifteen and twenty-one were fraught with danger and pitfalls, especially for boys.

As if mesmerized, she continued staring at the picture. Then a strange thing happened. It was only a feeling, just the barest hint of familiarity, but the longer she stared, the more convinced she became that she'd seen Alex somewhere before.

At first she thought that it was just another instance of her imagination playing tricks on her, but the more she tried to convince herself that she was imagining things, the more she came to believe that there was definitely something there.

Maybe it was his eyes. She squinted her own eyes in an attempt to block out everything but his eyes. Yep, that was it. Somewhere, at some time, she'd seen those eyes before. She was sure of it. But when? And where?

A hand descended on her shoulder from behind, and she almost jumped out of her skin.

"Sorry," Benny said with a pat to her shoulder. "I didn't mean to startle you, but I did call out several times."

Her heart still pounding and unable to keep the excitement out of her voice, she said, "Look — look at this." She pointed to the screen. "Please tell me I'm not imagining things. I could swear that I've seen this person before."

Benny stared at the picture. After several long moments, he finally shrugged and shook his head.

"He doesn't seem familiar to you?"

Again, Benny shook his head. "Sorry, not really."

"You're sure?" she persisted.

Benny nodded. "Yes, ma'am, I'm sure."

Charlotte sighed. "Phooey, and here I thought that I was on to something." With one last look at the picture, she turned off the machine, then stood and stretched. "Any luck at the computer?"

"No, ma'am." He gave her a sheepish

look. "Maybe if I was more computer literate or had several days to read all of the hits, I could find him, but —"

Charlotte squeezed his arm. "Hey, don't beat yourself up over this. I didn't have much luck either, except for confirming what Dawn told us about the Scott boy being railroaded for his sister's murder."

Benny grimaced. "Guess there's nothing left to find here, then." Through gritted teeth, his tone angry with frustration, he said, "This whole trip — nothing but a complete waste."

"Not a complete waste," she insisted. "We're not giving up yet. As for finding him through the computer, my sister, Maddie, is great at that kind of stuff."

Brave words, she thought, but truth be told, she wasn't quite sure what to do next. While it was true that Madeline had helped her find articles written by Bruce King, she had no idea if her sister could help them locate Alex Scott using the computer. Or even if Maddie would try.

Charlotte glanced up at Benny. "I need to visit the ladies' room; then how about that cup of coffee? I don't know about you, but I could use a shot of caffeine about now."

"Yes, ma'am. Me too."

After her trip to the ladies' room, Charlotte gave a little wave to the librarian who had helped them, smiled, and mouthed the word "Thanks," then followed Benny out of the library to where he had parked the limo.

By mutual consent, they agreed to return to the Coffee Corner. There, over coffee, they would discuss what to do next. Though the drive was short and took very little time, for some reason the picture of Alex Scott haunted Charlotte. No matter how many times she told herself that she was just imagining things, she couldn't shake the feeling that she'd seen him before. But again, when and where had she seen him?

CHAPTER 13

As they entered the Coffee Corner, it smelled just as good as Charlotte remembered from earlier that morning. Unbelievably, almost every table in the little café was occupied. Suddenly, all conversation stopped, and all eyes turned to stare at them as they headed for the counter.

"Not a good sign," Benny said beneath his breath. There was dead silence another moment; then slowly, the buzz of conversation began again, and Charlotte breathed a sigh of relief.

Once they had their coffee, Benny led the way to one of the only two empty tables, the one farthest from the counter, near the entrance. After they had seated themselves, in a low voice Benny said, "Wonder what's wrong with him?" He tilted his head toward Joe Harper behind the counter.

Charlotte chanced a quick look at the proprietor, but the man had turned his back to them. "Probably the same thing that's wrong with everyone else in here?"

"What's that old saying? If looks could kill?"

Charlotte shuddered. Though neither Joe Harper nor the other patrons were exactly hostile, it became increasingly obvious that none of them were thrilled with her and Benny's presence in the coffeehouse.

Charlotte took a drink of her coffee. The café au lait was strong and hot, just the way she loved it. She leaned across the table and in almost a whisper, said, "The only thing I can think of is that Mr. Harper's cold-shoulder attitude has to have something to do with me trying to get in touch with Dawn. As for the rest, who knows how they found out? News travels fast in a small town." She frowned. "Still, why would me asking the whereabouts of Alex Scott be a problem?"

"You've got me. Like you said, 'Who knows?' But I guess that answers our question."

"About whether to stay or leave?"

Benny nodded.

Charlotte stared down at her cup. "Yeah, I'm beginning to get the feeling that we've worn out our welcome in Oakdale."

"Guess it's time to pack our bags and hit

the road."

"Might as well," she replied. "Given what I've seen so far, I doubt seriously if anyone will be willing to talk to us now."

"Yeah, you're probably right."

Charlotte stared down at her coffee for long seconds, her mind racing. They'd come so close to finding out something important. She could feel it in her bones. Too close to just walk away. Somebody in this town knew something. She was sure of it. Then, like the proverbial lightbulb switching on in her head, she knew what they had to do.

"Unless . . ." She raised her gaze to stare at Benny.

"Unless what?"

"There is one more person who might talk to us." When Benny gave her a puzzled look, she lowered her voice to a whisper, and said, "Remember our waitress at Karen's Café? You know — the one who flirted with you? I believe her name was Sally."

When Benny rolled his eyes, she kept her features deceptively composed, and in the most serious voice she could conjure, she said, "I figure you could use your manly wiles on her —"

"My what?" Benny stared at her as if she'd suddenly grown two heads.

The people at the next table glanced their

way, so Charlotte cupped her hand around her mouth. "Manly wiles," she repeated softly, hard-pressed to keep from grinning.

"What the heck is that?"

"Well, folks usually say feminine wiles, but I figure what's good for the goose is good for the gander." Benny's expression reminded Charlotte of someone who had just sucked a lemon. Unable to contain herself any longer, she burst out in laughter.

When several people around them turned to stare, Charlotte covered her mouth in an attempt to smother her laughter. "Just teasing," she told him, fighting for control. "But —" She held up her forefinger for emphasis. "All you'd have to do is flirt with her a little and she'd be putty in your hands."

Benny shook his head. "I'm not believing this."

"Aw, come on, Benny. 'Take one for the Gipper' — or in this case, take one for Angel."

"That's 'win one for the Gipper.' "

"Whatever." Charlotte waved her hand in a dismissive gesture. "Will you do it?" she hurriedly added. "All you'd have to do is stand there looking all manly and smile at her. I'd do all of the talking."

"And this is the best you can come up with?"

"At the moment, yes, unless you have a better idea."

With a grimace of distaste, Benny shrugged, then muttered, "Maybe she won't be working tonight."

Ignoring him, Charlotte glanced at her watch. "It's still a bit early for dinner. Maybe we can catch her before she begins her shift."

A few minutes later when they neared the restaurant, Charlotte said, "Try to park so that we can keep an eye on the front entrance."

"But what if the wait staff goes in and out a back door?" Benny slowed the limo to turn into the restaurant's small parking lot across the street.

Just as he turned into the parking lot, Charlotte spotted a car pulling up alongside the curb in front of the restaurant. The passenger-side door opened, and she recognized the woman who climbed out as the hostess. The woman blew a kiss at the driver, then turned and went inside the front entrance. "I think they go in through the front entrance," Charlotte said.

Grumbling about know-it-all women, Benny parked the limo so that it faced the front of the restaurant. Two more vehicles pulled up and dropped off passengers in front, and both women were dressed in the black-and-white waitress uniforms.

"Maybe she got to work early and is already inside," Charlotte said after several minutes had passed. "We might have to go inside after all."

"I don't think so," Benny retorted. "Isn't that her?" He pointed at a lone woman who was walking toward them from down the block.

Unless her eyes deceived her, Charlotte couldn't believe their luck. The woman was Sally the waitress, and she looked as if she was headed straight for the limo.

"Hurry, roll the windows down," she told Benny.

The second the windows were down, Sally's face split into a huge grin, and she waved.

"Wave back," Charlotte urged quietly. "And smile." Though Benny groaned as if in pain, he dutifully smiled and waved.

Within seconds, Sally walked right up to the driver's side. "Well, hey there," she drawled as she bent over and braced her arm along the window ledge, her face within inches of Benny's. "I didn't expect to see y'all again so soon."

To Benny's credit he didn't back away. Charlotte leaned toward him and smiled at

Sally. "What time does the restaurant open for dinner?"

"Not for another thirty minutes or so," Sally responded, her eyes never leaving Benny's face. "Say, I was just wondering, would it be okay if I could see the inside of your car? I've never been inside a limo before."

This was almost too good to be true. "Of course it would," Charlotte answered quickly before Benny could object.

Unlike the cool reception they had received back at the coffeehouse, it was evident that no one had bothered to tell Sally that she wasn't supposed to talk to the strangers in town. Either that or Sally was just too enamored with Benny and his limo to care what the rest of the town thought.

"In fact," Charlotte said, "if you have a few minutes, Benny could drive us around the block. Couldn't you, Benny?"

When Benny turned to stare at Charlotte, a shadow of annoyance crossed his face. After a moment, though, he nodded. "Sure, why not?"

Sally's eyes widened, and she backed up a couple of steps. "That would be terrific," she gushed.

Taking his time, Benny slowly opened the door, and with the enthusiasm of a man suffering from arthritis, he climbed out and

265

opened the back door. With a stiff little bow and a wave of his hand, he motioned for Sally to climb inside.

"I think I'll join you back there," Charlotte said, and before Benny had time to close Sally's door, Charlotte hopped out of the passenger's side, opened the back door, and climbed inside, seating herself in the seat opposite to Sally.

"This is just gorgeous," Sally said in awe as she smoothed her hand over the sumptuous leather seat, then eyed the minibar. "Is that one of those compact refrigerators?" Without waiting for a response, she opened the small door next to the minibar. "It is. Oh, my goodness. Just look at that."

Inside were a variety of drinks including soft drinks, water, and wine.

"Help yourself," Benny told her as he firmly shut the door, then climbed back inside the driver's seat.

Sally glanced over at Charlotte as if waiting for Charlotte to give her permission as well. "I think I'll take a bottle of water," Charlotte told her with a smile, then leaned forward and selected a bottle of the special brand of water that Angel kept on hand.

"If it's okay, I'd like a Coke," Sally said.

Once they had their drinks and Benny had pulled out of the parking lot, Charlotte cleared her throat and said, "When we met the first time, you said that you went to high school with Marti. Would you mind me asking you a few questions?"

"About Marti?"

"Yes and no," Charlotte responded. "Benny and I need your help."

"My help?"

Charlotte nodded. "I don't guess you've read today's newspaper yet."

Sally laughed. "No, I don't read the newspaper — not the local one anyway. It's more of a gossip rag and social tabloid about the uppity-ups who run this town."

Charlotte sighed. How to begin? "Listen, Sally, Benny and I came here in hopes of helping Marti out of a jam."

Sally frowned. "Are you talking about Marti being arrested for murdering that no-good sleaze Nick Franklin?"

"You know about that?"

Sally smiled. "I may not read the local rag they call a newspaper, but I keep up with what's going on in the outside world. I subscribe to several *real* newspapers, but unfortunately, I'm always a day or so behind, thanks to our local post office. I didn't really know about Marti's arrest until after I finished work last night. And since I plan to study law one of these days and I know her personally, Marti's whole case really interested me."

Charlotte nodded. "That's wonderful — that you want to study law, I mean. And that you're interested in Marti's case." Even in the dimness of the limo, Charlotte saw Sally smile.

"I don't intend to be a waitress forever," she told Charlotte. "Not that there's anything wrong with it," she quickly added. "Some of the nicest, hardest-working women I know are waitresses. But just one more year and I'll have enough saved to go to law school. I've already taken all of my prelaw courses, but law school is expensive. So, what can I do to help you guys?"

Never judge a book by the cover. Yes indeed, there was definitely more to Sally the waitress than what appeared on the surface. Having been a maid for over forty years, more so than most people, Charlotte knew that people often were stereotyped by others and weren't always what they seemed to be.

Now comes the hard part, thought Charlotte. Even though Sally seemed like a really nice, honest, hardworking woman, she also seemed a little too eager to help. Some might think she was simply being paranoid, but Charlotte had learned early to trust her instincts about people. With Sally, her instincts were yelling for her to tread lightly. Charlotte took a deep breath. *Here goes nothing.* "First, let me say that neither Benny nor I think that Marti is guilty. We're convinced that the real killer has framed her. We were hoping that by coming here where she grew up, we might get a better idea of who might have a grudge against both Marti and Nick. Only problem, once the good citizens of Oakdale realized why we came here, no one wants to talk to us."

Sally nodded thoughtfully. "Yeah, this is a pretty tight town, especially where Marti is concerned. But you have to realize, she's the only real celebrity we've ever had. Plus, she's made some pretty hefty contributions to the town over the last few years."

Sally paused a moment to take a drink of her Coke, then slowly shook her head. "I can't think of anyone who would have a grudge against Marti. Besides being the town's only celebrity, she was always Miss Goody Two-shoes growing up — you know, the preacher's daughter and all. Now, Nick, he's a whole other story. The list of people who might hold a grudge against him is a mile long."

Disappointment washed through Charlotte. Now what? She needed in some way to work the conversation around to Alex Scott without seeming obvious about it. But how? Time was getting short. Though Benny had driven slowly, they were almost back to the restaurant.

Only one way, Charlotte decided. "What about the Scott family? We heard some rumors about their son Alex and Marti and Nick. It had to do with Alex's sister's death," she quickly explained. "I wanted to talk to Alex, but no one seems to know where he is."

Sally laughed. "Oh, they know all right, but it doesn't surprise me in the least that no one will talk about him. Never mind that he was convicted and served time, no one in this town believes he was guilty and they protect him almost as fiercely as they protect Marti. After all, he was the town's golden boy, their star quarterback, not to mention that his daddy has more money than Solomon."

At that moment, Benny turned into the parking lot across from the restaurant, and desperation clawed at Charlotte's insides. "So, do *you* know where Alex is now, or how I could get in touch with him?"

"Humph! Wish I did. I'd thank him. It's because of what happened to him that I decided I wanted to study the law. But to answer your question, no, I don't know where he is. And other than his family, the only person who could tell you is Dawn Sanders, but good luck trying to get her to talk."

Charlotte was suddenly confused. Hadn't Dawn admitted that she didn't run in the same social circles as the Scotts? "So Alex and Dawn were friends, as in boyfriend and girlfriend?" Charlotte asked.

"Dawn wished she was that lucky, but no, not back in high school. Then things changed once Alex got sent to prison, though. Dawn made a point of visiting him as often as allowed, and I guess poor Alex was desperate for any kind of connection to the outside."

Suddenly, Sally groaned. "Yikes, look at the time. I'm late." Before she could reach the door handle, Benny hopped out and opened the door for her.

"Thanks for talking to us," Charlotte called out.

"Sure thing," Sally said. "And you —" She poked Benny in the chest with her forefinger. "Don't be a stranger. I still need a date for the reunion."

Back at the hotel, Charlotte and Benny briefly debated whether to stay another night or go home.

"I don't think staying will do any good," Charlotte told him, "and I'd really like to sleep in my own bed tonight. But we've already missed the hotel's checkout deadline, and I hate to pay for another night without using it."

"Don't worry about that. Angel's picking up the tab for this trip. If you want to go home, then we'll go home."

During the trip back to New Orleans, the gloom that filled the limo was thick enough to cut with a knife. Benny said very little and seemed resigned to the fact that there was nothing more they could do to prove Angel's innocence. Oh, how she wished that there was something she could say or do to snap him out of his blue funk, but for one of the few times in her life, no words of encouragement came to mind. Truth was, she was just as depressed as he was about the whole matter.

Charlotte turned her head to stare out of the passenger window. The Mississippi landscape of green, forest-filled rolling hills along the interstate flashed by and seemed to go on forever and forever. In her mind's eye, though, she kept getting a different kind of flash. For some reason she kept seeing the newspaper picture of Alex Scott.

If not for the strange reaction of Dawn's stepfather, not to mention the townsfolk, after her inquiry about Alex Scott, she probably would have passed it off as just another case of her imagination working overtime. But their reactions, along with what Sally had told her about Dawn and Alex, explained a lot. If what Sally said were true, then Dawn was smitten with Alex. So why so open that first time, and yet she'd disappeared? If Dawn truly cared about Alex and believed in his innocence, one would think that she'd want the truth to come out.

Charlotte grimaced. She wished she could just forget about it, but like with a dog chewing on a bone, something about the whole thing kept gnawing at her very being.

CHAPTER 14

By the time Charlotte and Benny exited off Causeway Boulevard onto the interstate, the sun was fast sinking in the west, and Charlotte had come to a decision. More than ever, she was determined to find Alex Scott. Every instinct within kept insisting that he was the key to solving Nick Franklin's murder and proving Angel's innocence.

Except to ask her what she'd like to eat for dinner when they had stopped in Hammond, Benny had continued his brooding, silent vigil during the trip. He was busy negotiating through the heavy traffic because of road construction on the interstate when she turned toward him. "Just so you know, I'm not throwing in the towel yet," she told him. "I still think the key to all of this is Alex Scott."

"Maybe," he commented without much enthusiasm.

"No 'maybe' about it," she retorted. "It

may seem silly, but I know I've seen him before — or at least someone who resembles that newspaper picture of him."

Benny sighed deeply. "Miss Charlotte, I know you mean well, but that picture is at least ten years old. Most people change a lot in ten years. Besides — and I've been thinking about this a lot — none of that helps explain why Angel's fingerprints are on that letter opener."

She'd almost forgotten about the stupid fingerprints, mainly because she couldn't think of a logical explanation, other than Angel having used the letter opener in the scene that had been shot the day before the murder was discovered.

"As for the fingerprints on the letter opener," she said, "I haven't quite got that figured out yet, but I'm sure there's a logical reason for Angel's prints being the only ones found on it. And you're right, people do change over the years," she agreed.

She still remembered her ten-year high school reunion as if it were yesterday. If it hadn't been for the name tags that everyone wore, there were several people she would never have recognized.

"But that picture and Alex Scott are the best leads we've got right now," she continued. "Especially after what Sally told us.

Alex Scott is out there somewhere. Right now, other than Bruce King, the Scott boy seems to be the only other suspect who might have had a reason to murder Nick Franklin and set Angel up to take the blame."

"So, what next?"

"Remember me telling you that my sister is pretty good at finding stuff on the computer?"

Benny nodded.

"First thing tomorrow I'll go over to her place and see if she can get me that telephone list for all of the A. Scotts in the Hollywood area. I'd do it tonight, but it's been a long day, and frankly, I'm bone-tired."

Charlotte figured the phone list was a long shot, at best. There were too many variables to even think about it, but to add further aggravation, Benny's only response was a lackluster "Whatever" and a halfhearted shrug.

Charlotte felt her temper rising. What she'd like to do was shake some sense in him. Instead, she took a deep breath, prayed for patience, and then said, "Meanwhile, I want you to visit Angel and press her about Nick Franklin and what happened the night of Alex Scott's party. Maybe once Angel knows that we found out about that entire incident, she'll finally open up."

For several minutes Charlotte waited for a response from Benny. When he didn't give her one after what she deemed was plenty of time, she decided she'd have to pin him down.

"Will you do it?" she asked pointedly. "Will you go see Angel and question her about Alex Scott's party?"

Still, Benny hesitated. Then, after a moment, he sighed heavily and said, "Yeah, I'll go see her."

Charlotte narrowed her eyes. "And will you push her about that party?"

"I said I'd go see her," he retorted sharply.

Her patience about worn thin, Charlotte bit her bottom lip to keep from lashing back at him. She was tired and frustrated. Besides, none of this investigation stuff had been her idea in the first place. After all, Benny had been the one who had approached her about helping, not the other way around. The least he could do was cooperate. Even so, from experience, she knew that it took two to argue, and arguing would only further frustrate the both of them; plus, arguing wouldn't get the job done. Now that she was in this mess up to her eyeballs, she needed his help.

Instead of arguing, she threw his own words back at him. "Whatever," she replied.

When Benny finally pulled the limo into Charlotte's driveway, the first thing she noticed was the absence of Louis's car. Though she felt somewhat relieved, surprisingly she also felt an odd twinge of disappointment. She had dreaded having to explain why she'd reacted the way she had during their last phone conversation, mainly because she still wasn't sure why she'd done so. But she did owe him an explanation and probably an apology for the things she'd said. She was just relieved that she didn't have to do it tonight.

No probably about it.

Picky, picky. Okay, so she *definitely* owed him an explanation and an apology.

Don't put off tomorrow what you can do today . . . the sooner, the better.

Maybe she should call him instead of waiting until he got home. But what would she say? She set her chin in a stubborn line. Best to wait . . . at least until she came up with a viable explanation.

Coward.

Yep, that's me, she thought as Benny retrieved her luggage from the trunk of the limo and carried it to her front door.

She unlocked the front door and, with her

hand on the doorknob, turned to Benny. "Now, don't forget what I said about paying Angel a visit."

"I won't, and by the way, I'm sorry for being so snippy a while ago. I guess I'm tired too, but mostly I really, *really* hate going to see her empty-handed. I had hoped to have some good news for her."

Aha, so that was his problem. Almost immediately, like the thaw after a snowstorm, the tension between them melted. Now she understood. He had hoped to come back a hero, had hoped to find something that would set Angel free. Charlotte reached out and squeezed his arm. "Don't give up yet. There's still time. And who knows, maybe she'll slip up and actually reveal something helpful?"

Though Benny finally nodded, she could tell that he'd rather eat worms than have to visit Angel for the express purpose of pumping her for information.

"Whatever happens," he said, "thanks for trying, and get some rest."

"You too," Charlotte told him.

Benny turned away, and like a man being led to the gallows, he walked slowly across the porch and down the steps.

With a sigh, Charlotte shoved the front door open, then grabbed the handle of her suitcase and pulled it inside the living room.

Upon entering the room, she immediately spotted the birdseed scattered all over the floor. Immediate panic raced through her and all thoughts of Benny and Angel disappeared. She jerked her head toward Sweety Boy's birdcage. Thank the good Lord, the little bird was still there in his cage where she had left him, and he seemed to be just fine.

Charlotte let her breath out in a swoosh of relief. "Hey, Boy, what's all of this?" She motioned toward the floor. In addition to birdseed and hulls all over the floor, the little parakeet had also shredded the newspaper in the bottom of his cage. She shook her forefinger at him. "You nearly scared the daylights out of me."

Only months earlier, thanks to Louis's ex-wife, the little bird had come up missing and Charlotte had spent several agonizing days searching for him before he'd showed up on her doorstep. Ever since then, she had been a bit overprotective toward him.

Charlotte had heard of pets, mostly dogs and cats, getting angry with their masters for leaving them alone and destroying furniture and such, but she'd never heard of a bird acting out or trying to destroy anything.

Then, as if the little bird wanted to confirm why he'd done what he'd done, he chirped, "Missed you, squawk, missed you."

Charlotte's throat tightened a moment; then she laughed. "I missed you too, you little scamp," she muttered.

With a shake of her head, she deposited her suitcase near the doorway leading back to her bedroom, then walked over to the bird's cage.

"Yep, I missed you." She reached through the cage wires with her forefinger, and Sweety immediately sidled over close. "And I know you missed me too," she continued, gently rubbing his head. "But did you have to make such a mess? Just don't do it again or next time I'll leave the cover on." Just before she'd left with Benny for Mississippi, she'd purposely turned the air conditioner thermostat up. Since the house would be warmer than usual, she had decided to leave Sweety's cage uncovered.

"Yeah, next time I might just leave you in the dark," she told the little bird. Whether the bird understood anything she said, she hadn't a clue, but talking to him beat talking to herself.

With a shake of her head, she gave him one last rub, then headed for the kitchen, where she retrieved her broom and dustpan.

"Just what I wanted to do tonight," she complained when she returned to the living room. "Clean up a mess." Still, it was good to know that someone missed her, even if it was just her little bird.

As she passed by her desk, she noticed that the light on the answering machine was blinking like crazy. "Uh-oh, Sweety, looks like more than just you missed me as well." She counted the blinks and groaned. "Lots more." So why hadn't they simply called her on her cell phone?

She glanced over at her purse. Maybe they had and she hadn't heard it ring. Curious, she walked over to her purse. Propping the broom against the wall and setting aside the dustpan, she dug her cell phone out of her purse and flipped it open.

"Uh-oh," she groaned. No wonder she didn't hear it ring. She'd been so upset by Louis's phone call on Sunday, she'd completely forgotten that afterward she'd turned off the phone and had never bothered to turn it back on.

With another groan, she flipped the phone closed and dropped it back inside her purse. Grabbing the broom, she began sweeping up the birdseeds and hulls. Not only did she have a lot of calls to return, but more than likely, she'd have lots of explaining to do, especially since she hadn't bothered telling anyone about her impromptu side trip to Mississippi. It was a wonder they hadn't filed a missing person's report to the police.

" 'Lucy, you got some 'splainin' to do!' " Charlotte giggled at her own botched imitation of Ricky Ricardo's Cuban accent in the old *I Love Lucy* TV series. Yes, she had some 'splainin' to do, but not tonight, she decided, as she bent over and swept the birdseed and hulls into the dustpan.

Tonight, she intended on getting a good night's sleep, because once she did start making phone calls, she needed to be fresh with a clear, sharp mind. Tomorrow morning would be plenty of time to listen and respond to the messages . . . and get chewed out for not letting anyone know that she had decided to leave town for a couple of days.

Charlotte walked into the kitchen and dumped the contents of the dustpan into the trash. For tonight though, she was going to bed. The bed in her hotel room had been comfortable enough, but no bed, no matter how comfortable, was as good as sleeping in her own bed.

Back in the living room, she rechecked the deadbolt on the front door, then picked up her suitcase. "Good night, Sweety," she called out as she switched off the living room light.

Once she was in bed, though, Charlotte's mind raced. Mental images of Angel in her orange jumpsuit, the bloody letter opener lying on the floor beside Nick Franklin, his dead eyes staring into eternity, and the old newspaper picture of Alex Scott, all flashed through her mind over and over like a broken movie reel.

Overtired, Charlotte decided, squeezing her eyes tightly closed. She was too tired too sleep, if such a thing were even possible. With a groan, she flipped onto her back and stared up at the darkened ceiling.

Just breathe deeply and try to relax.

Charlotte took a deep breath and let it out slowly. Then she repeated the process. Outside, the Doberman across the street barked. In the distance the faint sound of a siren grew louder, then finally faded away.

Inside, Charlotte took another deep breath and let it out slowly, then flipped over onto her side again. Why on earth was it so hot and stuffy? Had she remembered to readjust the temperature of the air conditioner?

Just about the time she'd decided that no, she hadn't readjusted the air conditioner thermostat and she'd have to get up and adjust it, she suddenly froze. A second later, she sat straight up in bed.

"That's it!" she cried. "The pearl necklace — that has to be the answer." In the darkened room she grinned. She'd been obsessing about Angel's fingerprints on the letter opener being smeared. But it didn't matter whether her fingerprints were smeared or not, now that she'd figured it out. What was it that Heather had told her on that very first day?

"We always keep duplicates of a major prop in case they have to shoot the scene over."

Yep, that was it, and that meant that at least two other identical letter openers existed besides the one found by Nick's body.

Excitement thrummed through Charlotte. The killer could easily have stabbed Nick with one of the other letter openers, and then carefully smeared blood on the one that Angel had used in the scene shot the day before Nick's body had been discovered and placed it beside Nick's body. Just like in the movies, the killer had set up his scene.

She'd been so worried about telling the detective about Angel using the letter opener in the scene the day before the murder that she'd completely forgotten to tell him about the identical props . . . and evidently, no one else had thought to tell him as well.

What was that old saying? Something about things are seldom what they seem. What she needed to do now was locate those other letter openers.

Yeah, right. What makes you think that the police are going to just let you waltz into Bitsy's house and snoop around?

"Good point," Charlotte whispered as she slipped out of bed and headed for the thermostat located in the living room to check the temperature.

While it was true that the police wouldn't let her snoop around their crime scene, there were still other ways to find out what happened to the duplicate letter openers without setting a foot on the property. She could ask Dalton the prop manager. Surely he would know, since taking care of the props was his job. And Benny would know how to get in touch with Dalton, since she never had been told Dalton's last name.

But what if Dalton is the killer?

Charlotte swallowed hard. Who better would know how to manipulate the props?

Probably anyone who worked around the set, she decided. Then, a moment later, she shook her head. Off the top of her head, she couldn't think of any reason Dalton could have to kill Nick and set Angel up to take the blame. Evidently, neither could Benny, since Dalton had never been mentioned when they had made up their list of possible suspects.

"Hmm, better talk to Benny about Dalton first," she murmured. "Just to be safe," she added.

Even without consulting Dalton, though, there was still another alternative. Calling Judith was out of the question, but though it really galled her to think about it, she could always call Detective Gavin Brown and tell him about the duplicates. After all, it was his case. Whether he would do anything about it was anybody's guess, but he had told her to call him if she thought of anything else. Well, she had thought of something else, and it was a doozy.

In the living room, Charlotte squinted at the thermostat. Sure enough, she had neglected to readjust it. After resetting it to seventy-five degrees, she glanced over at Sweety Boy's cage and decided that, with the cooler temperature, she should really cover the little bird's cage. "Just for tonight, Boy," she told him as she slipped the cover over his cage. "Wouldn't want you to get cold."

Satisfied that the little parakeet would be protected, she headed back to the bedroom, back to bed.

Only problem, once back in bed Charlotte tossed and turned. No matter what position she tried, she couldn't seem to get comfortable, nor could she relax enough to fall asleep.

Throughout the seemingly endless night of tossing and turning, the last thing she remembered hearing was the clock in the living room cuckooing twice.

Charlotte! Charlotte, wake up.

Still half asleep, Charlotte wondered why in the world she was dreaming about Louis. Whatever the reason, the dream was aggravating her. All she wanted was to keep sleeping.

Charlotte!

There it was again, she thought sleepily. "Go away," she groaned. The words had barely passed her lips when she suddenly realized, this was no dream. Louis was there. In her bedroom. But how? And more to the point, why?

CHAPTER 15

Charlotte snapped open her eyes just as Louis reached out towards her. "Louis!"

Louis jerked his hand back; then, with a grim, foreboding expression, he crossed his arms against his chest and glared down at her.

"What are you doing here?" she demanded as she grabbed the covers and pulled them up to her chin. "How — how did you get inside my house?"

"I did knock first," he retorted, his tone not the least bit apologetic. "Several times," he added. "And loudly."

"Well, you don't have to be so snippy about it. Once again, what are you doing in my house?"

Louis's eyes narrowed. "Just get up. You've got some explaining to do."

Whether she was simply nervous or still in shock, hearing Louis say the same thing she'd thought the night before, minus the fake Cuban accent, made her giggle.

Louis's mouth took on an unpleasant twist. "I'm glad you find this funny. Frankly, I don't see anything funny about any of it. Now get your butt out of bed before I drag you out."

"You wouldn't dare!" she shot back.

"Try me," he warned. For several moments more, he continued to glare at her. Then, without a word, he suddenly did an about-face and marched out of the bedroom.

Charlotte stared at the empty doorway. She should be angry. No, not just angry, but furious. So why wasn't she?

With a shrug, she threw the covers aside. Probably because she trusted him and knew he would never knowingly do her harm. And probably, on some level, she was still feeling guilty about that awful phone call on Sunday. Then again, it was still early, and having been so rudely awakened, she couldn't think straight. She licked her dry lips. What she needed was coffee, lots of coffee. A good jolt of caffeine always went a long way in helping her think straight.

"Hey, Louis," she yelled out. "The least you could do is make a pot of coffee. Three heaping scoops to a twelve-cup pot." She slid to the edge of the bed and reached for her housecoat draped across the footboard. He never had answered her question. "Probably on purpose," she muttered. "Definitely on purpose," she added. He knew good and well that not answering would make her curious enough to get up . . . which was what he wanted in the first place.

So just how had he gotten inside her house without a key? To open that deadbolt from outside required a key. She'd never given him one, and she'd removed the extra one from the flowerbed, especially after what had happened the previous November. Always before then, she'd left an extra key hidden in the front flower bed. Mostly only her family and a couple of friends, including Louis, knew about the key. After Joyce's murder, though, she had decided that leaving an extra key hidden outside was just asking for trouble.

Charlotte frowned as she shoved her arm into the sleeve of the housecoat. Now that she thought about it, had the police ever returned her missing key? Then she remembered. They had returned the key, but after the incident with Joyce she'd had a locksmith change all of her locks.

Charlotte paused, her housecoat half on and half off. "That's it," she murmured. More than likely, that's why Louis had a key. She'd had to work the day the locksmith came and had asked Louis to be there while the locks were being changed. He'd probably kept a spare key for himself.

Again, she should be angry, she thought, and again, for some strange reason, she wasn't. "Whatever," she muttered, as she finished pulling on the housecoat and belted it. He'd eventually tell her how he got in and why.

Slipping into her moccasins, she headed for the bathroom, where she brushed her teeth and her hair. Forget the makeup, she decided, peering at her face in the bathroom mirror. "What you see is what you get," she muttered, thinking of Louis. Besides, putting on makeup would be just a bit too obvious. She sure didn't want to give Louis the idea that she was primping for him.

Why not?

Charlotte chose to ignore the irritating voice in her head, and with one last look in the mirror, she stepped out of the bathroom.

Suddenly, the ring of the phone broke the silence. Though she was tempted to ignore it as well, at the last minute she changed her mind. With a grimace, she hurried to the living room and snatched up the receiver.

"Maid-for-a-Day, Charlotte speaking."

"Are you okay, Mom?"

Hank. Uh-oh.

"Where in the devil have you been?" he demanded without giving her time to reply. "And why haven't you been answering the phone?"

"I'm fine, son. My goodness, I wasn't gone but a couple of days."

"Gone where?" he retorted.

The aroma of freshly brewed coffee drifted into the living room, and Charlotte's mouth watered. "Listen, I appreciate your concern, and I promise I'll explain everything, but I'll have to explain later, okay? Right now, I really, *really* need a cup of coffee first. And I have company."

"Company? At this time in the morning?"

"It's just Louis."

"And what's Louis doing there this early?"

From Hank's insinuating tone, she knew exactly what he was thinking. Well, he could just think again. Her love life, or lack of it, was no one's business but her own. Time to nip that in the bud. "That's just what I'm about to find out," she replied. "Thanks again for your concern, and I promise I'll call you later. Love you." Charlotte quickly hung up the receiver and sighed. For Pete's sake, why was everyone in such an uproar? You'd think that she'd been gone for weeks instead of just a couple of days.

"And what's Louis doing there this early?"

Charlotte suddenly grinned. Unlike Madeline, at least her son didn't think she was too old. With a shake of her head, she walked into the kitchen. Louis was already seated at the table with a cup of coffee. In front of him was the newspaper . . . her newspaper.

"That was Hank on the phone," she told him. "He wanted to know what you were doing here so early in the morning." When Louis simply shrugged and continued reading the newspaper, she said, "Thanks for getting in my newspaper and for making coffee." When he still remained silent, she rolled her eyes and turned to pour herself a cup.

Only once she was finally seated in front of him on the opposite side of the table did he carefully fold the newspaper, and lift his gaze to stare at her. For several moments, he said nothing, but continued staring at her with a troubled but resigned expression on his face. Finally, with a deep sigh, he said, "Look, I don't know what the deuce is going on or where you've been, but I'd be willing to wager a month's pay it has something to do with the Nick Franklin murder. Am I right?"

She gave a one-shoulder shrug. "So what?"

"So what?" he repeated, narrowing his eyes. "Just where in the devil have you been the last two days, and why haven't you answered anyone's phone calls? Oh, and one more thing. What was all that about when we did talk on Sunday?" When Charlotte didn't offer an explanation right away, he said, "Does this mean we're going to play guessing games?"

Charlotte leveled a no-nonsense look at him. "Tell you what. I'll answer yours if you answer mine."

"Your what?"

"My question."

"Ask away."

"I assume, since there are no broken windows, that you have a key to my house. Well, do you?"

"Do you have a key to *my* house?" he shot back, with a question of his own, a ploy that she suspected he was using to keep from answering her.

"Yes," she replied. "But I'm your landlord. So, what's your excuse?"

A slow grin pulled at his lips. "Guess I don't have one. But to answer your question, yes, I have a key to your side of the house. I kept the extra key when the locksmith installed the new locks."

It was just as she'd thought. When Charlotte continued to stare at him and didn't say anything, he reached down inside his pants pocket and pulled out a key ring full of keys. Within seconds he'd worked one particular key off the key ring. He placed the key on the table, and with his forefinger, he pushed it across the table to her. "Feel better now?"

Her eyes flashed a gentle but firm warning. With her own forefinger she slid the key back across the table to him. "You keep it. Just don't make a habit of letting yourself in."

"Sounds fair." He picked up the key and slipped it back onto his key ring. "Now, my turn," he drawled.

Feigning ignorance, she said, "Your turn? Does that mean that you want the extra key I have to your half of the house?"

"Just answer the questions."

"Oh, all right. Where have I been? I went to Oakdale, Mississippi, for a couple of days to do some background research on Nick Franklin. Why didn't I answer anyone's phone calls? Because I turned my cell phone off and forgot to turn it back on."

Louis waited several moments until it became obvious that she wasn't going to answer his third question. "And that Sunday phone call?" he finally asked.

Charlotte stared down into her coffee cup. "I'm sorry about that." She glanced up. "I was going to apologize, but I wanted to apologize in person instead of over the phone."

Louis shrugged. "Just tell me one thing. What did I say to set you off?"

"It wasn't so much what you said, but your attitude. It's like — like, you don't think I've got enough sense to come in out of the rain." Charlotte swallowed hard. While she was at it, she might as well get it all out in the open. "I'm a grown woman, Louis. I've run my own business now for more years than I care to remember. A business — I might add — that's paid the bills without help from anyone. And I raised a son, by myself, without his father or the help of family. I don't like being treated like I'm an idiot. And I don't like others trying to run my life for me."

"By others, I suppose you mean me."

Charlotte threw up her hands. "You, Hank, Judith —"

"It's just because they love you and because you live alone."

Did "they" include him?

Don't even go there.

"Believe it or not," Louis continued, "if I

297

don't check in with my son at least every other day, I get a lecture."

A smile pulled at Charlotte's lips. "No way."

Louis nodded. "Yes, way." He paused; then, giving her a stern look, he said, "So — what have you got?"

Charlotte frowned. "What do you mean?"

"The Nick Franklin murder. What did you find out?"

She narrowed her eyes suspiciously. "Why?"

Louis sighed with exasperation. "Did it ever occur to you that maybe I could help? After all, I *was* a police detective for a lot of years. And, evidently, for you to get involved means you believe that Angel Martinique is innocent. I know you'll find this hard to believe, but like it or not, I've learned that you've got pretty good instincts about these things."

What? A compliment? Charlotte's mouth dropped open in surprise. "Hard to believe" didn't begin to describe her feelings.

"Close your mouth, Charlotte, before you catch flies."

Charlotte snapped her mouth closed, and as wary excitement hummed through her veins, a sudden wave of weakness washed over her. Charlotte ignored the weak feeling for the moment. "Are you serious?"

"As serious as a heart attack. But start from the beginning. Sam filled me in on what she knew, but I want to know what you know."

"Sam? As in Samantha O'Reilly, the security guard?" When Louis nodded, Charlotte frowned. "That reminds me, what on earth was that boss of yours thinking when he hired her? Why, she's just a little bitty thing."

"Don't let her size fool you. I once saw her take down a man who outweighed her by a good hundred pounds. She's a tough cookie, but stick to the subject — what do you know?" Louis suddenly frowned. "Hey, are you okay? You look a little pale and a bit green around the gills."

Another wave of weakness washed through her. "I'm okay. Just a bit weak and need to check my blood sugar level and eat a bite."

"The diabetes?"

Charlotte nodded, then asked, "Have you had breakfast yet?"

He shook his head. "I came straight from the airport, and I've got to leave again to catch the noon flight back to Houston."

"Why so soon?" Or better yet, why come back home at all? She thought . . . unless . . . unless she'd been right and he'd made a turnaround trip just to check up on her.

Louis shook his head. "Never mind that, for now. Just take care of yourself. What can I do to help?"

"If you could just hand me that little blue bag on the counter and get me a glass of orange juice, the juice will hold me until breakfast."

Once Louis handed her the blue bag, she unzipped it, and after removing the items she needed, she checked her blood sugar. Just as she'd thought, it was way too low.

"Here's the juice." Louis handed her the glass and she drank it down. "Does this happen very often?"

Charlotte shook her head. "Not often — just when I neglect to do what I'm supposed to do. I'll be fine in just a few minutes."

"So — in the meantime, what can I do to help with breakfast?"

"You don't have to do that."

"Just tell me what to do, woman."

In spite of her weakness, Charlotte smiled. "Okay, you can get the ingredients ready: eggs, butter, bacon, and milk in the refrigerator. There's bread in the bread box, and instant grits in the pantry. Oh, and there's a small skillet in the bottom cabinet next to the stove."

By the time Louis had gathered all of the ingredients, the weak feeling had passed. Once Charlotte prepared breakfast, over the course of the following hour they ate and she brought Louis up to date on everything that she knew about Angel Martinique and Nick Franklin.

"This Benny fellow sounds like an okay guy," Louis said as he helped Charlotte clear the table.

"Yeah, he is, especially considering his background." Then she gave him a brief rundown of Benny's past.

When she'd finished, Louis handed her the last of the dirty dishes, then stood next to the sink while she loaded them into the dishwasher. "I think you're right on about this Alex Scott character," he said. "But I also think that you'd be wasting your time trying to find a location for him out in California. If he did do this thing, it means he's been planning it for a long time, and you can bet he's taken on a different identity. And since both Angel and Nick Franklin knew him, he might have even taken on a disguise."

Charlotte closed the dishwasher and turned toward Louis. "I hadn't thought of that — the disguise thing — but you're probably right. So how on earth can we find him?"

Louis threw up a hand, as if to ward her off. "Now, don't get your back up, but truth is, you probably won't find him. The best thing you can do right now is take the information you have to Gavin Brown and let the police deal with it. They've got the resources to find him. Besides which, if this Scott fellow gets wind that you're on to him, he's liable to come after you."

"Yeah, I guess you're right. I also thought about telling Detective Brown about the duplicate letter openers."

Louis nodded. "Good." He abruptly glanced at his watch. "I hate to, but I've got to leave. Before I go, I want your promise that you'll at least talk to Brown." When Charlotte grimaced, he said, "I know you, Charlotte. If I don't make you promise, you won't do it."

At this point, there wasn't a whole lot else she could do, unless Benny was able to get Angel to open up. "Oh, okay, I'll talk to him."

Louis leveled a no-nonsense look at her. "Soon!"

"Yeah, yeah, soon," she retorted. "Now get going, before you miss that flight."

"Just one more thing," Louis said, placing

his hands on her shoulders. "Promise me that you'll be careful."

Unable to do anything else, Charlotte nodded. "I promise."

"Good." He suddenly bent down and kissed her hard on the lips. Before she could think to respond, he released her and headed toward the door. Just as he reached the doorway, he paused and said, "And I still have something I want to talk to you about when I finish this Houston job." Then he was gone.

CHAPTER 16

Long after Louis left, Charlotte sat at her kitchen table, nursing a cup of coffee and replaying their conversation in her mind. What he said about Alex Scott changing his identity made sense, but even if he had, surely either Nick or Angel would eventually have recognized him.

Charlotte suddenly went stone-still. Maybe Nick Franklin *had* recognized Alex, even in disguise, thus the need for Alex to kill him. Then again, if her revenge theory was right, Alex Scott had intended on killing one of them anyway and setting up the other one to take the blame. Of course, Nick made a much easier target than Angel did, since Angel had a bodyguard.

Charlotte squeezed her eyes shut. Problem was, she had no proof of anything, just speculation. She'd promised Louis that she'd talk to Gavin Brown, but after past dealings with the surly detective, she wasn't sure she could keep that promise. There was also the possibility that Benny was right when he'd said it was unlikely that the police would check further, since they thought they already had the killer in custody.

But you promised.

"Yeah, yeah," she muttered. After all, the detective had been thoughtful enough to warn her about the media, and, according to what Benny had said, he'd paid her a compliment . . . of sorts. Maybe she would keep her promise to Louis and talk to Brown after all, but right now thinking about it was giving her a headache.

Louis.

Charlotte opened her eyes and stared out of the window. Though he hadn't outright admitted it, she still suspected that he had flown back from Houston for the express purpose of checking up on her. What other reason could he have had?

A part of her was flattered that he cared that much. Yet another, more cynical, part figured that his actions were further confirmation that he didn't think she had sense enough to take care of herself.

From the living room, Charlotte heard Sweety Boy squawking. "Great," she whispered. She'd completely forgotten that his cage was still covered. With a sigh, she shoved back her chair. "I'm coming," she called out. Given the little bird's wild reaction whenever Louis was around, it was probably just as well that his cage was still covered.

After placing her empty cup inside the dishwasher, she hurried to the living room and straight to Sweety's cage. "Sorry, little guy. I completely forgot."

Out of the corner of her eye, the blinking light of her message machine caught her attention, a reminder of yet another thing she had to do. "Once I get dressed, then I'll return those calls," she told Sweety Boy.

Dreading having to return calls and explain herself, Charlotte took her time showering and dressing. Once dressed and knowing she was procrastinating, she made up her bed and gathered a load of clothes to be washed.

"Oh, for Pete's sake," she muttered on the way to the laundry room. "Just do it and get it over with."

In the living room, she seated herself at her desk and took out a writing pad and pen. Pen poised above the pad, she hit the Play button on the machine. Between Maddie, Hank, Judith, and Louis, there were seven messages, all with the same theme.

"Where are you? Why haven't you called me back?" And so forth and so on, she thought, getting more aggravated the longer she thought about it. Then the eighth and last message played.

"Ms. LaRue, this is June at the flower shop. Remember, you asked me to call you if that same person came in and ordered flowers? Well, he did come in, and I have another bouquet of flowers to deliver to you, but this time I got his name. His name is Delbert O'Banion. If you'll just give me a call when you get home, I'll send the flowers over."

As Charlotte stared at the answering machine, a slow smile pulled at the corner of her lips. Delbert — Bert — O'Banion had been in the same hospital that Joyce had stayed in for a while, but for different reasons. Because of the loss of his beloved wife, Bert was being treated for depression. And because he'd helped Charlotte when she'd been trying to find out who had murdered Joyce, he'd put himself in danger.

Charlotte's smile widened. Bert had offered to make a trade. He'd been willing to give Charlotte some vital information for her promise to call and persuade his daughter to get him out of the hospital.

Evidently, her phone call to his daughter

had done the trick. The fact that he was able to go to the florist and order flowers had to mean that his daughter had listened and that he was well enough to be out on his own again, thus the flowers and the thank-you note.

"Well, that's one mystery solved," Charlotte told Sweety. Her smile suddenly faded. "Oh, dear," she whispered. One bouquet of flowers was enough to say thank you, but two bouquets . . . was it possible? "Oh, no," she murmured. Surely Bert hadn't decided that he wanted some kind of romantic relationship with her. "Just what I need," she groaned. "Or I should say, just what I don't need."

Charlotte knew that just thinking about such a thing would drive her crazy, so she made a concerted effort to shove all thoughts of Bert aside for the moment. Mentally rehearsing what she'd decided to tell all of her callers, she tapped out her sister's phone number. She'd decided to stick as close to the truth as possible, and simply say that she had to make a quick overnight trip to Mississippi for business purposes and forgot to turn on her cell phone.

Her sister answered on the third ring, and then she began her explanation. Just as she hung up after returning the last of her phone calls, her telephone rang. "Now who could that be?" she murmured, not recognizing the caller ID. Since she'd just talked to almost every member in her family, she decided that the caller had to be either a prospective client or someone trying to sell her something. "Or someone wanting a donation," she grumbled.

One way to find out. She picked up the receiver. "Maid-for-a-Day, Charlotte speaking."

"Ms. LaRue, I'm calling for Tom Rolland, the producer for Mega Films. We realize this is short notice, but Mr. Rolland is calling a cast and crew meeting this afternoon for three o'clock at the Duhè house to discuss the status of the movie. Can you make it?"

Charlotte glanced over at the cuckoo clock. It was almost noon, plenty of time. "Yes, I can be there."

"Great, and thanks."

Charlotte noticed that all of the street barricades had been removed when she parked in front of Bitsy's house at a quarter to three that afternoon. All of the storage vans but the one that held Bitsy's household items were gone as well.

"Not a good sign," she murmured as she

walked to the front porch and climbed the steps.

At the front door stood Samantha O'Reilly. "Hey, Charlotte, how are you?"

Charlotte smiled at the young woman. "I'm fine, and you?"

"I'm okay."

Charlotte leaned close to Samantha, and in a voice barely above a whisper, she said, "So, any clue about this meeting?"

Samantha shrugged. "Nothing official, but between you and me, I think they're shutting it down."

"My thoughts exactly."

Samantha opened the front door for her. "Everyone's gathering in the front parlor."

"Thanks. See you later."

Inside the parlor, every chair was occupied, so Charlotte joined several of the crew members who were standing near the back of the room. Most of the people she recognized, but some she didn't.

As they waited for what seemed like forever, the building tension seemed to grow thicker as each minute passed. For at least the third time Charlotte glanced at her watch. Almost three, thank goodness. Then the door opened, and to her surprise she saw Heather Cortez, Toby Russell, and Simon Clark enter the room. Upon realizing that the room was almost full, all three lined up against the wall near the door.

Why on earth would Angel's entourage show up? she wondered. Possibly to give Angel a firsthand account of the meeting, she finally decided, then frowned. But if that was the case, then where was Benny and where was Angel's chef? Why hadn't they showed up as well? She could understand why the chef wouldn't have showed. Where and when he cooked was of no significance, and with Angel in jail, there was no reason for him to cook — period. As for Benny, since she hadn't heard from him, she figured that he hadn't got around to visiting Angel yet and probably didn't want to chance having to explain why. Or he had visited Angel but was unable to persuade her to talk.

Charlotte's frown deepened. Come to think of it, what about Angel's lawyer? Shouldn't he be the one to report back to Angel? She glanced around the room again, but didn't see him. So why wasn't he here?

Again, her gaze went to Angel's entourage. The three that had showed had such somber expressions on their faces that anyone watching them would think they were attending a funeral instead of a business meeting. Of course in a way, it was a funeral of sorts, she decided. Unless the producer pulled off some kind of miracle, the movie was essentially dead as long as one of the main stars was in jail.

At three o'clock on the dot, a short balding man whom Charlotte didn't recognize entered and walked to the front of the room. The minute he reached the front, the buzz of voices died out. Had to be Tom Rolland, she decided.

"Thank you," he said. "I appreciate everyone showing up, and I'll be as brief as possible. Unfortunately, due to circumstances beyond our control, Mega Films has made the decision to put production on hold indefinitely."

Charlotte sighed. No big surprise there. It was just as she'd thought. Even though she'd expected that the movie would be shut down, just thinking about it and it actually happening were two different things. With the exception of herself, most of the people in the room were now out of a job. Even worse, Angel was still in jail for a crime she didn't commit, and this meant that, like Benny had said, Mega Films had truly abandoned their main star.

And what about Hunter Lansky? He wasn't getting any younger, and it had been a long time since she'd heard of him making a movie. What if this was to have been his last chance on the big screen?

While Charlotte listened with half an ear as Tom Rolland continued talking, she glanced around the room for one last look at the movie star that she'd idolized. Unable to find him the first time, she began searching for him again. With a twinge of disappointment, she finally realized that he wasn't there. It would have been nice to see him just one more time, but whom could she ask about him? Max Morris, the director, might know, but so far she hadn't seen Max either. Maybe Heather knew where Hunter was and what would happen to him.

Charlotte shifted her gaze to Heather Cortez. Beside Heather, Toby Russell had leaned down and was whispering something in her ear. As if sensing that Charlotte was staring at her, Heather glanced her way, smiled, and gave her a little wave.

Charlotte smiled back. Then Toby turned his head to see who had caught Heather's attention. Though his dark eyes flickered in recognition, it was as if his somber expression had suddenly turned to stone.

As he continued to stare at her, Charlotte willed her smile to stay in place and nodded at him. When Toby gave no reaction whatsoever but continued staring at her with his cold, dark eyes, an ominous, uneasy feeling whispered through her. A bit unnerved, she quickly looked away.

What on earth was his problem? she wondered, and was tempted to take another peek at him, just in case her imagination was playing tricks on her again. Resisting temptation for the moment, she tried instead to concentrate on what Tom Rolland was saying, but she couldn't shake the strange feeling she'd experienced when Toby had looked at her.

"And in conclusion," Tom Rolland said, "we will be in touch if anything changes. Now, are there any questions?"

When the producer searched the room for anyone who might have a question, Charlotte took the opportunity to glance at Toby again. As if he'd read her mind, he looked straight at her.

Though Charlotte quickly looked away, the sudden shock of recognition shook her to the core. In that moment, she realized why the old newspaper picture of Alex Scott had looked so familiar.

In spite of the bodyguard being at least ten years older and seventy-five pounds of pure muscle heavier, and in spite of his head being shaved and his nose a bit different, there was definitely something about him that bore resemblance to that picture of

Alex Scott. Not a smack-you-in-the-face resemblance, but it was there. Possibly the eyes were the giveaway, she decided.

"Since there are no questions," Tom Rolland said, "then that concludes our meeting. Again, thank you."

Chairs scraped, the buzz of voices grew louder, and the crowd surged toward the door, but Charlotte stood frozen to the spot, her mind racing.

Toby Russell and Alex Scott were the same person. She was sure of it. But how had he slipped detection? She could understand him not being recognized. Ten years was a long time, and to be fair, it had only been a couple of days since she'd seen the picture of the teenage Alex Scott. Even so, surely, Angel's people would have run a background check on him. While she didn't doubt Louis's suggestion that he could have forged a new identity, it was still hard, if not impossible, to believe that Alex Scott could have gotten away with such a thing.

Even worse, though, she couldn't shake the feeling that somehow he suspected that she'd recognized him. Why else would he have been staring a hole through her?

"Ms. LaRue?"

Charlotte gave a start, then jerked her head around to see who had called out her name. Tom Rolland was making a beeline straight for her.

"May I speak to you a moment?" the producer asked.

Get a grip, Charlotte. Snap out of it. Toby could be watching you. Just act natural, for Pete's sake.

She swallowed hard, finally remembered to nod, and blurted, "Sure."

"Could you be available tomorrow?"

"To-tomorrow?"

"The crew will be moving out our equipment and putting Mrs. Duhè's stuff back. I'd like for you to help oversee the placement of Mrs. Duhè's things. Then, once the crew is finished, the house will need a good cleaning. Is that okay with you?"

"Ah, well, sure. Wh-what time should I show up?" she asked.

"I think midmorning would be early enough, say around ten or so. Now, if you'll excuse me, I need to speak to Dalton before he leaves."

Before she could say anything further, he turned away and hurried to where Dalton had gathered his crew in the corner of the room.

Chancing a glance over to where Toby had been standing, she was relieved to see that the space was empty. The last thing she wanted was to run into him. After a quick search of the room to reassure herself that he had truly left, she was able to breathe much easier.

Aren't you being a bit paranoid? the annoying voice in her head accused.

Not this time, she argued.

Sure, her revelation about Toby was just a feeling, but a feeling based somewhat on fact. Charlotte shivered. Besides, experience was a hard taskmaster, and she'd learned a long time ago to trust those types of feelings. Better safe than sorry was her motto.

Now, if she could just make it home and place that phone call to Detective Gavin Brown, like she'd promised Louis, she'd feel a whole lot safer. Too bad she hadn't had the foresight to make a copy of that picture of Alex that she'd found in Oakdale.

"Hindsight's a wonderful thing," she murmured sarcastically.

And what if Detective Brown doesn't believe you?

One step at a time, she argued. *I'll cross that bridge when I come to it.*

Hoping that Samantha O'Reilly was still standing guard at the front door and could be persuaded to walk her to her van, Charlotte left the room. Only a few people still lingered in the foyer, but no sign of Toby, thank goodness.

Charlotte hurried to the entrance door.

What if she's gone, and he's just waiting for you to step outside?

That thought brought her up short. At the door, she cautiously peeked outside, first to her right and then to her left. Toby was nowhere to be seen. Then she saw Samantha O'Reilly on the porch just a few feet away talking to another security guard, and relief washed through her.

Samantha smiled when Charlotte approached her. "Well, I'm told that they're shutting it down; just exactly what we expected, huh?"

Not exactly, Charlotte thought. She certainly hadn't expected Toby Russell and Alex Scott to be the same person. But she nodded anyway. "Yeah, they're shutting it down."

"That's too bad. Guess that old saying 'The show must go on' doesn't apply in situations like this one."

"Guess not," Charlotte agreed absently, her gaze searching the front lawn and farther to where her van was parked. So far, so good. Still no sign of Toby. She turned her attention back to Samantha. "Ah, Sam, listen, could you do me a favor? Could you escort me to my van?"

318

Samantha frowned. "Sure, no problem. Is something wrong?"

Should she confide in Samantha or not?

What? So she can run and call Louis?

Not, she decided. Charlotte had no doubt that Samantha would call Louis, and if she called him, then he'd probably hop the next plane back to New Orleans . . . again. Besides, hadn't she made a big deal out of being able to take care of herself? Well, it was time to put up or shut up.

Searching frantically for a viable excuse, Charlotte summoned a smile that she hoped looked reassuring. Then the perfect excuse popped into her head. "No, nothing's wrong, not exactly; but I am a little worried about running into that pesky reporter again." Not a lie, not exactly. Though she hadn't thought of the reporter until that moment, it was true that she didn't want to cross paths with him again. "And speaking of Bruce King, will you be here again in the morning? I've been asked to work tomorrow," she explained, "and I'd feel a lot safer if you were here."

Samantha nodded. "Yes, ma'am. I'll be here with bells on, right up until the time that Ms. Duhè returns home."

Charlotte nodded. "Thanks. That's a relief."

Samantha motioned toward the steps. "Ready to go?" she asked.

Charlotte scanned the distance between Bitsy's house and where she'd parked. There were several cars and vans lined up alongside the curbs on both sides of the street, but still no sign of Toby. Taking a deep breath, she said, "I'm ready."

Once at Charlotte's van, Samantha stood near the driver's side and waited until Charlotte was safely inside and had locked the doors. The moment Charlotte cranked the engine, Samantha called out, "See you tomorrow," and, with a wave to Charlotte, headed back to the house.

Before Samantha reached the porch, Charlotte was well on her way, headed down the street toward Magazine. Before she reached the end of the block, she glanced into her rearview mirror and noticed that a black SUV was following her from a distance.

Charlotte narrowed her eyes suspiciously. If memory served her right, that particular SUV was the same one that had been parked not far from her van in front of Bitsy's house. Then again, she could be a bit paranoid. Nope, not paranoid this time, she decided. It had to be the same one. The one parked in front of Bitsy's had sported a fleur-de-lis sticker on one side of the front bumper, and an I LOVE NEW ORLEANS sticker on the other side. Even as far back as the SUV was, the stickers stood out, just one of the reasons she'd noticed it in the first place. Ever since Hurricane Katrina, the fleur-de-lis had become known as the symbol for New Orleans's recovery. For months she'd been thinking about getting one of the stickers for her van.

By the time Charlotte reached the next block, the black SUV was still behind her, only much closer. At the stop sign, she peered into the rearview mirror, hoping to see the driver, but the windows were tinted too darkly.

"I thought that was against the law," she murmured as she drove through the intersection. In fact, she was sure that several years back the Louisiana legislature had passed a law against tinting windows that dark, mostly to protect the policemen from being taken unaware when stopping vehicles for suspicious activity or traffic violations.

Coincidence, she told herself. Surely it was just coincidence that the SUV happened to be traveling the same route. So why the ominous feeling in her gut?

There was one way to find out for sure, she thought, as she approached Magazine

Street. Charlotte flicked on her blinker, indicating she was turning left, and stopped at the intersection. A moment later, behind her, the turn signal of the SUV began blinking, indicating a left turn as well.

Keeping her eyes on the passing traffic, she waited for just the right moment. Suddenly, there was a brief break in traffic. Charlotte gunned the motor and turned right. Brakes squealed and a horn blared from the car she'd cut off, but Charlotte ignored it. The important thing was that the SUV was stuck back at the intersection momentarily.

Keeping a wary eye on the rearview mirror, Charlotte breathed a tentative sigh of relief when a few moments later there was still no sign of the SUV. As she approached the intersection of Magazine and General Taylor, she began to breathe even easier. Then as she approached Marengo Street she glanced into the rearview mirror yet another time, and instant fear shot through her. The SUV again, and only two cars separated it from her van.

Along with fear, panic welled in her throat. Her street, Milan Street, was just half a block away. What to do? What to do?

You need to buy time to think.

Charlotte gripped the steering wheel

tighter, and eased her foot off the accelerator to slow the van down. Now what?

Think, Charlotte, think.

There was a good chance that the driver didn't know her address, else why would he be following her in broad daylight, especially since she was listed in the phone book, for Pete's sake, and anyone could find her? Had to be a spur-of-the-moment decision to go after her, she finally decided. Even so, there was no way she was going to lead him right up to her doorstep.

Charlotte continued driving slowly and passed up the turnoff to Milan Street. So what now? Should she just keep driving or . . .

Suddenly, out of the blue, she knew exactly what she should do, and she grinned. "I'll fix his wagon," she whispered.

CHAPTER 17

The next street past Milan was General Pershing, followed by Napoleon Avenue. About halfway between General Pershing and Napoleon Avenue was the Second District Police Station.

Just as Charlotte approached the police station, a police cruiser pulled away from the curb in the restricted parking zone in front of the station. Knowing she was probably inviting a traffic ticket, Charlotte immediately pulled into the empty space anyway. She'd gladly risk a ticket if it meant shaking the man tailing her.

"Now follow me, sucker," she muttered, watching as the SUV slowed when it approached the spot where she'd parked. Then, as if the driver suddenly realized why she'd stopped and where she'd parked, he gunned his motor and whizzed past her, continuing on up Magazine.

Her heart pounding with victory, Charlotte shook her fist at him. "Yeah, run, you coward!"

Once she was sure that the SUV wasn't going to stop, she immediately hopped out of the van and headed straight for the entrance door to the station. As long as she was here, she figured it was the perfect time to keep her promise to Louis and talk to Gavin Brown.

Inside the station, she approached the information desk.

"Can I help you?" the young officer behind the desk asked.

Charlotte nodded. "I need to talk to Detective Gavin Brown."

The officer tapped some keys on a computer keyboard in front of him, then shook his head. "Sorry, but Detective Brown doesn't work out of this district. He's with the Sixth District."

For a second Charlotte was speechless; then it hit her. Of course! Duh! Bitsy's house was located in the Garden District, which was policed by the Sixth District, thus the reason Gavin Brown had been assigned the case. This station was the Second District and policed the Uptown area, including her street.

"Can someone else help you?" the officer asked.

Thoroughly embarrassed for making such a gaffe, Charlotte backed away, shaking her head. "Ah, no — no, thank you." She'd lived in New Orleans all of her life, for Pete's sake, and should have known better. "I really need to speak to Detective Brown," she reiterated.

Fear, she decided. Coming on the heels of her revelation about Toby's real identity, and then being followed, she'd immediately assumed that the driver was Toby, out to get her. She'd been so frightened that everything else, including common sense, had gone right out of her head.

"In that case, you'll need to go to Felicity Street, off of Martin Luther King Boulevard. The address is —"

"I know the address," she blurted, cutting him off. Of course she knew the address, knew exactly where it was located. "But thanks so much anyway," she quickly added, not wanting to appear ungrateful.

Outside the station, Charlotte searched up and down the street as she dug her keys out of her purse. With no sign of the black SUV in sight, she walked quickly to her van.

Now the big question, she thought, as she locked the doors and shoved the key into the ignition. Should she go home or head directly for Martin Luther King Boulevard?

Charlotte glanced at her watch. Neither, she decided. No way was she taking a chance that the driver of the black SUV might have gotten hold of a telephone book, and even now be parked, waiting for her in front of her house. But, at the same time, it was getting late, and there was a good possibility that Gavin Brown might not be working. Why drive over there if she didn't have to? Her best choice would be to call the detective first and decide where to go after she'd talked to him.

She opened up her purse. Now, where had she put his business card? She searched the inside of her purse, her thoughts going back to when he'd given her the card. If she remembered right, she'd dropped it inside her apron pocket. But had she ever transferred it from the apron to her purse?

It would be a cold day in Hades before she ever called him.

Charlotte swallowed hard, remembering her thoughts when the detective had handed her his card. "Guess it finally turned cold in Hades," she murmured.

Now, what did she do with that card? Just as she rezipped one of the inside pockets, she suddenly recalled that she'd slipped the card inside the small zippered pocket located on the outside of her purse.

Sure enough, it was there, right where she'd put it. There were two phone numbers listed on the card: his office number and a cell number. As she pulled out her cell phone, she glanced around again, just to make sure there was still no sign of the black SUV. Satisfied that there wasn't a black SUV in sight, she turned her attention back to the card. She'd try the station number first. After six rings, his voice mail kicked in, inviting her to leave a message.

"Detective Brown, this is Charlotte LaRue, and I need to talk to you as soon as possible. It's urgent," she added, and then gave him both her home phone number and her cell phone number.

Next, she tapped out his cell phone number. As it rang, she glanced nervously up and down the street. So far, so good. Still no black SUV.

"Yeah, this is Brown," a voice interrupted the ringing.

"Detective Brown, this is Charlotte LaRue. I need to see you right away."

"Is this an emergency?"

"No, I don't guess it is, but I still need to see you right away. I've got some information you should hear."

"Can it wait until tomorrow?"

Charlotte sighed impatiently. What part of

"right away" did he not understand? "No, it can't."

"Where are you now?"

"I'm on Magazine near the Second District Police Station."

"Okay, how about I meet you at Joey K's, say, in about thirty minutes?"

Charlotte glanced around again, making sure that there was still no sign of the SUV. "Okay, I'll be there."

Joey K's was a neighborhood restaurant on Magazine Street, located not far from where she was at the moment. Charlotte looked at her watch. The restaurant was open for dinner at five; since it was close to five, maybe she'd go ahead and get there early enough to order something and eat while waiting for the detective to show. One thing for sure: she'd be a lot safer inside the restaurant, surrounded by people, than simply sitting in her van. She also figured that since she would be doing most of the talking, it would be better if she were done eating by the time he got there.

When traffic permitted, Charlotte pulled the van out onto Magazine, then turned at Napoleon and U-turned back to Magazine. Turning left, she retraced the route she'd taken to get to the police station. A few minutes later, she couldn't believe her luck when she spotted a parking spot that was almost directly across the street from Joey K's.

Still a bit jumpy about the SUV, she took a good look around before she finally unlocked her door and slid out of the van.

Inside the homey restaurant, wonderful aromas filled the air and served to fuel her hunger pangs. She chose a table close to the entrance. Since it was early, there weren't that many customers, but Charlotte knew that would change the later it got. Joey K's was always busy.

Charlotte didn't even look at the menu. She already knew what was on it and knew what she was going to order. When the waitress approached her table, the temptation to throw caution to the wind and order her favorite, an oyster po' boy with a side of onion rings, was really strong. Caution prevailed, though, and she ordered her next favorite item. "I'll have the grilled chicken salad and a cup of gumbo," she told the waitress. "Unsweetened iced tea to drink, please."

By the time Gavin Brown arrived, Charlotte's food had also arrived. "That looks good," he told her, seating himself across the table.

Charlotte nodded and swallowed the bite of salad she'd been chewing. "It is good," she said, and forked up another bite.

While she finished up her salad, the detective signaled for the waitress, then placed an order. "I'll have coffee and a catfish po' boy dressed," he told her. Once the waitress left, he turned his attention to Charlotte. "Okay, what's so urgent that it can't wait until tomorrow?"

Charlotte blotted her mouth with her napkin. "I know who killed Nick Franklin, and it wasn't Angel."

Gavin Brown rolled his eyes. "Oh, boy, here we go again." He leaned forward menacingly, and in a voice dripping with sarcasm, he said, "And this is your big revelation that couldn't wait until tomorrow?"

Charlotte stiffened at his contemptuous tone. Sudden anger ripped through her. "Look," she lashed out, breathless with rage. "I'm tired, I'm scared, and I need help. What I don't need is some egotistical jerk who has to belittle someone else to make himself feel important. I am not an idiot and I'm not a fool. If you don't want to listen to what I've got to say, then I'll find someone in the Sixth who will."

The detective narrowed his eyes and

glared at her. "Okay, you've got my attention."

At that moment the waitress brought the detective's coffee. By an unspoken mutual consent, neither spoke, both waiting for the woman to leave. Charlotte used the moment to get her temper under control. Now that he was actually listening to her, she didn't want to blow it.

When the waitress walked away, the detective nodded at Charlotte. "Okay, now why don't you start from the beginning and bring me up to speed?"

Feeling somewhat calmer and choosing her words carefully, she began her story with Benny's visit and his plea for her help. She told him about the overnight trip to Mississippi and what she and Benny had uncovered about Alex Scott, Nick Franklin, and Angel. Then she told him about the old newspaper picture of Alex Scott that she'd seen in the library. "When I saw that picture, I knew I'd seen him somewhere before, but I just couldn't remember where. So then I started thinking and came up with a theory." While she explained her theory about Alex Scott getting his revenge by murdering Nick Franklin and setting up Angel to take the blame, Gavin sipped his coffee. Though he'd yet to say a word or offer a comment, she could tell that he was listening . . . finally, really listening.

When the waitress appeared with the detective's sandwich, Charlotte stopped a moment, long enough to take a sip of tea. Once the waitress left, she continued. "Like I said, the moment I saw that old newspaper picture, I knew that it reminded me of someone I'd seen before. Then today Tom Rolland, the producer of the movie, called a meeting of the cast and crew and announced that they're shutting it down indefinitely. Some of Angel's entourage was there, including her bodyguard, Toby Russell. The moment I saw him, everything clicked. Though he looks completely different now and is using a different name, Toby Russell and Alex Scott are the same person."

When a look of skepticism crossed Gavin Brown's face, Charlotte rushed on. "Only problem, somehow he knows that I know. I could tell from the way he kept glaring at me. Then, when I left the meeting, a black SUV followed me. I'd be willing to bet my last dime that Toby Russell was the driver."

Charlotte paused a moment and took a deep breath. Suddenly, she remembered something else she needed to tell him. "I almost forgot. You know that letter opener — the murder weapon?" When he nodded, she said, "Nobody probably bothered to tell you, but they always have at least two duplicates of each main prop."

Gavin suddenly stiffened, and he didn't look quite as skeptical as he had in the beginning.

Satisfied that she was finally making headway and really had his attention, she said, "I've thought about it and thought about it, but couldn't come up with anything to dispute Angel's fingerprints on that letter opener. Then I remembered about the props, and finally figured it out."

"Figured what out, and what about the props?"

Charlotte quickly explained. "The prop department always supplies at least two duplicates of an important prop. The day before the murder was discovered, Angel shot a scene where she had to use the letter opener. It would have been easy for anyone who had access to the props to take one of the other two, stab Nick, then replace it with the one that Angel had handled the day before. All the killer had to do was" — Charlotte shivered at the thought — "smear a little blood on the prop that had Angel's fingerprints."

When Charlotte didn't say any more, Gavin asked, "Is that it?"

Her lips thinned in aggravation. "Are you still being sarcastic?" she shot back.

The detective sighed deeply, and after a moment, he slowly shook his head. "No," he answered. "No sarcasm this time."

"Then, yes, that's it."

He nodded, stared at her a moment more, then pulled out a notebook and pen. "Okay, then, once more from the beginning."

Charlotte was so thrilled that he was actually interested enough to go through it again that she didn't mind getting grilled for the next half hour, while he jotted down names and information.

When he finally closed the notebook, he said, "Do you have someone you can stay with tonight?"

"Then you really believe me?" For some perverse reason, she needed to hear him admit it out loud.

"Let's just say that there's a lot here —" He tapped the notebook with his forefinger. "A lot that I need to check into before this goes any further. Now — once again — do you have someone you can stay with to-night?"

Not exactly an admission out loud, but pretty close, she decided. Charlotte nod-ded. "I can stay with my sister, but I'll need a couple of things from home — some medications I take."

He nodded. "Okay. I'll follow you home, then follow you to your sister's house. One thing, though, if, at any time, you see that black SUV, don't stop. Just keep driving, and remember, I'll be right behind you."

During the drive to her house, Charlotte phoned her sister. "Maddie, are you up for company tonight? I need a place to stay."

"What's happened?" Madeline asked, a note of alarm in her voice. "Are you okay?"

Shades of déjà vu, thought Charlotte. The last time she'd stayed at her sister's house overnight had also been because of her involvement in a murder investigation. "I'm fine, Maddie, and I'll explain everything when I get there. Okay?"

A few minutes later Charlotte pulled into her driveway, and Gavin Brown pulled in right behind her. When she slid out of her van, he stuck his head out of the window and said, "I'll wait out here for you."

With a nod, she hurried up the steps to the front door. Once she was inside, the first thing Charlotte noticed was the blinking light on her answering machine. Ignoring it for the moment, she rushed around and, using a couple of tote bags, gathered the few things she needed for her overnight stay. She also adjusted her thermostat and made sure that Sweety Boy had plenty of food and water.

Ever aware of the passing time, she quickly replayed her messages: one from Bitsy, one from Hank, one from Louis telling her that if things went well, he'd be home on Thursday, and the last one from Bert O'Banion. *Bert!*

"Hi, Charlotte. Bet you're surprised to hear from me. Listen, there's something I need to talk to you about, so give me a call. I'll be waiting. My number is —"

Charlotte quickly grabbed a pen and pad and scribbled down his phone number. "Humph!" she grunted. So Bert had something he needed to talk to her about. And Louis had something *he* needed to talk to her about. "Well, stand in line, boys," she drawled. "Stand in line."

With a shake of her head, she stuffed the phone number into her pocket. After erasing the messages, she grabbed her tote bags and purse, and headed for the door. Right now, her biggest worry was staying alive.

By the time Charlotte arrived at her sister's home the sun was setting and there was still no sign of the black SUV. True to his word, Gavin Brown had followed her all the way.

Gathering her bags, Charlotte slid out of

the van and locked the door. To her surprise, Gavin got out of his car and walked over to where she was standing.

"Thank you," she said.

His only response was a nod. Then he said, "Don't go back home until you hear from me. Once we check out your story and locate this Toby Russell character, I'll let you know. Also, I need a number for Benny Jackson." He pulled a small notebook and a pen out of his pocket.

Charlotte nodded. "His number is on my cell. Just a second." She set down her bags, then dug her cell phone out of her purse. After pressing some numbers on the phone, she showed him the number on the tiny screen and he jotted it down.

"Now give me the number here at your sister's house."

Charlotte told him Madeline's phone number, and he wrote it down. He slipped the notebook and pen back inside his pocket, and said, "Don't discuss this with anyone else. The fewer people who know about this, the better chance we have of locating Toby Russell and solving this thing."

"Okay." Charlotte dropped her cell phone back inside her purse. "But I'll have to tell my sister something."

Gavin chuckled. "With your imagination, I'm sure you can come up with some kind of reason."

Charlotte grimaced and picked up her bags. In other words, she was going to have to lie to Madeline.

"One last thing," he cautioned. "Don't go anywhere without checking in with me."

"Okay, but —"

"No buts."

"Just listen," she insisted. "Tom Rolland, the producer, asked me to work tomorrow. They're dismantling the set and moving Mrs. Duhè's stuff back in. Once that's done, the place will need a good cleaning, which is why they hired me in the first place. I know for a fact that Lagniappe Security will have someone there, a guard named Samantha O'Reilly," she added. "My friend Louis Thibodeaux says she's one of the best guards that Lagniappe has. Do you know Louis?"

"Yeah, I know him, and yeah, Sam is pretty capable, but that doesn't alter the fact that a man got killed on their watch. Lagniappe really dropped the ball on that one."

He had a point, a really good point, so what was she thinking? After what she'd been through, it was pretty stupid to even consider going anywhere until Toby Russell, a.k.a. Alex Scott, was firmly in custody. Charlotte shivered just thinking about what could happen.

"Look, Mrs. LaRue, it would be easier all around if you just stayed put until we find this guy."

"You're right," she agreed, somewhat relieved. "And I know it doesn't seem that important, considering the circumstances; it's just that Mrs. Duhè is an elderly lady and a long-time client who depends on me. Besides which, Mega Films is paying me a lot of money for this job. But only if I actually do the job," she emphasized.

"Believe me, I understand, but right now your safety is more important than a job or the money."

Both relieved and disappointed, Charlotte sighed. "Yes, I do realize that."

"Tell you what, just as soon as I know anything, I'll call you. And if it helps, I can contact Tom Rolland too. I can always come up with a reason why the crime scene shouldn't be disturbed yet. Meanwhile, I'll put in a call and request that a patrol car be assigned to make extra rounds by this address."

Charlotte smiled, amazed at the complete change of attitude in the detective in such a short time. "Thanks," she said, and really meant it. "As for Tom Rolland, I'll handle him. A delay for a day or two won't make that much difference." At least she hoped it wouldn't. Bitsy wouldn't be pleased with a delay and neither would Tom Rolland, especially since she couldn't explain why she was going to have to miss work tomorrow, but oh, well, too bad. She really had no choice in the matter.

"Okay, then, I'll be in touch. Now get inside so I can get to work."

Charlotte nodded and headed for Madeline's front door. At the door she only had to knock once before Madeline immediately opened it. "Well, it's about time," Madeline said. "I've been waiting on pins and needles for you to get here."

"Nice to see you too, Maddie." As Charlotte stepped through the doorway, she glanced over her shoulder. Gavin Brown was still standing where she'd left him, watching and waiting to make sure she was safely inside before he left. With a sigh, she firmly closed the door behind her.

When Charlotte set down her bags, then turned and locked the door and slid the safety chain into place, Maddie's eyes widened in alarm. "What in the devil is going on?"

Buying time to think of what she was going to tell her sister, Charlotte said, "Can I at least put my pajamas on first? And I'd love a glass of iced tea, if you've got some made."

With a grunt of disbelief, Madeline waved her hand toward the guest bedroom. "By all means, sister, dear, make yourself at home. But I want an explanation."

"Okay, okay," Charlotte retorted. "No need to get all huffy about it."

"Well, hurry up."

Rolling her eyes, Charlotte grabbed her bags and headed for the bedroom.

Feeling much more comfortable in her pajamas a few minutes later, Charlotte left the guest room and went in search of her sister. Though she'd come up with a couple of outright lies to tell Maddie, she'd finally decided to simply tell her sister the truth.

She found Madeline waiting for her in the kitchen. "Here's your tea." Maddie handed Charlotte the glass. "Now sit!" She pointed to a chair at the kitchen table.

Charlotte smiled at her sister. "Yes, ma'am." Once they were both seated at the table, Charlotte said, "All I can tell you is that I can't tell you anything."

"What? You've got to be kidding!"

Charlotte shrugged. "Nope. I was told not

to tell anybody."

Madeline narrowed her eyes. "This has something to do with that movie business job you took and that man being murdered, doesn't it?"

CHAPTER 18

Suddenly unsure again what to tell her sister, Charlotte took a sip of her tea. Now what?

Just stick to the truth.

Yeah, that's probably best. She gave her sister a no-nonsense look. "Like I said, all I can tell you is that I can't tell you anything."

Madeline glanced up at the ceiling as if seeking guidance for a hopeless cause. "I knew it! I just knew it!" She jerked her head forward and glared at Charlotte. "When none of us could get in touch with you Sunday or Monday, I told Judith then that I bet you were somehow involved in that mess. I swear, Charlotte, you're like a magnet when it comes to murders."

Charlotte simply shrugged, since there was nothing she could say. On the outside, she was sure it appeared that way, but what was she supposed to do? Let a murderer go free?

Suddenly an old quote used by John F. Kennedy in some of his speeches chased through her head. *All that is necessary for evil to triumph is for good men to do nothing.*

Charlotte sighed. Nope, this particular murderer wasn't going free, not if she could help it. But right now, she needed to somehow placate her sister. "Maddie, I really do appreciate you letting me stay here. I know you're upset with me, and I'm sorry about that." Unable to help herself, she yawned. "Oh, my goodness," she said. "I think I'm done for tonight. If you don't mind, I really need to go to bed."

Without waiting for her sister to respond, Charlotte shoved out of her chair and walked over to the sink. She poured out the remaining tea into the sink and put the glass in the dishwasher.

Charlotte turned to face her sister. "Just one more thing. I'm expecting a phone call either tonight or tomorrow, so if the phone rings late tonight, don't get upset." Not that she was really "expecting" Gavin Brown to call, not exactly. More like hoping and praying. The sooner this mess was over, the sooner she could get back to her real life.

Madeline's expression was a mask of stone, but she finally stood up. "Like I said before, make yourself at home."

"Don't be mad at me," Charlotte pleaded. Madeline was her only sibling, and she hated it when they argued or disagreed. "I promise that I'll explain everything when I can." Though her sister's expression still didn't change, Charlotte walked over and hugged her anyway. "Good night, hon. And thanks again."

When the phone did actually ring, Charlotte groaned. What time was it anyway? She forced her eyes open. Since it was dark outside, it had to still be night. She rolled over in the bed and glared at the illuminated dial of the clock on the bedside table. Three o'clock.

With another groan she reached over and turned on the lamp, then grabbed the telephone. "Hello?"

"Mrs. LaRue?"

"Yes, Detective. It's me."

"Good news!"

"Well, I should hope so, given the time of night — or should I say morning? — that you're calling me. Did you get him?"

"Yes and no."

"What do you mean, 'Yes *and* no'?"

"He checked out of his hotel, and we've traced him to the airport. According to Southwest Airlines, he boarded a plane headed for Hollywood around midnight. We contacted the California FBI and they'll be at the airport to take him into custody just as soon as his plane lands."

"The FBI?"

"Yeah, well, besides murder and unlawful flight to avoid prosecution, we're charging him with attempted kidnapping as well."

"Who did he try to kidnap?"

Gavin Brown laughed. "Why, you, of course. Yeah, I know, it's a stretch, but we wanted to throw everything we could at him."

"Okay, that's great. So, does this mean that I was right about Toby and Alex being the same person?"

"Yeah, it sure looks that way. The lab finally got back to us, and we got a set of fingerprints back that matched Alex Scott's. Our boys are still going through all of the movie props to find those other two letter openers, but *we will* find them, one way or another."

"A man named Dalton was in charge of all of the props," she offered.

"Yeah, well, we're still trying to get in touch with him."

"He should be at Mrs. Duhè's house in the morning," she told him. "And speaking of tomorrow, does this mean it's okay for me to go to work?"

There was a slight hesitation; then Gavin said, "I'd rather you didn't — not until we actually have this Scott guy in custody — but I guess it won't hurt. One of our crime scene guys is going to go through the house again, just in case those props are still there. If you do go, make sure that Sam knows what's going on."

"Oh, don't worry. I'll make good and sure she knows."

"Well, I just wanted to let you know what was happening. Be careful and be cautious."

"Good night, Detective."

"Night, ma'am."

Charlotte turned off the phone and placed it on the bedside table, then switched off the lamp. She should be feeling a huge relief, she thought as she turned over onto her side and pulled the covers up to her chin. So why wasn't she? Probably because she was still half asleep and still so very tired. Yep, she decided. That had to be the reason.

She should also call Benny and let him know what was going on. She snuggled down farther in the bed. Too late tonight. She'd call him tomorrow. What she needed now was a good night's sleep. After a good night's sleep, she was sure she'd feel better about everything in the morning.

When Charlotte woke up the following morning, any relief that she'd expected to feel was buried beneath a horrific headache. In the bathroom, she splashed water on her face. After a brief, fruitless search for Tylenol, she figured that the kitchen was the most likely place Maddie would keep medications. Besides, if she wasn't mistaken, she could smell coffee.

Charlotte entered the kitchen and found it empty. So where was Maddie? Maybe she was still asleep. Then, on the cabinet in front of the coffeepot, she spied a piece of paper. Charlotte picked up the note and read it.

Charlotte, I forgot about my hair appointment this morning. I should be back around noon.

What time was it anyway? And where did Maddie keep her Tylenol? She glanced at the clock on the microwave. "Nine o'clock," she cried. Oh, for pity's sake. She couldn't believe she'd slept that long.

Heaving a sigh, Charlotte began opening cabinets. First Tylenol, then coffee. Then a shower and breakfast. She finally found the Tylenol, along with various other medicines, in a narrow cabinet next to the sink. Swallowing two of the capsules, she decided she should probably have a glass of juice and take a shower *before* breakfast and coffee. The last thing she needed was one of those weak spells again.

In the shower, Charlotte kept thinking back to her conversation with Gavin Brown. Parts of the conversation were a bit hazy, but there were parts of it that kept nagging her.

Though the detective didn't mention it, the fact that Toby knew that she knew about his masquerade was puzzling. And he did know. Had to. Why else would he have come after her?

Charlotte stepped out of the shower, and as she dried herself off, she finally figured out that the other thing nagging her had to do with the duplicate letter openers. Why hadn't anyone found them? While she dressed, she thought back to the day Nick Franklin had been murdered. Maybe the crime scene team didn't find them in the beginning because, for one, they didn't know about the duplicates, and two, if they didn't know about the duplicates, they wouldn't have searched for them. Since they had already found the so-called murder weapon on the floor beside the body, there was no reason to look any further?

Her head feeling somewhat better after the Tylenol and shower, Charlotte headed back to the kitchen. So, how did Toby know about her learning his secret? No way could he have figured it out just because she was staring at him during that meeting. And where on earth would he have stashed the other two letter openers? More importantly, where would he have stashed the one he'd used to murder Nick Franklin?

Charlotte grimaced. "Not my problem now," she muttered as she fixed herself a bowl of Cheerios and poured a cup of coffee. She'd done her part by pointing out the real murderer. It was up to the police to do the rest. Still, like a mosquito bite that wouldn't stop itching, the unanswered questions wouldn't leave her alone.

Charlotte shook her head. *Stop it! Just forget about it.* What she needed was to think about something else, get her mind on something more positive. Setting the bowl of cereal and coffee on the table, she glanced at the microwave clock again. Instead of worrying about stuff that no longer concerned her, she needed to decide if she was going to work today.

By the time she'd finished the cereal and coffee, she decided that going into work would take less effort than having to phone Bitsy and Tom Rolland, and make up some lie to tell them. Besides, just the thought of having to placate Bitsy was enough to bring back her headache.

When Charlotte parked the van in front of Bitsy's house, the place was a beehive of activity. Not only was there a crew moving stuff in and out, but the NOPD Crime Scene Van was also parked just down the street.

Though she knew she was being paranoid and in spite of Gavin Brown's reassurances, Charlotte glanced around, just to make sure there was no black SUV parked nearby. She didn't see one, but she did see Samantha O'Reilly standing near the door on the front porch.

When Charlotte got out of the van, Samantha waved at her. Charlotte waved back, and after unloading her supply carrier, she locked the door. Halfway between her van and the front porch, out of the blue she suddenly remembered that she'd totally forgotten about returning the phone calls on her answering machine. She definitely needed to call Hank, but Bitsy could wait. Bert could wait too. As for Louis, there was nothing in his message that required her to return the call.

With the phone calls on her mind, thoughts of Benny popped into her head. "Oh, shoot," she whispered, her footsteps slowing. She'd meant to call Benny . . . really *needed* to call him.

Charlotte frowned, and her footsteps slowed even more. She found it pretty strange that she hadn't heard a word out of Benny since he'd dropped her off at her house on Monday evening. Her frown faded. She did need to tell him what was going on, though, and this would be the perfect reason to call him.

"Don't discuss this with anyone else." Gavin Brown's voice echoed in her head.

But that was before they'd tracked down Toby, she silently argued. Now that they knew where he was, surely it was okay to tell Benny, of all people.

Still mulling over her dilemma, Charlotte climbed the steps to Bitsy's house.

"How's it going, Charlotte?" Samantha called out.

A grin tugged at Charlotte's lips. "That's a loaded question. Are you sure you really want to know?"

When Samantha simply shrugged, Charlotte said, "Just kidding. I do have a few things I need to tell you, though."

"Sounds serious." Samantha motioned toward a bench near the end of the porch. "Step into my office and let's talk."

"Some office," Charlotte commented teasingly, once they were seated on the bench.

Samantha simply smiled, then said, "So, what's going on?"

Charlotte filled her in about everything that had happened since the murder, as best she could. When she'd finished, she added, "Even though the police think they'll catch him, Detective Brown wanted me to let you know what's happening, just in case."

A puzzled look crossed Samantha's face. "Just in case what?"

Charlotte shrugged. "Your guess is as good as mine." She paused a moment. "I've been thinking about the reasons why Toby followed me yesterday."

Samantha nodded. "Yeah, that's a bit weird. How did he even know that you were on to him?"

"I'm not really sure, but he did know — that I'm sure of. I guess he thought that he needed to get rid of me before I told anyone. But once I told the police about him, he wouldn't really have a reason to bother me. At least I hope not."

Samantha nodded. "Sounds logical. But if I were you, I'd still want to know how he found out about you."

"I do want to know." She paused, lost in thought. Then the answer came to her. "Off the top of my head, I figure that someone in Oakdale had to have tipped him off."

Samantha pursed her lips. "Anyone in particular?"

Charlotte thought about that for a moment. "I'd say that the Scotts' housekeeper would be the most likely person, but I was very careful not to give her my name when I talked to her. My best guess is Dawn Sanders — the nurse — but what I can't figure out is why she would be so eager to give us information that first time we talked to her, then simply disappear."

"If it were me, I'd try calling her again and outright confront her about it."

"Maybe, but I'll have to add that call to a long list of calls I need to make." Out of the corner of her eye, Charlotte noted that two of the moving men were headed up the front steps with one of Bitsy's sofas.

"Hey, guys," she called out to the men. "Please be careful with that. It's a really expensive antique."

Though the men seemingly ignored her, she noticed that they did slow down to ease the sofa through the entrance door in an attempt not to scratch it. To Samantha, she said, "I guess I need to get to work, but first I should probably go in and see what kind of damage has been done so far. Bitsy will never forgive me if they damage any of her stuff."

"Bitsy?"

Charlotte smiled. "Mrs. Bitsy Duhè, the owner of the house."

"Oh, yeah. I knew that the house belonged to a Mrs. Duhè, but I didn't know that her first name was Bitsy. Say, didn't we once have a mayor with the last name Duhè?"

Charlotte nodded as she stood up. "We did, and Bitsy was his wife."

Samantha stood up as well. "Listen, Charlotte, about that other stuff, thanks for clueing me in. And, 'just in case,' I'll be extra vigilant today." She grinned. "Besides, Louis would have my hide if anything happened to you."

Charlotte forced a brittle smile, then headed for the entrance door. *Louis, Louis, Louis.* That man was going to drive her crazy.

But in a nice way.

Yeah, yeah. I guess.

The moment she stepped inside into the center hall, she froze in disbelief. Boxes and furniture were stacked everywhere, leaving only a narrow path in the wide hall. After a moment, she made her way over to the doorway leading into the front parlor. None of Bitsy's furniture was where it was supposed to be. Everything was such a mess that she wasn't quite sure where to even begin cleaning.

Time to find Dalton, she decided as she edged her way down the hall through the boxes and furniture toward the kitchen.

The kitchen wasn't in much better shape than the rest, but Dalton was there, standing at the breakfast table and peering down at what looked like at least a hundred photographs covering the top of the table. The prop manager was so absorbed in studying the pictures that he didn't notice Charlotte until she walked over and stood right beside him.

He glanced up from the pictures. "Oh, hey, Charlotte, glad you could make it." He motioned at the photos. "Afraid this is going to take a while, though. It will probably be later on this afternoon before you can actually start cleaning."

Charlotte peered down at the pictures and immediately recognized that they were photos taken at every possible angle of each room in Bitsy's house before Mega Films changed things. Charlotte turned her attention back to Dalton. "So, should I come back later?"

"You could do that." He paused and eyed her with a calculating expression. "But — since you know the layout of the house so well, if you're willing, I could actually use your help now."

Charlotte shrugged. "Doing what?" she asked.

He gathered up several of the pictures. "Right now we're trying to place the furniture back where it belongs, as well as make sure that all of Mrs. Duhè's possessions are returned. If you'd be willing to help, we could get this done a lot faster and probably a lot more accurately. You could take the upstairs, while I take the downstairs."

Sounded simple enough, so again Charlotte shrugged. "Okay." Besides, she'd much rather be doing something than just sitting around waiting.

A huge grin split Dalton's face. "Great! That's great!" He handed her the stack of pictures. "In addition to making sure that all of her stuff is returned, we want to make sure that all of her paintings, knickknacks, books, lamps, and such, are put back in place where they belong." He picked up a clipboard and removed some papers stapled together, then gave them to Charlotte. "This is an inventory of her things upstairs.

Anything left over should belong to Mega Films and needs to be packed and loaded in that moving van outside. Just tell the moving team what you want them to do."

Charlotte worked fast and furious for the rest of the morning, took a hasty lunch break, and then went back to work. It was late afternoon before everything had finally been placed where it belonged. Once she was satisfied with the second story of the house, with Dalton's encouragement she double-checked what he had accomplished downstairs.

All of the boxes had been cleared out, and out of the full crew, only Dalton and a couple of other men remained. Except for a few minor adjustments in the parlor and a mix-up with some of Bitsy's gadgets in the kitchen, the bottom story of the house was pretty much back to normal.

Charlotte was still rearranging Bitsy's kitchen gadgets when Dalton walked into the room. "We finally got the moving van squared away," he said. "Guess that about wraps things up for me, so I'm about to take off. Before I leave, though, I just wanted to thank you again."

Charlotte nodded. "Glad I could help."

Dalton motioned toward her supply carrier on the floor near the pantry. "Why don't you take a break before you start cleaning?"

Charlotte shook her head and laughed. "I'm afraid if I stop now, I might never get started again."

Dalton made a face. "Didn't mean to wear you out."

"You didn't. Besides, there's not a whole lot left to do. Mainly, just some dusting and vacuuming."

"Okay — if you say so. Then I guess I'm out of here." He gave her a two-fingered salute. "You take care now."

With Dalton and the remaining men gone, the house was eerily quiet inside. Charlotte glanced at her watch and sighed. It was almost five. If she hurried, she should be finished by eight at the latest. She really should eat a bite of something now, though, so maybe she would take that break that Dalton suggested, after all.

All she had with her was a pack of peanut butter crackers in her purse. She glanced over at the refrigerator. "Wonder if they left any food," she murmured. When she opened the refrigerator door and saw the small plastic container of mixed fruit, she smiled. "Perfect."

After devouring the fruit, she washed it down with a bottle of water. Eyeing the assortment of gadgets piled on the counter with distaste, she said, "Upstairs first, then finish the kitchen last." Grabbing her supply carrier on the way out, she headed for the stairs.

An hour later, Charlotte had completely dusted and vacuumed all of the rooms, including the bedroom that Angel had used. She glanced around the room one last time.

Cleaning that particular room had been really difficult, especially when it dawned on her that today was the one-week anniversary of the day that she'd found Nick Franklin's body. The memory of Nick Franklin lying on the blood-soaked antique rug was still vividly etched in her mind and had disturbed her more than she would have thought it could.

Charlotte shook her head, as if the action would make the image in her mind disappear. "Enough already," she whispered. "Get back to work."

In the hallway, just outside that room, she checked her watch, then grimaced. Almost six. This was taking longer than she'd thought it would. She still needed to Windex the dresser mirrors and the ones in the bathrooms. They weren't that dirty, though, so she could let that slide and move on to the ground floor.

She stared at the bottle of Windex in her supply carrier. She never had been the type to do a job halfway. Besides, it wouldn't take but a few minutes more to clean the mirrors.

She bent down and removed the Windex, then frowned. Strange, she thought, staring at the roll of paper towels wedged lengthwise in the bottom of the supply carrier. The carrier wasn't terribly big, so to conserve room, she always stood the roll up on end.

Setting the Windex aside, she grabbed the roll and tugged, but it was really jammed. Frowning, she got down on her knees, and using one hand to push against the edge of the supply carrier and the other hand to grasp hold of the roll of paper towels, she yanked hard.

When the roll suddenly popped loose, and two metal, oblong objects fell out from the cardboard tube in the middle of the roll, a startled cry escaped her.

For long moments, all she could do was stare in shock at the two missing letter openers. She swallowed hard. How on God's green earth had they ended up stuffed inside the tube of her paper towel roll . . . in *her* supply carrier?

No wonder no one had been able to find

them, but again how? And why *her* supply carrier?

Almost as soon as the questions popped into her head, so did the answer. "Duh," she retorted, a bit disgusted with herself for not having thought of it before. It was the perfect place to hide them, and the perfect place to make sure that the police didn't find them, especially if Toby couldn't risk getting them off the premises without detection.

Charlotte shivered, and her mind raced, as it all began to make sense. Someone got word to Toby that she was snooping around, and when he'd seen her at the meeting and realized that she knew about his secret, he'd panicked. Or maybe he'd even thought that she'd already found the letter openers.

No wonder he'd followed her. Either way, he knew that, once she found them, she'd turn them over to the police. If that happened, then the police might decide to start digging into Nick's murder a little deeper.

Her mind still racing, she thought of an additional possibility. What if he'd been careless, or in a hurry, when he'd hidden them? What if he was afraid that he'd left a fingerprint on them? If that were the case, he had to get the letter openers back, so he could dispose of them permanently.

Charlotte could feel a dull ache building behind her eyes. She squeezed her eyes closed for a second, then opened them again. "Who knows?" she whispered. "Maybe he'd planned on retrieving them all along, but for whatever reason, he hadn't done so."

Right now, though, she needed to call Gavin Brown. The sooner, the better, she thought as she got to her feet. She glanced through the open doorway of the nearby bedroom. If she remembered right, there was a telephone in there.

"Oh, shoot," she muttered, remembering that Gavin Brown's business card was in her purse, and her purse was downstairs in the kitchen pantry. Carefully stepping over the letter openers, she walked quickly to the staircase, then hurried down the stairs.

Once in the kitchen, she retrieved the card from her purse and quickly dialed the first number listed on the detective's card, his office number.

"Great," she muttered when she got his voice mail instead. She tapped her foot impatiently, waiting for the beep to sound. When it finally sounded, she said, "Detective Brown, this is Charlotte LaRue. I'm at Bitsy Duhè's house, and I just found those other two letter openers. They were stuffed in the middle of the roll of paper towels that I keep in my supply carrier. Please come right away."

Charlotte ended the call, then dialed the second number listed on the detective's card, his cell phone number. Again, she got his voice mail, and again, she left him a message, then disconnected the call.

"Never a cop around when you need one," she complained, and stuffed the card and her cell phone into her pants pocket. "Now what?" She stared into space for several moments and tried to decide what she should do next.

Samantha! Go tell Samantha.

"Good idea," she murmured, and took off for the front door. When she reached the door, she opened it and stepped out onto the gallery.

Charlotte frowned. Where was Samantha? "Sam?" she called out tentatively. Then, louder, "Hey, Sam, where are you?" She strained her ears, listening for any sign that Samantha was still around. When several minutes passed and there was still no response, unease crawled up her spine.

Where was she? Surely she hadn't left without letting Charlotte know, especially after what Charlotte had told her. Besides, she'd said she would be there until Bitsy came home.

Calm down. Just take a deep breath and calm down.

Obeying the voice of reason, Charlotte breathed deeply until she felt calmer and could think more rationally. Spooked. She was spooked because of the letter openers. There had to be a logical reason why Samantha wasn't around front. More than likely, she was making rounds and was probably around back instead.

Still uneasy, but feeling a bit more calm than before, Charlotte went inside the house. Just for good measure, she closed and locked the front door.

Retracing her steps, she returned to the kitchen and headed straight for the back door. "Please let Sam be in the backyard," she whispered.

Just as Charlotte reached for the doorknob, the door burst open. Her eyes widened with fright. *Oh, dear Lord in heaven, I need help!* Screaming at the top of her lungs, she stumbled backward.

Run, Charlotte! Run!

She wanted to run, but her legs refused to cooperate.

CHAPTER 19

"Scream all you want," Toby Russell yelled, slamming the door behind him. Before Charlotte had time to even think past her panic, he locked the door and threw the deadbolt. Jerking back around, he advanced toward her. "No one's going to hear you."

Charlotte's scream froze in her throat. He wasn't supposed to be here. He was supposed to be in California, in custody by now.

"And by the way, I took care of your little security buddy out there," he continued, "and you're next if you don't tell me where those letter openers are."

Fear, laced with anger, knotted inside her. What had he done to Sam?

"You just couldn't let well enough alone!" he shouted, his face purple with rage. "I've spent years planning this, but oh, no, you had to go snooping into my business. Where are they?" he demanded.

"Wh-what did you do to — to Sam?" she

blurted out, her voice little more than a croak.

He stepped even closer. "Where are those letter openers?"

Why hadn't he answered her about Sam? Charlotte swallowed hard, suddenly afraid of the answer.

"Where?" he shouted.

She couldn't tell him. Once she told him, he would kill her. He'd have to, to keep her quiet. What she needed was a weapon, something, anything, to defend herself.

Think, Charlotte, think.

In her mind's eye, she saw the top of the counter behind her. Scattered over the counter were several of Bitsy's cooking gadgets. That big new hammer-looking meat tenderizer might work. It was heavy enough. Maybe, if she could just keep him talking, buy a little time . . . if she could just get closer to the cabinet . . .

"Wh-why should I tell you anything?" she retorted, her voice shaky with fear as she eased backward toward the cabinet. "You're just going to kill me anyway."

Fury mottled his face. "I don't want to kill you!" he yelled. "You weren't supposed to come back to work this soon. I thought I had time. I'll do it, though. I'll kill you if I have to. What's one more?"

She eased back another step. Almost there. "If you kill me, you'll never find them."

"Oh, I'll find them," he said, sneering, " 'cause, one way or another, you will tell me where they are."

She took another step backward. Then, quicker than she would have thought possible, he reached out and clamped his hands around her throat. The edge of the cabinet bit painfully into the small of her back. But what good was being near the cabinet if she couldn't breathe?

At first, she tried scratching at his eyes, but he easily turned his head, dodging her attempts. Then she clawed at his hands, but his hands were like iron shackles. She tried kneeing him in the groin, but he easily pinned her body between his and the cabinet.

"Where are they?" His hands tightened, shutting off her air.

Within moments the edges of her vision turned dark. Just as the darkness closed in, he loosened his hold, just enough for her to breathe again. "Tell me what you did with them," he demanded.

"Can't —" she gasped. "Can't breathe." When he eased his grip even more, she sucked in as much oxygen as her lungs would hold. With one hand still pulling on his hands, she reached behind her with the other hand, her hand sliding back and forth, her fingers searching and grabbing for anything she could get.

"Where are those letter openers?" he demanded as his hands began tightening around her neck again.

Suddenly, her fingers connected with a hard metal object. From the rough surface, she immediately recognized that she'd grabbed Bitsy's brand-new cheese grater. It was a flat oblong type with a wooden handle. Praying that she had it turned the right way, she took hold of the wooden handle. Aiming for his eyes and using every bit of strength she had left, she swung her arm upward. When she smashed it into his face, she yanked it down hard, then pushed it upward again.

Toby screamed with pain, released her, and covered his raw, bleeding face with his hands.

She was free, but not for long, she figured. Her eyes swept the room for an escape route. He'd be on top of her before she could unlock and unbolt the back door, and he'd catch her before she could make it to the front door.

The laundry room.

It had a lock on the door, and it was the closest. At least it would buy her some time.

Ducking low, she ran. Behind her Toby was stumbling around, trying to find something to use for pressure to stop his face from bleeding.

When Charlotte reached the laundry room, she slammed the door and locked it. The flimsy lock wouldn't keep him out for long. She figured that she only had a couple of minutes, at the most, just enough time to call the police. She reached in her pocket for her cell phone. Then what? He'd burst in and kill her before the police could get there.

What she needed was something else to defend herself with. She searched the room frantically, looking for anything she could use. Then she spotted the half-gallon bottle of bleach sitting on top of the dryer. If she remembered right, it was a brand-new bottle. With Toby's face already raw, the bleach just might do the trick; it would at least buy her enough time to get out of the house, so she could call the police.

On the floor near the washing machine she spied a small plastic mop bucket. *Perfect.* She uncapped the bleach, then poured all of it into the bucket.

The sudden pounding on the door made

her jump. Throwing the empty bleach bottle aside, she bent over and picked up the bucket. With one hand clutching the top rim and the other hand braced against the bottom, she waited.

The pounding suddenly stopped. Charlotte's breath caught in her throat, and fear and anticipation coursed through her. A second later, the door crashed open. Toby's wild eyes were filled with fury and hate, and a swath of his face and nose looked like raw hamburger.

Do it! Do it now!

Charlotte swallowed hard and bit back tears. With a firm grip on the bucket and aiming for his raw face, she swung the bucket back, then thrust it forward. The bleach flew out and hit him squarely in the face.

Toby screamed in agony. Clutching his face and still screaming, he fell to his knees.

Wasting no time, Charlotte quickly edged around him. Once she was out of the laundry room, she ran flat-out for the front door. Outside the door, she eased it closed behind her. That way, if he came after her again, he might think that she was still inside the house somewhere.

She tilted her head and leaned close to the door. Even with it closed, she could still hear Toby screaming and cursing inside.

Spurred on by the thought that he'd soon begin searching for her, Charlotte hurried across the porch and down the steps. She was tempted to take off running down the middle of the street, but she'd be in plain sight. He'd be able to see her and come after her. Best to hide and call 911.

Looking around frantically, she searched for some place to hide. She shot a brief, longing look at her van, but without keys, it was useless. She could hide behind it, but she'd still be in the open.

After a moment, she decided that the thick clump of azaleas at the end of the porch was her best bet. As she hurried to the bushes, she shoved her hand into her pants pocket and pulled out her cell phone. Without hesitation and ignoring the scrapes from the limbs, she pushed her way through the bushes, and wedged herself in the small space between the side edge of the porch and the azaleas. Then she dropped to her knees.

Charlotte peered through the bushes. They had looked a lot thicker from a distance. Unfortunately, since she could somewhat see through them, she figured there was a good possibility that she could be seen as well.

Too late now. She didn't figure she had enough time to find a better hiding place. All she could do was hope and pray that, if and when Toby came out of the house, he wouldn't look her way . . . if he could see at all after the bleach. Besides, she needed to use what time she had to call the police.

Breathing hard, she flipped open her phone. Her fingers trembling, she tapped out 911. When the operator answered, Charlotte told her, "Please send someone now! A man is trying to kill me." She'd no sooner finished giving the operator Bitsy's address than the front entrance door burst open.

"I know you're still here," Toby bellowed above her.

In her ear, the operator said, "Ma'am, don't hang up. Stay on the phone."

Charlotte didn't dare answer for fear Toby might hear her. She breathed as shallowly as possible, afraid that the slightest movement would give away her hiding place. Above her, she could hear Toby cursing and heard his heavy footsteps as he stomped from one end of the porch to the other end.

Not far from above her hiding place, the footsteps abruptly stopped near the front edge of the porch. Charlotte held her breath. Could he see her? Had he spotted her?

Suddenly, she heard the sound of running footsteps coming from the opposite end of the porch. Not Toby. Someone else. Then there was a guttural shriek of fury, followed by a thud and a crash. Above her, Toby flew off the porch and landed on the ground within mere feet of her hiding place.

"Take that, you son of a snake! I'll teach you to mess with *me!*"

A woman's voice. A *familiar* woman's voice. Charlotte's eyes grew wide. Samantha!

Then everything seemed to happen at once. In the distance, police sirens screamed, growing louder each second. In front of her, Toby struggled on the ground to get to his knees. Above her on the porch, Samantha let loose another guttural shriek, vaulted off the porch, and ran straight at Toby. Then, with a flying leap, she kicked him in the head.

Toby went down again. Samantha fell to the ground, but rolled to her feet. Then she jumped on top of his back. With one hand, she yanked his arm behind him. With her other hand, she grabbed a handful of his hair and pinned him facedown on the ground.

The ear-piercing sirens suddenly died when several police cars screeched to a halt in front of the house. Officers with their guns drawn poured out of the vehicles.

"Hands in the air," they shouted. "Get your hands in the air!"

While two of the officers pulled Samantha off Toby, Charlotte struggled to her feet. One of the officers handcuffed Toby, and the other one pulled out handcuffs and grabbed Samantha's wrist.

"No, stop!" Charlotte shouted as she fought her way out from behind the bushes.

At least three officers jerked guns toward her.

Charlotte threw her hands up in the air. "Hey, I'm the one who called you in the first place," she cried. With her head, she nodded toward Samantha. "She's a guard with Lagniappe Security." Then she nodded at Toby. "*He's* the one who tried to kill us."

Only then did Charlotte notice Samantha's black eye and swollen cheek. Charlotte frowned with concern. Was that dried blood near her nose?

Out of the corner of her eye Charlotte caught sight of Gavin Brown jogging toward them. Benny followed a few steps behind the detective.

"Hey," the detective yelled, holding up his

badge. All eyes turned his way. "You can let the ladies go." To Charlotte he said, "And you can lower your arms."

Benny walked over to Charlotte. "You okay?"

"I think so."

Gavin Brown took one look at Samantha, and shaking his head, he told her, "You need to get checked out by the EMTs."

"I'm fine," she snapped.

The detective shrugged. "If you say so."

The officers pulled Toby to his feet, and when Gavin Brown saw his face he gave a low whistle. "Ouch, that must hurt, huh?" He turned to Samantha and Charlotte. "Which one of you did that to him?" When neither replied, he said, "Never mind for now, but don't go anywhere yet. I've got some questions."

Once Toby was taken away, Gavin Brown turned his attention to Samantha, Benny, and Charlotte. Charlotte immediately launched into a tirade. "You told me he was on his way to California," she yelled. "And where have you been? I tried two different times to —"

The detective threw up his hands. "Now, just hold on. If you'll calm down, I'll explain."

Still breathing hard, Charlotte muttered,

"You'd better."

Taking a deep breath, Gavin Brown said, "I was told that he'd checked out of the hotel, that he'd turned in his rental car, and that he'd boarded the plane headed for California. And he did all of that. Only problem, we didn't learn that the flight had a short layover in Houston until it was too late. Instead of continuing on to California, he caught a flight back to New Orleans.

"Now, if you don't mind and if neither of you needs to see a doctor, then you two wait on the porch." He pointed to Charlotte and Benny. "And you" — he pointed to Samantha — "you come with me."

Samantha followed the detective inside the house. Charlotte and Benny walked up the steps, then headed for the bench. Once they were seated, Charlotte faced Benny. "Where have you been?" she demanded. "Why haven't you called me?"

Benny hung his head. "I'm sorry about that, and" — he lifted his head to look at her — "I'm sorry about all of this as well. I did go see Angel yesterday, just like you and I talked about. I told her what we'd found out in Oakdale, but it didn't make a difference. She still wouldn't talk. I guess I was so ashamed that I'd failed in the one thing you asked me to do, I just couldn't face you right then. Especially after all you've done," he added. "And with me dragging you into this mess in the first place."

Charlotte sighed. "Don't be so hard on yourself. I've got a feeling that even without Angel's help, things are working out."

"Yeah, but I almost got you killed."

She shook her head. "Stop that. Stop it right now. Besides, I'm tougher than you think. It will take a lot more than that jerk to do me in." She smiled. "Besides, I had some great backup."

Benny finally cracked a smile. "Yeah, that security officer chick is pretty tough too."

"Well, yes — her too — but I was referring to a much bigger ally." She tilted her head upward, then lowered it again.

Benny nodded solemnly. "Yes, ma'am."

A few minutes later, Samantha emerged from the house and pointed to Benny. "Your turn."

Benny went inside and Samantha seated herself by Charlotte on the bench. "May I join you?" she asked.

Charlotte nodded. "Guess so. After all, this is *your* office," she added teasingly.

Samantha managed a tremulous smile. "Listen, I just need to apologize."

"For what?"

"For not doing my job better. For not

protecting you."

"Don't be ridiculous. From where I was hiding, you were doing a bang-up job."

Samantha shook her head. "It should never have gone that far and doesn't excuse me letting that snake get the drop on me the first time. He ambushed me while I was making my rounds in the back. Knocked me out cold for a while there."

"Speaking of which, are you feeling okay now?" Charlotte reached up and tentatively touched Samantha's swollen cheek.

Samantha shrugged. "A slight headache, but I've had worse. I'm just glad that I came to in time to take him out before he found you." She suddenly grinned. "Of course you weren't doing too badly on your own."

At that moment, their attention was drawn to the front door, where Benny sauntered out, a wide grin on his face. With a brief wave to both of them, he ran down the steps and jogged across the front lawn toward a car.

"Wonder where he's going," Charlotte murmured.

"Mrs. LaRue?"

At the sound of Gavin Brown's voice, Charlotte jerked her attention toward the front door.

"Could you come in here, please?" he said.

"Sure," she answered, still a bit puzzled at Benny's behavior. She stood, and with an oh-well shake of her head, she turned her attention back to Samantha. "And you, young lady — you go home and put some ice on that cheek."

Samantha nodded. "Will do. See you around."

Inside the house, the detective directed Charlotte to the front parlor. After they were seated he said, "Are you okay?" He motioned to her neck. "You're already bruising up."

"I'm okay."

"Good — that's good. I sure don't want Thibodeaux or your niece giving me a hard time. So — tell me what happened here today."

"I will, but first, you never did tell me where you were when I tried to call you. I tried two different numbers and kept getting your voice mail."

The detective grimaced. "Sorry about that, and I promise, I will explain, but let's get this other matter out of the way first."

Charlotte grudgingly nodded, then told him how she'd found the extra letter openers and explained her theory about how they came to be in her supply carrier. "You know? Just before I found Nick's body, I was in the master bedroom. I always do a walk-through before cleaning," she said, "so I'd left my supply carrier at the top of the stairs. I remember thinking that I heard a noise, like a creaking stair or something, but dismissed it as just the creaking of an old house. But maybe it wasn't that at all. Maybe that's when Toby hid the letter openers." She paused a moment. "Of course I brought the supply carrier downstairs with me and left it on the floor near the staircase. He could have planted the letter openers then as well. Anyway, they're still up there on the floor right where they fell. And just so you know, I didn't touch them."

Gavin Brown grinned. "That's great."

Then, with a shudder, she told him about her harrowing ordeal with Toby, and how she'd escaped.

A puzzled frown came over his face. "Now, tell me, once again, what you used on him."

"A cheese grater and some bleach."

The detective visibly shuddered. "Humph, remind me never to get on your bad side."

Charlotte's lower lip trembled. "I didn't *want* to have to hurt him," she cried.

"Hey —" He reached over and patted her hand. "There's nothing wrong with defending yourself. With what you've told me, along with Ms. Sanders's testimony, he'll be lucky if he doesn't get the death penalty."

"Ms. Sanders? As in Dawn Sanders?"

He nodded. "Yep, that's why I didn't answer your calls right away. Dawn Sanders showed up this afternoon and turned herself in. More than likely I was interrogating her when you called. Seems she knew all along that Toby — Alex Scott — was planning something, but she didn't realize that he was going to murder anyone, not until you and Benny showed up and started asking questions. She thought he was out to prove that Nick and Angel killed his sister. After she talked to y'all, she got to feeling really guilty and decided that this time, she'd do the right thing."

"That sure explains a lot," Charlotte said, thinking of the second time that she had tried to talk to Dawn and the way Dawn's stepfather had acted toward Benny and her.

"Yeah, well, it explains more than you know. Seems that Toby, a.k.a. Alex Scott, has been planning this for years. While he was in prison, he learned how to forge a new identity from another inmate. Through yet another inmate's outside connections, he was able to get a recommendation when he applied for the job of being Angel's bodyguard."

"I had wondered about that," Charlotte admitted.

Gavin Brown nodded, then continued. "It seems that once Ms. Sanders started visiting him and he found out that she had been hired to take care of Angel's mother, he had the perfect way of keeping up with Angel and Nick — their whereabouts and such. So he strung her along, letting her think he really cared about her. After he got out of prison, though, he disappeared. That's when Ms. Sanders realized that he'd probably been using her all along."

"Poor Dawn," Charlotte murmured, truly feeling sorry for the young woman. Then she frowned. "Seems like Toby — Alex — really perfected the art of using people. I wonder if it's possible that he was using that tabloid reporter, Bruce King, as well. I can't prove it, but I think Bruce King is the one who leaked my name to the press."

"He was," the detective confirmed. "After that leak happened, I brought him in for questioning. Let's just say that after I got through with him, he won't be bothering you anymore."

"Good. Serves him right. But back to Dawn. What's going to happen to her now?"

"If what she's told us checks out, then nothing will happen to her, except that

Angel will probably fire her."

"Too bad," Charlotte said. "She really seemed to care for Laura Pate. So, what about Angel?"

Gavin Brown checked his watch. "I'd say, right about now, Benny is picking her up at the jail."

"Oh, wow, that's great!" Charlotte grinned. No wonder Benny had been in such a hurry. Then another thought occurred to her and her grin slid into a frown. "I've got a question," she said. "If it turns out that Nick and Angel *were* the ones who ran over Alex's sister, what will happen to Angel?"

"Afraid I don't have an answer for that one. That would be up to the county prosecutor where the murder occurred." He glanced at his watch and stood up. "Guess that's about all the questions I have for now, but as the case progresses, I may have more."

Charlotte nodded and stood as well. "Ah, I hate to bring this up, but I never did finish cleaning the downstairs."

The detective shook his head. "Not today. I've got the crime scene team on their way back over here. Give me a call in the morning, and I'll let you know then if you can finish up here."

■ ■ ■ ■

All the way home, Charlotte kept telling herself that it was just as well that she didn't have to work anymore that evening. For one thing, she was bone-tired, physically and emotionally; for another thing, all she could think about was a hot shower, her pajamas, and her bed.

Once inside her house, Charlotte saw that, for a change, there were no new messages on her answering machine. She sighed. She still needed to call Hank and Bitsy.

"And Bert," she grumbled, dreading that particular call. "But first, a nice glass of iced tea," she told Sweety Boy.

After spending an hour on the phone with Hank and Bitsy, Charlotte decided to wait to call Bert the next day. The call to Hank wasn't as bad as she'd expected, but the call to Bitsy was a nightmare. Bitsy was still upset about her antique rug being ruined.

"Might as well throw it away," she had complained. "And I've been thinking about something else as well. Now that someone was actually killed in my house, I'm not sure I want to live there anymore."

It had taken Charlotte more time than she'd wanted to spend calming Bitsy and reassuring her that no, ghosts weren't going to haunt her house just because someone was murdered there.

Even more tired after her phone conversations, Charlotte headed for the shower.

In the bathroom, she glanced in the mirror and frowned. "Great. That's just great," she murmured, stretching her head first to one side, then the other, as she inspected the wide purple bruises around her neck.

Unexpectedly, tears filled her eyes. Up until that moment, she hadn't let herself think about how close to being murdered she'd come. With a sob, Charlotte reached up and swiped at the tears running down her cheeks. Both Hank and Louis would have a conniption once they saw those bruises. Maybe she could wear a scarf until the bruises faded.

"Yeah, sure," she murmured, stepping into the shower. Since she didn't own any scarves, she'd have to buy some first. Maybe makeup would hide the bruises.

A good twenty minutes later, she felt a lot more human after her extra-long shower, but her crying jag had completely drained her.

"Bed," she whispered, turning back the covers of her bed. And sleep. Things always looked better after a good night's sleep.

Suddenly, the ringing of the telephone broke the silence. With a sigh, Charlotte went into the living room and picked up the receiver. "Maid-for-a-Day, Charlotte LaRue speaking," she said into the receiver.

"Are you okay? You don't sound so good."

Louis. "Why wouldn't I be okay?" she countered.

"Well, I hear that you did some major damage to Angel's bodyguard this afternoon."

Samantha O'Reilly. Had to be. The woman might be a tiny thing, but she sure had a big mouth. "I would suspect that by now he's Angel's *ex*-bodyguard," Charlotte said. "I did what I had to do."

"I know you did, Charlotte. I mostly just wanted to make sure that you were okay and congratulate you."

"Congratulate me?"

"Yeah. After all, you solved a high-profile murder, freed an innocent woman, and beat up the bad guy."

"Sam did most of the beating up the bad guy," she retorted.

"Not the way I hear it. Anyway, I also want to ask you out to dinner tomorrow evening — kind of a celebration. And before you say no, I've already made reservations at Commander's."

Commander's Palace, one of her most favorite restaurants in the city. A warm fuzzy feeling spread within her. What a sweet gesture.

"Would about seven be a good time?"

Would it be a good time? Charlotte thought back over the past several days. Seeing and talking to Laura Pate had made her realize, more than ever before, that life is short. Laura's predicament had also made her rethink her life, specifically. Yesterday was gone; Hank's father was gone. Had been gone for almost a lifetime. Maybe it was high time — past time — for her to stop holding on to something that never could be. And just maybe it was time for her to start living for today and looking forward to the future.

"Hello? Charlotte, are you still there?"

"Yes, Louis. And yes, I'd love to go to Commander's with you."

"So it's a date?"

She managed a smile. "See you tomorrow evening."

"Now, go get some rest, woman."

"Good night, Louis."

First thing Thursday morning, Charlotte phoned Gavin Brown. "Well? she asked. "Is it okay to finish up at Mrs. Duhè's house this morning?"

"Yes, it's okay. We've got everything we need from there."

"Great! Just one thing, though. What about that antique rug, the one Nick was on top of?"

"Sorry, but we're going to have to keep that for a while."

Charlotte sighed. "Well, when you're finished with it, you can check with Mrs. Duhè, but I don't think she wants it back."

"Will do. Now, you take care, Charlotte LaRue, and try to stay out of trouble, if you can."

"Bye, Detective Brown." Charlotte hung up the receiver, but she could hear him laughing before the call disconnected. "Ha! Ha! Ha!" she told Sweety Boy. "He thinks he's so funny."

She stared at the phone. She still needed to call Bert. "Might as well get that over with," she said, dreading the call. She tapped out his phone number. After several rings, the phone switched to voice mail.

"Hey, there, this is Bert. I'm busy right now, so leave a message."

Charlotte grinned. Maybe this wouldn't be so bad after all. It was the coward's way out, but it would be much easier to simply leave a message than to actually have to tell

Bert that she wasn't interested in a relationship with him.

"Hi, Bert. This is Charlotte LaRue, returning your call. Listen, the flowers you sent were beautiful. But just knowing that you're doing well is all the thanks I need. And, Bert, don't close yourself off from people. Out there somewhere is someone who is just as lonesome as you are. Now I really must go. Best of luck to you."

Charlotte hung up the receiver and sighed. Had she been too subtle? Surely her message was clear enough to get the point across. At least she hoped it was. As for the second bouquet of flowers he'd ordered, maybe she'd have the florist deliver them to her church or to a local hospital.

"For now, though," she told Sweety Boy, "I've got to go to work."

That afternoon, Charlotte treated herself to a hot bubble bath, and languished in the tub until most of the bubbles were gone. By six thirty she was fully dressed and getting more nervous by the minute. Would Louis notice the bruises on her neck? She hoped not.

She walked over to her dresser and looked at her reflection in the mirror for the third time in the last five minutes. Satisfied that the bruises didn't show, thanks to the makeup she'd used, she turned a bit to check out her silhouette. Though the solid navy, silk dress she'd chosen to wear was a few years old, it was a classic, the kind that never went out of style. The dress, along with her pearl earrings and the matching pearl necklace, always made her feel elegant and sophisticated.

"You look just fine," she told her reflection. "For Pete's sake, it's just Louis, so get over yourself."

It was ten till seven when Louis knocked on her door. "You look really nice," he told her when she opened the door.

"Thank you," she replied. "You don't look so bad yourself.

The short drive to Commander's didn't take long. Once there, Louis requested that they be given a table in the Garden Room.

Charlotte smiled as the maître d' escorted them up the stairs to their table. Commander's was divided into several different dining areas on two floor levels. Some were small, others large, some private, some open, but of all the rooms, Louis knew that the one on the second floor called the Garden Room was her favorite.

Once they were seated at one of the small tables, Charlotte glanced around. The large, spacious room, with its walls of mirrors, white latticework, and huge windows had been designed to enhance the outdoor setting of oaks and palms visible through the windows. She hadn't been there for dinner since the renovations after Hurricane Katrina, so she was pleased to see that it was just as beautiful and elegant as ever.

When the waiter asked for their drink order, Charlotte was surprised to hear Louis request a bottle of champagne.

"You really meant it when you said we were going to celebrate, didn't you?"

For an answer, he simply smiled.

Several minutes passed, and Charlotte realized that she was perfectly content with the silence. With Louis, she didn't feel the need to keep up an ongoing conversation.

At that moment the waiter arrived with the champagne. Once he'd popped the cork and poured them each a glass, Louis told him, "Give us a few minutes; then we'll order."

The man nodded, then left.

"This is really nice," Charlotte said. "Thanks for inviting me."

Louis reached across the table and took both of Charlotte's hands in his. His warm hands swallowed hers, and for the first time that evening, a prickly feeling of suspicion tiptoed up her spine.

"What's going on?" she asked.

Louis sighed and gently squeezed her hands. "I'm a little nervous. Just give me a minute."

Louis nervous? About what? Then, suddenly, like the winds of a category-five hurricane, it hit her, and she knew what all of this was leading up to. At least she thought she knew. If her suspicions were right, then how could she have been so clueless, what with all of those phone calls to check on her, the good-bye kisses, and such? Whether her suspicions were right or wrong, deep within a feeling that she'd long thought dead blossomed. "Now you're making me nervous," she told him.

"Don't be. I'm nervous enough for the both of us." He cleared his throat, then looked deep into her eyes. "How long have we known each other now?" he asked.

Her voice barely above a whisper, she said, "Several years, I guess."

"Long enough for me to tell you that I love you?"

Charlotte's breath caught in her throat, and all she could do was stare at him.

"Long enough for me to ask you to marry me?" he persisted.

She managed a shrug. "I — I suppose so."

"I do love you," he told her. "I've known it for a while now, but couldn't work up the courage to tell you. I'm not the greatest catch in the world, and you probably deserve a lot better than some old, worn-out, retired detective, but will you marry me?"

Tears sprang to her eyes as the realization swept through her that she loved Louis too. But marriage? At her age? For Pete's sake, she'd just started drawing her Social Security.

So what? Big deal. What does age have to do with it?

For once, she didn't want to argue with the aggravating voice in her head. In fact, she decided that the voice was absolutely right on.

"You're not that old or worn out," she told Louis. "If you are, then I am too. I — I'm no spring chicken, though. That's for sure," she finished in a whisper.

He simply smiled. "Neither am I."

He gently released her hands, and then slipped one of his into the inside pocket of his suit jacket and pulled out a small black velvet box. He opened it and removed a solitaire diamond ring. "So, how about it?" He held the sparkling ring out to her. "Are you going to marry me?"

Charlotte swallowed hard. The gold ring

was gorgeous in its simplicity. The diamond was large enough to be noticeable, but not so large that it looked fake.

"Yes," she said firmly, and held out her left hand for him to slide the ring on.

Hank's father would always be her first love, but there was more than enough room in her heart for Louis as well. God willing, Louis would be her last love.

This time she reached out across the table for his hands. Her heart overflowing with joy, she squeezed them tightly, and whispered, "Just so you know, I do love you too."

A Cleaning Tip from Charlotte
The next time you clean mirrors or something made of glass, use a single coffee filter with your window cleaner instead of a paper towel. Unlike paper towels, coffee filters are lint free. Also, a package of coffee filters costs a lot less than a roll of paper towels.

RECIPE

Each year Charlotte bakes her son, Hank, a special cake for his birthday.

RED VELVET CAKE
Makes 12 large or 16 small slices.
1 1/2 cups sugar
1/2 cup vegetable shortening
2 ounces red food coloring
2 eggs, unbeaten
2 cups flour
1 teaspoon salt
1 tablespoon cocoa
1 cup buttermilk
3 teaspoons vanilla
1 teaspoon baking soda
1 tablespoon vinegar

Cream sugar and shortening together until light and fluffy; add the food coloring and unbeaten eggs, 1 at a time, beating well after each addition. Set aside. Sift together 3 times: flour, salt, and cocoa. Add dry ingredients alternately with buttermilk to the sugar mixture and mix well. Add the vanilla and beat well at least 2 minutes. In a separate bowl, dissolve soda in vinegar, and then gently fold mixture into cake batter. Don't beat. Pour batter into 2 (or 3) well-greased and floured round cake pans, then bake in a 350-degree F oven for approximately 35 minutes. Cool completely before icing.

RED VELVET CAKE ICING
3 tablespoons cornstarch
1 cup milk
2 sticks margarine
1 cup sugar
1 teaspoon vanilla

Cook cornstarch and milk in a double boiler and stir constantly (mixture must not be lumpy). After mixture thickens, cool completely. In separate bowl, cream margarine, sugar, and vanilla; then add to first mixture and beat until fluffy. (Note: if you're very careful, you can cook cornstarch and milk mixture in the microwave instead of a double boiler, but stir often. Remember, it must not be lumpy.)

ABOUT THE AUTHOR

Barbara Colley is an award-winning author whose books have been published in sixteen foreign languages. A native of Louisiana, she lives with her family in a suburb of New Orleans. Besides writing and sharing her stories, she loves strolling through the historic New Orleans French Quarter and Garden District, which inspired the setting for her Charlotte LaRue mystery series. Readers can write to Barbara at P.O. Box 290, Boutte, LA 70039 or visit her website at www.barbaracolley.com.

We hope you have enjoyed this Large Print book. Other Thorndike, Wheeler, Kennebec, and Chivers Press Large Print books are available at your library or directly from the publishers.

For information about current and upcoming titles, please call or write, without obligation, to:

Publisher
Thorndike Press
295 Kennedy Memorial Drive
Waterville, ME 04901
Tel. (800) 223-1244

or visit our Web site at:

http://gale.cengage.com/thorndike

OR

Chivers Large Print
published by BBC Audiobooks Ltd
St James House, The Square
Lower Bristol Road
Bath BA2 3SB
England
Tel. +44(0) 800 136919
email: bbcaudiobooks@bbc.co.uk
www.bbcaudiobooks.co.uk

All our Large Print titles are designed for easy reading, and all our books are made to last.